# Wrong Turning

## Catherine MacDonald

Copyright © 2016 Catherine MacDonald

All rights reserved, including the right to reproduce this book, or portions thereof in any form. No part of this text may be reproduced, transmitted, downloaded, decompiled, reverse engineered, or stored, in any form or introduced into any information storage and retrieval system, in any form or by any means, whether electronic or mechanical without the express written permission of the author.

This is a work of fiction. Names and characters are the product of the author's imagination and any resemblance to actual persons, living or dead, is entirely coincidental.

The views expressed in this work are solely those of the author and do not necessarily reflect the views of the publisher, and the publisher hereby disclaims any responsibility for them.

ISBN: 978-1-326-61255-9

PublishNation
www.publishnation.co.uk

catherinemacdonaldauthor.com

*With special thanks to James, Penny, Liz and Maggie.*

# Chapter One

## July 1998

I stood helplessly in the middle of a throng of people, and wondered why on earth I had thought that shopping in Chester was a good idea.

It was summer, and in addition to the usual crowds, I was jostled by camera-wielding tourists, intent on recording every quaint detail of the black and white buildings and the tiered rows of shops. Foreign language students spilled over the pavements, laughing and chattering, careless of the natives who were trying to go about their daily business.

I couldn't help thinking that everyone seemed busy and contented, and this only added to my feelings of frustration. It wasn't that I was so very unhappy or unoccupied, but my life as a mother whose children were fast flying the nest meant that I was conscious of time slipping away from me, and I wanted something to reaffirm my status as an individual again. Today, I simply felt like a lowly ant in a populous anthill.

I stepped into the middle of the street, to avoid a pack of loud-voiced Liverpool lasses, mincing over the cobbles in short, tight skirts and killer heels. Something struck me hard in the small of the back. I turned round crossly to remonstrate with the person responsible, and my mouth dropped open.

'My God – is that you, Ian?'

My assailant put down the briefcase whose sharp edge had caught me, and a bewildering kaleidoscope of expressions passed over his face.

'I don't believe it. It's Eithne ...' he said, his gaze sweeping over me from head to toe.

It is always a little awkward when you meet someone you have not seen for many years in an unexpected place. It's doubly awkward, when you were once engaged to them, and then disengaged, under very unfortunate circumstances. I couldn't believe my eyes, and I was temporarily at a loss for words, as long-buried memories rose up and threatened to overwhelm me.

Ian was the first to recover his equilibrium.

'I do apologise,' he said stiffly. 'It's so crowded here today. I hope you're not hurt.'

'Well, you did give me a shock.'

I began to regain my composure, and took a proper look at him. Although Ian was in his mid-fifties, he was still an extremely handsome man. His brown hair was greying, and life had etched lines around his eyes and jaw, but his tall figure was athletic and trim. He had always worn the most beautifully tailored suits, and today was no exception – he was immaculately dressed. I suddenly felt very conscious of my casual trousers and top and windblown curls.

'What on earth are you doing in Chester, Ian?' I asked, assuming a bright tone to cover my confusion.

'I live locally,' he informed me.

This was another surprise. I found it hard to believe that he would have left London, and his successful career in advertising, and wondered what unexpected events could have taken him away from his southern roots.

Ian was examining me intently in his turn. I realised that I must appear very different to the young woman he had known twenty years previously, and hoped that he would not think the years had treated me unkindly. At forty-eight, I felt neither young nor old, but I was conscious of the passage of time in a way which I had not been in my thirties, and did not always appreciate what I saw in the mirror nowadays.

Then he smiled at me, and I remembered how I had so often been disarmed by that engaging, confident regard. It seemed genuine, but with Ian, you could never be entirely sure.

'You haven't changed so much,' he said softly. 'I'd forgotten that you moved to Cheshire after you left work. I suppose this is your usual stamping ground.'

A flock of Spanish students surrounded us, like twittering sparrows, and for a moment, we both stepped back under the onslaught. When they had passed by, Ian glanced at his watch. He seemed to be making a decision.

'Do you think we could lunch together?' he asked. 'It would be good to catch up, and maybe lay a few ghosts to rest. I don't think that either of us were very happy with the way we parted at Mackerras Mackay. There's a cosy little Italian restaurant in the next courtyard. Please say you'll come.'

I had intended to snatch a baguette in a coffee shop. It would be a treat to have a more leisurely meal, and I was curious about my ex-fiancé, now I had got over the initial shock of seeing him. He was right. The last months of our earlier acquaintance had been a period of conflict and stress. However, the time was surely past when he could affect my life in any adverse way, and I felt suddenly that I would like to be on better terms with him. It would go some way to assuaging the guilt I still felt about causing the original rupture between us.

'Yes. I think I'd like that.'

Ian picked up the offending case, and took my arm in an authoritative grip, which I remembered well. I felt a tiny frisson run down my spine.

'This way, then.'

The restaurant was very quiet, and the waiter made us comfortable at a corner table. We ordered our food, and Ian asked for a bottle of wine.

'I feel we should mark the occasion,' he said, laughing. 'I hope you're not driving, are you?'

'No, I came on the bus. It's so difficult to park in Chester. Wine will be nice.'

The waiter filled our glasses, and we both said 'cheers' in a self-conscious kind of way. It seemed unreal to be sitting there with him. I remembered dozens of meals out in London when we had been together, but none of them had felt as awkward as this.

'So why did you move to Cheshire?' I asked, searching for an innocuous beginning.

'Well, I'm contemplating retirement now. My wife's elderly parents live here, and she wants to be closer to them now they're getting on. We've bought a place called Delamere Court, near a village called Fenwich. It's a pretty spot.'

'*You've* bought Delamere Court!' I exclaimed, not quite suppressing a note of apprehension in my voice. 'How extraordinary. We live at the Old Rectory in Fenwich.'

All our friends had speculated about the identity of the recent purchasers of the Court, a rambling 1930s property set halfway up a hill amongst dense woodland. It was reputed to have beautiful views across the Cheshire plain, but I thought the steep and winding drive would be a nightmare in winter. The place had extensive grounds and a swimming pool, and required a lot of upkeep. Ian was obviously very well off to be able to take it on.

'You know it?'

'I know of it. I've never been inside. The Ramsays, who lived there before you, spent most of their time in Spain, and they kept themselves to themselves when they were here.'

It dawned on me that life might well become more complex with the advent of these new neighbours. Ian was gazing at me in a very reflective way, as he toyed with his glass.

'Remind me,' he said in his deep voice. 'You married an old friend of Nick's, and your son Nicholas must be in his early twenties now. What's he doing with his life?'

I had married my husband Peter when Nicholas was just over a year old. Nick DeLisle, Nicholas' father and my first love, had been killed in Africa just before Nicholas was born, and I had a terrible year in London coping with bereavement, a baby and a difficult situation at work. I would always be grateful to Peter for carrying us off to a more settled and serene life at the Old Rectory.

'Nicholas is at Oxford, and he's just finished his second year. Peter and I have two daughters together,' I said. 'And your son must be a year or so older than Nicholas. Do you and Jane have any more children?'

A faint grimace crossed his face, and he put down his glass.

'My marriage to Jane was very short-lived,' he said. 'It was a mistake all round. You are partly to blame for that.'

He was alluding to the fact that I had broken my engagement to him and resumed my relationship with Nick all those years ago. Ian and I had worked at the same advertising agency, and in order to put some distance between us after our split, he had moved to America for a few years. He met Jane there, and they had married because of her pregnancy.

'I'm sorry,' I said, feeling genuinely sad that things had not worked out for them.

'But I have a son and a daughter with Laura, my second wife,' he said quickly. 'Sam's about to go to Edinburgh University. Maudie is sixteen. She's sitting GCSE at present.'

The waiter brought our starters and we ate in silence for a few minutes, both digesting the information we had shared. One thing was very clear to me. Given the proximity of our houses, it was going to be impossible to avoid Ian and his family socially. I would have to make sure we agreed that certain details from our past remained secret. I didn't want our history circulated in the neighbourhood, as a subject for gossip.

Despite my earlier apprehension, I began to relax as I drank my second glass of wine, and Ian seemed more at ease as well. For a moment, I wondered whether a marriage between us would have worked, or whether it might have foundered along the way. It was impossible to speculate now.

'I've never really understood why you threw me over.' Ian took the bull by the horns. 'Was it simply that Nick came along again at an opportune moment? Or was there some other reason; was he a convenient excuse? It all happened so suddenly, and at the time, it wasn't possible to have a rational discussion. I would really like to know what you were thinking back then.'

I didn't want to recall those turbulent times in too much detail. I had been very happy, and then very unhappy, and my life had been filled with drama and tragedy. However, I recognised that Ian deserved an answer. I had tried to be honest with him at the time, but we had parted on very bad terms, and perhaps the truth had been difficult to distinguish amidst the confusion.

'I had begun to be afraid of you,' I said hesitantly. 'You became very controlling after we were engaged, and I was worried about what that might mean for the future. I was flattered when you proposed to me, but I was taken by surprise, and perhaps I wasn't thinking straight.'

'Afraid of me?'

Ian put down his fork. He looked disturbed.

'Yes. You know you like to have your own way, Ian, and you were being impossibly dogmatic about the wedding, and other things. I began to think I wouldn't be tough enough to stand up to you.'

I gulped. It was hard to put into words, and the memories had a painful edge. 'Nick coming back when he did was sheer chance, but when I saw him again, I had to accept that my feelings for him had never really gone away. He was the love of my life. He always will be.'

Tears pricked at my eyelids as I said this. A vivid memory haunted me. Even after all these years, there were moments when I thought I would never get over Nick's untimely death. I had fallen in love with him at a very young age, and although our relationship had its ups and downs, we had been close and blissfully happy together at the end.

Ian stirred uncomfortably in his chair, and his face grew sombre.

'That must be consoling for your husband,' he said, after a short silence.

'I've had a good marriage with Peter. He knew he couldn't replace Nick, but we've been happy together, and we get along very well.'

I thought briefly of my sensible, supportive husband, and counted my blessings. It hadn't been possible for me to love anyone else with the passion I had felt for Nick, but there are different degrees of love, and on the whole, I felt that a less consuming affection was an easier way of coping with everyday life.

'I was certainly afraid of you when I went back to work at Mackerras Mackay, after my maternity leave was over,' I told Ian. 'You were back from America then, and I really felt you had it in for me.'

'I was hurt, and angry with you. I wanted to hurt you too,' he admitted. His eyes darkened, and a shadow passed across his handsome face.

I felt shaky. That was a time of horrible incidents I really didn't want to remember. Our present meeting was so unexpected, and it was painful to dredge up the past. I think Ian realised this, because he said, more gently,

'A lot of water has flowed under the bridge since those days. I'm very glad to have this opportunity of talking to you now, especially as we're going to be neighbours. I don't know whether I really understand, Eithne, but I would like to put all the ill feeling behind us. Please forgive me for any hurt I may have caused you back then. I hope we can genuinely be friends in future.'

He reached for my hand, and squeezed it gently. The gesture pleased me. He sounded sincere, and I wanted to believe him. But there was one thing I needed to clear up, something which had happened in our past, the memory of which still bothered me. It was during an event from the last days of our joint working life, when we had been part of an agency team staying away from home to brainstorm for new business.

'Ian – please tell me – did you spike my drink at the hotel in Sevenoaks?'

He gave me a look of utter blankness, and I blushed furiously.

'What on earth are you on about?'

'You remember when we were having that new business session? The barman told me he thought he saw you put something in my drink when you were at the bar. I didn't know whether to believe him or not.'

An incredulous smile crept over his face.

'Is that why you rushed off into the night in that dramatic way? Eithne, I'm disappointed in you. Surely you knew I wouldn't do something so utterly unclassy? Not to mention criminal. What did you think ... no, better not tell me.'

My face was flaming now.

'I did wonder if I'd over reacted, but I was upset at the time. I'm sorry.'

There had been other reasons to doubt his motivation towards me, but I believed he was telling the truth about this. For a moment, it crossed my mind that the incident had been pivotal in my decision to marry Peter, and I wondered just how much my judgment had been at fault in those emotionally charged times.

The waiter hovered once again, and we fell silent as the plates were cleared.

'I've always been ashamed of the way I behaved towards you, Ian,' I said, glad to get this off my chest. 'I didn't mean to hurt you.

If Nick hadn't come back .... well, it's too late to think what might have happened. Surely we can get along now without too much trouble, can't we? The only thing is – how much do you want people to know? Obviously Peter is aware of our past history, but we've never spoken about it to the children.'

He sighed. I wondered if it was equally painful for him to recollect the events of those distant years.

'Laura knows I was briefly engaged before I married Jane. I think it will be as well to tell her about our connection,' he said. 'But there's no necessity for the children, or anyone else to know. We can merely say that we worked together in the seventies. That's true, in any case.'

The waiter delivered our plates of pasta with a theatrical flourish, garnishing the food liberally with black pepper and parmesan. I began to feel better, and picked up my fork with renewed appetite. As we ate, Ian told me that Mackerras Mackay, the agency where we had been employed, no longer existed.

'We sold out to the Americans in the early nineties,' he said. 'I made a lot of money from my equity, but it was sad to see the name disappear. Afterwards, I worked in consultancy. I still have a few executive directorships. It's good to keep one's hand in.'

Then he asked me about Peter, and I explained that he managed the family engineering business, based just outside Manchester.

'Somehow, I never went back to work,' I said. 'Olivia was born within a year of my marriage, then I had Louisa two years later. Three children were quite a handful, and Peter really wanted me to be at home with them.'

'Didn't you miss working?'

'Yes, sometimes I did. But in any case, it would have been difficult to continue in the same line outside London. I know there are agencies in Manchester, but it's hard to get back into the industry after a break.'

'Shame. You had a good brain,' he commented.

'I like to think I still have.'

'Aren't you ever tempted to try a different career?'

'I'm really fully occupied at home,' I retorted, although this wasn't entirely true any more. I didn't want to pursue the topic. 'Does your wife work, or is she too busy with family commitments?'

He smiled. Of course, there would be no financial necessity for his wife to contribute to the family exchequer, and perhaps the question was superfluous.

'Well, she works hard at the gym and the business of looking good. And she runs the household very efficiently.'

I concentrated on my pasta for a while. It was really delicious, and it was a treat to have a meal in a restaurant. Peter had been so very busy lately that we hardly ever managed to go out together, and I thought suddenly, and with a twinge of irritation, that this state of affairs needed to change.

'How did you meet your second wife?' I asked, when I had finished.

'Laura? She came to work as a secretary at the agency, just after you left. My marriage was on the rocks by then and we suited each other,' he replied.

'Were there ever any secretaries at Mackerras Mackay you didn't sleep with, Ian?'

Perhaps this was cheeky of me, but in those days, he had a reputation for amassing a huge number of notches on the bedpost. He gave me a reproving glance.

'One or two, I suppose,' he said, deadpan. 'Actually, Laura reminded me of you – not physically, but her way of dealing with things was similar. And we've also had a good marriage. She knows when to look the other way.'

What did he mean by that? Perhaps he had never been able to shake off his philandering habits. I wouldn't have liked that at all. However, I didn't feel able to ask him to elaborate.

Neither of us wanted a pudding, and we ordered coffee.

'So here we are,' he said, as the meal drew to a close. 'I certainly wasn't expecting to be revisiting the past today. But I think it's been a good thing, meeting you like this. As we're going to be such near neighbours, I expect we'll be seeing you socially, and there won't be any embarrassment now.'

'No. It's been good to see you, Ian.'

I never would have thought I would hear myself say that, but I realised it was true.

Ian asked for the bill. I opened my bag, but he waved away my offer of payment, and opened a wallet heavy with credit cards.

The manageress came to the table with the payment machine, and Ian smiled at her. I noticed her taking in his well-cut suit and striking face, and she gave him a sexy little look from under her eyebrows. Then she glanced at me, and it was obvious from her disdainful manner that she couldn't understand my connection with this Romeo in the slightest.

For a moment, I wanted to slap her. I was hit by an unexpected pang of chagrin, as I realised that this desirable man had once been mine, and I had discarded him. Quickly, I repressed the feeling, before it could harden into something which might stay with me. I might be a little bored from time to time, but I was perfectly happy with my life, wasn't I?

'Thank you for lunch, Ian. I'm looking forward to meeting your wife and family,' I said politely, as we strolled back towards the main street, and I prepared to do battle with the hordes once more.

'It's not a bad little restaurant,' Ian said. 'You must fill us in on the good eating places locally. We had a nice meal in Fenwich the other day. What's the pub called?'

'The Three Feathers? My daughter Olivia works there at weekends as a waitress. I wonder if you saw her?'

He stopped, surprised.

'Tall, curly blonde hair? I knew that girl reminded me of somebody, but I couldn't think who.'

He smiled suddenly, a rather wolfish smile. 'My son Alexander certainly took a shine to her. Is she still at school?'

'She's in the process of leaving. She took her A levels last month, but she doesn't know what she wants to do as yet.'

It was hard to keep the irritation out of my voice. At her age, I'd been on my way to university. Olivia's casual approach to life was another reason why I felt frustrated at present, although her father didn't appear to be worried about her.

Ian continued to smile to himself.

'Well, I expect you'll soon be meeting my elder son,' he said. 'It looks as though our lunch today was very well timed. I think we may be seeing quite a lot of one another in future.'

My heart missed a beat. Despite all the friendly overtures which had been made today, I didn't know whether I was pleased about that or not.

# Chapter 2

When we said goodbye, I received a firm kiss on each cheek. I wondered whether the kisses were bestowed as a kind of benediction, as if I had done penance by confessing to past misdeeds, or whether they were merely social. There was nothing in the way Ian grasped my shoulders to suggest he still retained any affection for me, and I felt that little pang again.

'Stop being silly,' I told myself.

I sat, gazing out of the window on the bus home, thinking hard about the events of day. Peter would need to be told in full about what had occurred, but the children would receive an expurgated version. Perhaps Ian was planning something similar in his turn.

I had found it unexpectedly exciting to see Ian. Although I had almost hated him when we last had dealings with each other, I believed that he was sincere in his desire to put that episode behind us. Sometimes, that early part of my life seemed to have happened to a completely different person compared to the Eithne of today. If Nick had not returned from America to claim me, I would have become Mrs Inglis – but perhaps I would have lasted no longer in that position than Jane had done.

What startled me was my reaction to Ian's physical presence. He was still as magnetic as the younger version to whom I had become engaged. I had forgotten what a strong personality he possessed, and felt sentimental, which made me question old decisions in a way which I had not done for years. I was in danger of forgetting that age and experience may well cast a different perspective on earlier circumstances.

Back at the Old Rectory, I found my daughter Olivia preparing for her shift at the Three Feathers. She was working some extra hours because of staff holidays, and as she had more or less finished with school, I was relaxed about her having a few late nights during the week.

She strolled into the kitchen, slim and self-possessed in a black T-shirt and criminally short skirt. Olivia had inherited my curly hair, much to her fury – Louisa had dead straight locks, which were much easier to manage – and tonight, she had piled her curls up on her head, which made her look sophisticated, and older than her eighteen years.

'Can you run me to the pub, Mum?' she asked. It was about a mile away at the other end of the straggling village, and just a bit too far for easy walking.

'I suppose so,' I said reluctantly. 'Does Terry mind you wearing such a short skirt at work? What happens when you have to bend over?'

'The customers can see my bum – or at least, they would, if I wasn't wearing tights,' she responded. 'Terry likes it. He says it's good for business. It certainly helps get me great tips.'

Despite her laid-back approach to life, there was a steely core in Olivia, which went undetected by most people. She had her own decided views on things, and the only person who had the slightest influence on her was her father.

Recently, a degree of friction had intensified between us. I knew Olivia felt that I favoured her elder half-brother, and she was also jealous of the fact that Nicholas had glamorous relations on his real father's side.

The DeLisles were very well-to-do, and Nicholas would inherit a third of his grandparents' estate in due course. Rosine, Nick's sister, was married to a wealthy banker, and they often carried Nicholas off for exotic holidays and visits. Now the Oxford summer term had finished, he was staying with them in the South of France, and I missed him very much.

I was an only child, and Peter's sister Janet was a good sort, but not particularly stimulating company, so I had some sympathy for Olivia in this respect.

I tried very hard not to show partiality amongst the children. It wasn't made easier by the fact that Nicholas was insouciant and charming, and he was also my only link with someone I had loved very much indeed. Olivia was a prickly person, and we argued about many things – education, clothes, boyfriends – until there were days when we found it hard to communicate at all. Peter could do no wrong in Olivia's eyes, and of late, I suspected her of playing the two of us off against each other with increasing skill. Sometimes I wished she would take a gap year, or do something which would take her away from home for a while.

I was searching for my car keys when I heard the scrunch of gravel, and Peter's Jaguar drew up outside.

'Good. Dad's back. I'll ask him to take me instead,' Olivia exclaimed.

I heard her laughing and joking with him, and watched as the car reversed round the garage before setting off again. At least that meant I could get on with the preparations for supper.

A few minutes later, the Jaguar returned, and Peter came into the kitchen. He walked across the room and kissed the side of my head.

'Hullo, darling. How was Chester?'

I paused in the act of peeling the potatoes. Where should I begin?

'I had a very interesting lunch,' I told him, watching the door carefully in case Louisa came in. 'I bumped into Ian Inglis – literally. He bumped into me in the street, and we ended up at Mazzaro's. He's retired up here, and his family have bought Delamere Court. You can imagine what a shock that was.'

'You lunched with him? I'm surprised you didn't punch him on the nose after the way he behaved towards you at Mackerras Mackay!' he exclaimed, indignant on my behalf.

'Peter, that was years ago. He had some reason to be upset with me then,' I remonstrated. 'We had a discussion to clear the air, and I've established that the incident in Sevenoaks was all in the barman's imagination. We're going to be neighbours, and think how awkward it would be socially if it got out that there was bad blood between us. I want things to be as normal as possible. He's on wife number two, and he has three children like us. He also told me that his elder son had met Olivia at the pub, and fancies her. I really do feel that he's sorry for what happened at Mackerras Mackay. We should leave the past in the past.'

Peter frowned, looking unconvinced. I went around the table, and put my arms around his tall, spare frame.

'If I can accept the situation, surely you can, too?' I murmured. 'Suppose Olivia likes his son. Are you going to forbid him to come to the house?'

'No, of course not.'

My husband gazed down at me with serious blue eyes. 'I don't believe in the sins of the fathers. But I don't think I'll feel comfortable with Ian Inglis, knowing about the way he treated you before you left work.'

He tightened his embrace, and held me close to him.

'For what it's worth, I did get an apology today. We've agreed not to tell the children, or anyone else, that we were involved with one another,' I said, my voice muffled against his shoulder. 'We were once colleagues, a long time ago. That's all anyone needs to know. Please don't stir up past problems.'

I knew that Peter would do as I asked, once he had thought things over. He sighed, and gave me another quick kiss.

'It seems such an unlikely coincidence. The Inglises buying Delamere Court ... I hope for his sake he's still well-to-do. Gerry Danvers told me that the Ramsays had really let the place go. However, that site's got a lot of potential.'

It was typical of Peter to be interested in the practical side of things, and I hoped that meant he would begin to come to terms with having the Inglises as neighbours.

Louisa came galloping down the corridor, and I returned to the potatoes. She was a straightforward, cheerful girl of sixteen. Animals still meant more to her than people. She had wanted to be a vet since she was a tiny girl, and I had no doubt she would achieve her ambition. It was strange that our two daughters were so very different in their attitude to life.

'When's supper, Mum? Have I got time to clean out the guinea pigs?' she demanded.

'Not for about an hour,' I told her. 'How was school?'

She paused, midway to the door.

'Okay. A new girl came to visit, and she was nice. She'll be starting next term. Her family have moved here from London.'

'Maudie Inglis,' I murmured, half to myself.

'Yes, that's right. How did you know?' she asked, looking mystified.

'I met her father in Chester today. We used to work together, years ago,' I told her.

'That's strange. Anyway, she asked me to go swimming at her house when she found out I lived in Fenwich – she lives at Delamere Court, now the Ramsays have moved. It'll be nice having a friend with a pool.'

She sauntered out to the old stables where the guinea pigs were housed, whistling to herself.

Peter observed all this with a wry grin. I looked across at him, comparing him with the older Ian I had met today, and thinking with some satisfaction that Peter also bore his years very well. He was approaching fifty, but he retained the spare figure of his youth, and still had a full head of close cropped fair hair.

'It's starting already,' he said. 'The invasion of the Inglises. At least forewarned is forearmed.'

I laughed. He picked up his briefcase, and went upstairs to change.

When Olivia returned from her shift later that night – she persuaded one of the bar staff to run her home – I asked her if she had come across the new occupants of Delamere Court at the pub. She frowned, trying to remember.

'Would those be the people who were in last Friday? Quite a large party; a good-looking, tall man, and his family. The elder son works in Manchester, and he had a long chat with me later on, when it was quiet. They were all pretty pukka. Dad's a very good tipper, so I hope they come again.'

It sounded right. I wondered what the son did in Manchester. Perhaps he was an ad man like his father.

Olivia's cheeks had grown slightly pink. She said,

'Alexander – the son – asked me when I was next off work. He might be running me into Chester at the weekend. I know you don't like the traffic, and I feel guilty pestering Dad. With Nicholas away just now, I need someone to give me a lift now and then.'

I wondered what had happened to Jane, Alexander's mother, and whether she was still in the UK.

'I met his father in town today. We used to work together years ago,' I told her.

'Did you? I should think it'll be fun knowing them. Apparently, they're converting the old stables to a proper games complex. Table tennis, snooker, the works. They're installing a gym, too.'

I hesitated for a second.

'What was Mrs Inglis like?' I asked, wondering why my voice sounded unnatural as I spoke.

'Can't remember really. Blonde, posh laugh, very well dressed. Didn't you know her as well?'

'No, Ian wasn't married to her then.'

Olivia glanced at me suspiciously. I wondered whether she divined that I had more than a passing interest in Alexander's household.

'It's a shame you didn't stick at your driving lessons. You could be independent if you passed your test, and Dad and I would get you a little runabout,' I said hastily, wanting to turn the subject.

'Well, maybe Alex will give me a few lessons.'

Olivia yawned, pulling her curls down around her shoulders, and looking very much younger as she did so. I looked at her, trying to recall the sweetly determined little girl I had been so close to once upon a time. I did wish we could recapture some of that closeness again.

'Anyway, I'm off to bed. See you in the morning.'

She poured herself a glass of water, and went out, humming to herself.

It had been an eventful day. As I snuggled up to Peter in bed, he sighed, and put his arms round me in a sleepy embrace.

He had been a wonderful husband, even though our marriage had come about through tragic circumstances. As I waited for sleep to claim me, I wondered how different my life would have been if Nick and I had married as we planned, or if I had stayed with Ian. It was a good job none of us knew at the beginning of our adulthood just how many challenges would be thrown at us. Life was hard enough on a day-to-day basis as it was.

I always found it difficult to get off to sleep until Olivia came home from her evening shifts. The next Friday night, I tossed and turned for a while, and then decided to come downstairs again about half past eleven to see if some camomile tea might help me to relax. I was brewing up a pot, when I heard the sound of car wheels, and muffled voices. A key scratched at the lock, and Olivia came in, accompanied by a young man who was a stranger to me.

They both looked very surprised to see me.

'Mum! Are you all right?' my daughter enquired, apparently displeased that I was still up and about.

'Yes, fine. I couldn't sleep, so I'm making some herbal tea,' I explained.

I looked at the young man, who immediately held out his hand politely.

'Hello. I'm Alexander Inglis.'

'I'm Eithne, Livvy's mum,' I replied, returning the handshake. 'I know your father. We used to work together many years ago – I expect Livvy's told you?'

'Yes. What a coincidence for you both to meet again like this.'

Alexander had an air of maturity compared to the local lads, and he definitely had better manners than the usual run of Olivia's young men. I looked at him, trying to trace something of Ian in his features. He was not so tall as his father, but he had the same thick brown hair and grey eyes, and his face was open and pleasant. However, he was not imposingly handsome like Ian.

Livvy was looking in the fridge for something to eat.

'Would you like a coffee, Alex?' she said over her shoulder.

'Coffee would be great.'

I poured myself a mug of tea, knowing that I should leave them to it, but feeling curious to find out a little more about Alexander and the rest of the Inglis family.

'Livvy tells me you work in Manchester, Alex,' I said.

'Yes. I work for a PR firm, and I've got a flat in Salford,' he replied. 'It's nice for me that my father has moved up here from London. I can see a lot more of them all now.'

I wondered again where his mother fitted in, but felt it would be impolite to ask.

'Did you go to Charterhouse like Ian?' I began, but Olivia cut across me impatiently.

'Mum! He just gave me a lift home – he doesn't need the third degree.'

She stomped away to the pantry in search of biscuits. I felt embarrassed.

'I apologise, Alexander, I was just making conversation,' I said smoothly. There would be words with Olivia in the morning about her rude behaviour.

He gave me a shy smile.

'It's fine. Yes, I did, and so did my brother Sam.'

He stepped back, and knocked against the edge of the dresser, sending a photo frame flying. Luckily, the glass didn't break. He retrieved it quickly and looked at it before handing it back to me.

'Sorry. Is that Olivia with her brother and sister?' he asked, sounding interested in his turn.

'Yes. That was taken at a family wedding last year. Louisa is the same age as Maudie, I believe. Nicholas is the girls' older half-brother – he's at Oxford.' I explained.

Olivia barged back in with the biscuits. Her hair was loose and curled around her shoulders, and she looked very pretty, despite her long evening's work. Alexander gazed at her with admiration written large upon his face.

'Nicholas is Mum's favourite,' she told him pertly. 'Lou and I come a poor second, but we're used to that.'

Whatever had got into her tonight? I gave her a reproving frown.

'Pay no attention to her, Alex,' I said. 'That's an ancient complaint, and has no basis in fact, but when you get to know Olivia a little better, you'll realise that she likes to stir things up.'

Poor boy. He looked slightly stunned as my daughter and I locked horns. It was definitely time for me to make my exit.

'Goodnight. Don't stay up too late,' I said, picking up my mug and moving towards the door.

I resettled myself in bed. The calming effects of the camomile tea had been undone by Olivia's rudeness, and this time, I felt really cross with her.

It didn't occur to me to worry about leaving her alone downstairs with a young man. At her age, I had been enjoying a full sexual relationship with Nicholas' father, so it would be hypocritical of me to object if she wanted to become close to someone. However, as I drifted off, I wondered if I really wanted her to get close to Ian's son.

# Chapter three

Saturday mornings were always a relaxed time at the Old Rectory. Peter had a well-deserved lie-in for a change, then showered, and came down to eat breakfast and read the papers amongst the ferns and climbing plants in the conservatory.

We had added the conservatory to the main house when the children were small. It gave us extra space for their toys, and also enabled us to get pleasure from the garden all the year round. Now the toys were gone, and it was a room where Peter and I spent a good deal of our time.

Louisa was out riding with her best friend, Carly. I pottered for a while, then joined Peter with a fresh cafetière of coffee. Olivia had not yet surfaced after her late night entertaining her swain, so things were peaceful.

'I met Alexander Inglis last night. He brought Livvy home from the pub,' I told Peter as I refilled his mug. He put the paper down.

'And is he as amazing as his father?' he asked in sarcastic tones, which pained me.

'Don't be like that. He seems to be a very nice boy, and he's certainly an improvement on Richard.'

Richard, Olivia's last boyfriend, was a wannabe rock musician whose conversation was limited to grunts, and we hadn't cared for him at all.

'That's something, I suppose.'

Peter returned to the paper. I remembered Olivia's behaviour towards me, and felt aggrieved.

'Olivia was very rude to me in front of him. I shall have to say something to her today,' I complained. 'I don't know why she carries on about Nicholas being my favourite child, especially to strangers. It's embarrassing. I try very hard to treat them all the same.'

He looked up quickly.

'Perhaps that's the reason,' he said. 'If you really felt the same about them all, you wouldn't have to try.'

This enraged me. Blood rushed to my cheeks, and I took a deep breath.

'Do you mean you think I behave differently towards Nicholas? That I love him more than the girls? You'll be telling me that you don't give Olivia any preference next.'

We stared at one another, both of us annoyed, both taken aback by this sudden confrontation. I thought to myself that Olivia would be pleased to see us arguing over her, and felt a spasm of dislike wash over me.

'Eithne. Don't let's fight,' Peter said, his face sad now. 'I wouldn't blame you if Nicholas has a larger part of your heart. Considering all the circumstances, that might be quite natural. But we must both be careful with the children, that they don't have any real cause to complain that we're favouring one over the other. I'll speak to Olivia. I'm sure she'll be sorry to have upset you.'

I thought angrily that the reverse was true. Snatching up part of the paper, I flounced down into a chair and hoped that my body language was revealing what I felt about my elder daughter and her special bond with her father. Peter was such an imperturbable person, and sometimes I wanted to shake him out of his easy-going ways.

An uneasy silence filled the room. Neither of us was comfortable after this conversation. Instead of the usual Saturday morning feeling of relaxation and family harmony, the air swirled with unspoken recriminations.

I put down the paper, and wandered into the garden. The day was cool but sunny, and the scent of roses and honeysuckle drifted on the breeze. I sat on the bench by the maple tree, and tried to let my anger melt away, but I could not escape a growing feeling that I was dissatisfied with life at the Old Rectory at present. I nursed my resentment about Olivia, and let it eat away at me.

A moving flash of colour in the conservatory indicated that Olivia was up. I thought that I would leave her and Peter to talk alone, because they were better to discuss things without me being there. I knew I would find it difficult to keep my temper if provoked.

Ten minutes went by. Then the flash of colour materialised as Olivia in her yellow bathrobe, and she sauntered across the lawn to where I was sitting.

I looked at her as she approached, wondering what mood she would be in this morning. Her cheeks were flushed, and she retied the belt of her robe with an angry gesture as she reached the seat.

'Mum. Sorry if I overstepped the mark last night. But you were being pretty irritating too. Why do you need to know stuff about my friends?'

Well, I supposed it was meant for an apology.

'Don't be so childish,' I said evenly. 'What's wrong with making conversation? Alexander didn't seem to mind.'

'No. He's too well-mannered to object.'

'You could do with following his example.'

Peter had also come outside, and he caught the last of this exchange. He gave me a resigned look.

'When is this boy picking you up, Olivia?' he asked.

'Just before midday,' she said sulkily, picking at a nail.

'You'd better get your skates on, then. I know how long you take getting ready, and if you make him wait, Mum's probably got a long list of questions for him today.'

If this was an attempt at humour, it failed to impress either Olivia or me. However, she skittered back into the house, glad of an excuse to leave us. Peter sat down next to me.

'Don't be too critical. She works hard at the Three Feathers, you know, they think highly of her,' he murmured, reaching for my hand.

'I'm sure she does – but I wish she would raise her sights somewhat higher,' I said waspishly. 'At least the other two seem to have some ambition.'

I thought with approval of Lou and her veterinary plans, and Nicholas, now approaching his last year at Balliol. Peter considered this, frowning.

'I know about Lou, but I wasn't aware that Nicholas had a particular career in mind,' he said.

'I didn't have a particular career in mind until I'd almost finished at Oxford,' I retaliated. 'But I did at least recognise the importance of further education.'

I could hear the telephone ringing in the house. After a minute, Olivia came to the conservatory door and called to me.

'Mum! Telephone for you.'

It was my mother calling for our usual weekly chat. I listened with scant attention to her tales of life in Beresford, where I had grown up, still conscious of inner rumblings of annoyance after my argumentative morning. Eventually, she ground to a halt, and I was able to get away. Then I felt guilty for being so unresponsive, and decided I would need to ring her back later, when I was in a better mood.

Peter had returned to the conservatory and the papers, and I sat down with him again. But before I could begin the crossword, a black Clio turned into the drive, its engine growling impressively.

'That must be Alex Inglis. I'll give Livvy a prod,' I said.

An irritated yelp from Livvy's room greeted my announcement that her beau had arrived. I went back downstairs, and found Peter and Alexander deep in conversation on the drive.

Alexander greeted me politely, and I was struck anew by his air of maturity.

'Livvy won't be long.' I told him. 'Please can you get her back in good time for her shift at the pub at six?'

'Yes, of course. I think my father's booked a table for tonight. They have friends visiting from London,' he said.

I felt slightly wistful, as I thought that the Inglises would undoubtedly have a much better social life than we did. It was definitely time for us to make more of an effort in that department.

After a few more minutes, Olivia strolled out, looking youthful and pretty in cropped jeans and a floaty top. She didn't appear to have a problem with her father asking Alex questions, and stood there, idly swinging her bag, while the two men chatted about cars and engines.

Peter got a kiss on the cheek. I got a wave over her shoulder as she got into the car. We stood there, watching, as they drove away.

'He seems a nice enough boy. I should think he'd look after Livvy when they're out together,' Peter said, with some satisfaction.

'I'm sure that Olivia can look after herself,' I said.

Later that afternoon, I heard noisy wheels outside, accompanied by brisk hooting, mingled with the barking of Labradors. My friend Maddy Potter was sitting at the wheel of her family Range Rover.

She made no attempt to get out, but lowered the window as I walked towards her, and I reeled back from the earthy onslaught of dogs, horsy bits and pieces and empty crisp packets which inhabited the interior of her car.

'Can't stop. Can you come to us for dinner next Saturday? The new owners of the Court are coming. You'll like them, they're madly glam.'

'I know one of them at any rate. I used to work with Ian in London many moons ago,' I said. 'We'd love to come, thank you.'

I was very fond of Maddy. She was a real scatterbrain, but being married to a senior partner in a Manchester legal firm enabled her to get through life with a whole tribe of au pairs, gardeners and cleaners to help her, and I envied that. Lou was very friendly with Carly, Maddy's eldest child.

Maddy's house, Pippins, was always overflowing with children and animals, and tidiness was a concept unknown to her. I found it rather refreshing.

'Well, that's great. About seven thirty, then? We'll look forward to seeing you both.'

She began to reverse out of the drive.

'Shall I bring a pud?' I called, as she turned the car with a series of bumps and stutters.

'No need. The new au pair's a fabulous cook.'

I waved as she drove off, clashing the gears, and almost colliding with the bus as it swayed down the lane between high hedges.

Peter came out to see what was going on, and I told him about the dinner invitation. His face grew downcast.

'Meet the Inglises! I suppose you know I'll find it very hard to be civil to that man. Do you really think this is such a good idea?'

He kicked irritably at a loose edging stone, maybe imagining it was Ian's head.

'Yes. Let's get it over with. You know very well you'll be perfectly polite when you see him. For my sake, you need to put these old feelings behind you now,' I said.

In fact, I was a little perturbed myself at the prospect, but we would have to do it sooner or later. Things would surely simmer down afterwards.

I began to worry about what to wear to the dinner party. If Laura Inglis was such a glamour puss, I didn't want to appear a dowdy country mouse.

'I'm going into Chester tomorrow,' I told Peter at supper on Monday. 'I need a new dress for Saturday, and the sales have started.'

Olivia looked up from her baked potato and cheese. She was going through a vegetarian phase, blithely heedless of the disruption this caused for the rest of her carnivorous family.

'I'll come and help you choose one, Mum,' she exclaimed. 'You need a bit of encouragement. Your clothes aren't exactly trendy, you know.'

I started to say I would go on my own, but then I caught sight of Peter's face. He was obviously delighted at the prospect of a mother-daughter outing, so I curbed my objections.

'Have lunch out as well. Make a day of it,' he said, smiling.

Funnily enough, I was quite pleased that Olivia was with me, in the end. She steered me firmly away from my usual black, and we found a pretty silk dress in a smudgy blue and grey floral print which was elegant and summery. The bodice was cut a little low, but she assured me it wasn't too revealing.

'Dad will like it,' she said firmly, and I knew that was the most important thing as far as she was concerned.

A pair of strappy blue sandals completed the outfit, and Olivia pronounced herself satisfied. We even managed lunch without getting into an argument, and I wished we could get on so well every day. Perhaps being away from the home environment had helped.

I had a hair appointment in the village on Friday morning, and there was a wonderful surprise waiting for me when I returned to the Old Rectory. Nicholas was home from France.

It was a delight to see him, and his half-sisters were also pleased to have their brother back. He had brought presents for everyone, and was in high spirits.

'This is for you, Dad. Keep it for yourself, it'll be wasted on the girls,' he said handing Peter a bottle of Pomerol. Having never known his real father, Nicholas regarded Peter as his dad, and they had an excellent relationship. Peter's only regret was that Nicholas had neither the talent nor the inclination to follow him into the family engineering business, which would now be sold when Peter decided to retire.

Nicholas had brought delicious chocolates for the girls, and a bottle of Chanel No 5 for me. I scolded him for his extravagance.

'Don't worry, Mum, I hardly had to pay for anything when I was away. Aunt Rosine and Uncle Andrew are very generous,' he assured me.

'Did you meet any nice French girls?' I asked, giving him a hug. He laughed, and looked a little shifty.

'One or two. I think my French has improved, anyway,' he said, returning the hug. I knew I would not get any further information, because he was extremely secretive as far as his love life was concerned. He was a very nice looking boy, although he was not as darkly, devastatingly handsome as his father. However, he had definitely inherited Nick's charm, and the phone never stopped ringing with girls wanting to speak to him when he was at home.

It had always been a disappointment to me that he did not look more like Nick. But as he became an adult, there were moments when I thought I saw sudden small resemblances, and my heart would turn over, as memories of his father flashed across my consciousness. It was a disturbing sensation, and I couldn't decide whether it made me happy or sad.

Peter was uptight about the dinner party. He spent Saturday afternoon closeted in his study, and emerged to get ready to go out with a very long face. I was conscious of the sartorial elegance to be expected on the Inglis front, and persuaded him, with some difficulty, to wear a suit, which didn't improve his mood.

However, he liked my new dress, and cheered up when Nicholas offered to drive us to Pippins and pick us up later, so we could both have a drink. Trying to soothe Peter's ruffled feathers meant I had not had time to be nervous myself about meeting Ian and his wife, but I didn't feel quite comfortable on the way there.

Several expensive looking cars lined the drive at Pippins, and a pack of enthusiastic dogs greeted us noisily as we got out of the car. I shooed them away, not wanting dirty paws on my frock, and we rang the doorbell.

Maddy's eight-year-old daughter, Kate, opened the door to us.

'Eithne! I do like that dress. What a pretty colour,' she exclaimed in a bright, social manner, older than her years, which made me smile. We followed her through the hall and out on to the terrace where the other guests were assembled. Alan, Maddy's husband, kissed me, and pressed glasses of champagne upon us,

'Eithne and Peter, meet your new neighbour, Laura,' he announced, with the air of a conjuror producing a rabbit out of a hat.

A tall, slender woman, clad expensively in a black halter-neck frock and elaborate gold jewellery, smiled at us, with a flash of very white teeth. Her ash blonde hair was styled in a long bob, and she appeared extremely well groomed and confident. Suddenly, I felt a bit too colourful, almost peasanty by contrast, with my flowery blue silk and loose tawny curls.

Laura had the tanned, slightly brittle look of a middle aged woman who concentrates on watching her weight and undergoing extensive beauty treatments to keep back the march of time, but I had to admit that the overall effect was good.

Peter certainly seemed to like it. He gazed at her with admiring eyes, and I was relieved to see his shoulders relax. We exchanged polite pleasantries, and I tried to look round unobtrusively for Ian.

'We've met your son, Alexander. He's a very nice boy,' Peter was saying.

'My stepson,' she corrected him, with a tight little smile. 'And we've met your daughter, I believe, the charming waitress at the Three Feathers.'

I detected condescension in her tone, and rushed to Olivia's defence.

'It's a holiday job. She's just finishing school,' I said firmly.

Laura's attention was fixed on Peter. I saw that she was one of those women who prefer to reserve their efforts for the opposite sex, and I moved away, on the pretext of admiring a large tub of geraniums. Then I caught sight of Ian, in conversation with Rick and Judy Ryan, the other guests, and walked across to their little group.

'Hullo Eithne. Ian was telling us that you knew each other aeons ago, in London,' Rick said, eyebrows raised in mock surprise.

'Yes. We worked at the same agency for a few years,' I confirmed. There was a polite murmur at this, and I looked at Ian. He gave me a quick, sardonic smile.

'It was very nice to meet Eithne again, even if I did nearly knock her over,' he explained, and there were further murmurs as he described our rendezvous in Chester.

'Has she changed very much?' Rick enquired, winking at me. He was a good friend of mine, and had a teasing way with him, which I usually enjoyed, although I didn't appreciate it so much tonight.

Ian looked at me gravely.

'No. She is as charming as ever,' he said softly and diplomatically.

What an old smoothie he was – he certainly hadn't altered in this respect. I was glad to see Alan approaching to top up our glasses.

From the corner of my eye, I could see Laura exercising her fascination over Peter like a stoat with a rabbit. I thought, hopefully, that this would help to reconcile him to Ian's presence. In fact, the two men only had time for a quick, cold handshake, before Maddy announced that dinner was ready, and ushered us into her dining room.

I was envious of the dining room at Pippins. It was long and panelled, with large windows down one side opening on to the garden, and the polished walnut table made a perfect circle in the middle of the room. The wood was beautifully grained, and I traced a whorl with my fingers as I took my seat. I found I was placed between Ian and Rick, which suited me fine.

Rick began to tell me of their holiday plans, as Maddy served a cold summer soup. He and Judy were childless, but this didn't seem to bother them, and they were always visiting exotic locations or voyaging with determination through parts of the globe which seemed distinctly challenging to me. Our holidays were much less adventurous, and the discussion was somewhat one-sided as a result.

Halfway through treating me to a little travelogue about Tibet, he looked over and saw Ian engaged in close conversation with Maddy on his far side.

Rick lowered his voice.

'Have you heard about the plans for Delamere Court yet? Your old colleague must be simply rolling in it, my dear. I never knew there was so much money to be made in advertising.'

'Well, if you have equity and then sell out, you can walk away with a lot of dosh,' I said.

'The wife looks as though she'd be expensive to run. But she's very charming, and they will be a definite acquisition for the neighbourhood, I'd say. It must be nice for you to have someone to talk over old days with, as well.'

I murmured a non-committal response. Laura, across the table from me, was now employing her charm on Alan, gazing at him intently as though she was fascinated by every word he said. I sensed that she was as tough and ruthless as her husband, and they were evidently very well suited.

Ian turned his attention to me as the roast beef was served.

'You look very nice, Eithne. Blue always was your colour,' he said, his eyes lingering on my chest. I flushed, and fidgeted at my neckline with nervous fingers.

'Your wife is very glamorous,' I replied. 'Is she the same age as me?'

'Yes, almost exactly, I think.'

He helped me to more wine.

'How are you settling in at your new house?' I asked, conscious that this was safe territory.

'Well, there's a lot to do. I'm afraid we're facing quite a few months with the builders in when we finally decide on the plans. But I hope it will be worth it in the end.'

The roast beef was delicious, rare and savoury, and I wondered whether the new au pair had helped with it. Maddy's cooking was usually a bit hit and miss. Peter and Laura were conversing again, interspersed with little bouts of laughter. I glanced across at them, and Ian followed my gaze.

'I can tell that Laura likes your husband. He seems a serious chap, not the sort of person I'd associate with you somehow,' he said.

'What's *that* supposed to mean?'

I didn't know whether to be amused or annoyed. It was easy for people who didn't know Peter to underestimate him, but underneath the austere, apparently solemn, exterior was a successful businessman and broadminded, intelligent person.

'Well, I never met Nick, but I understood he was a real charmer, and a live wire as well. I don't mean to belittle Peter, but he must be very different to the type of man you were attracted to when you were younger.'

I assumed he included himself in that category. The irritating thing was, he was right. In my young days, I had fallen twice for a particular type of handsome, charismatic alpha male, not always with the best results.

'Do you ever think about what your life might have been like if you and Nick had been able to marry?' he continued, in casual tones, as if we were discussing some everyday, ordinary topic. Now I was becoming cross.

'Don't you think that's a pointless exercise? Yes, obviously I have thought about it on occasions. Nick and Peter aren't at all similar, but someone with solid qualities like Peter was what I needed after Nick died and I was finding life so hard in London. In that sense, I've been lucky. Life doesn't necessarily work out the way one plans it.'

My voice wobbled a little. Ian glanced at me swiftly.

'I'm sorry. I don't mean to upset you,' he said, more gently. 'I'm glad that you've been happy, and I've had a similar experience. After we broke up, I made a bad misjudgement when I married Jane, but Laura and I have got on very well.'

An unspoken question – 'Would our marriage have been a success?' – hung heavily in the air, and we skirted uneasily round it.

'Tell me about your children,' I said, feeling that this was a subject less fraught with complications.

We chatted about the problems of life with teenagers as we finished the main course, and I was pleased to find that every family appeared to meet the same kind of obstacles along the way.

'Where is Alexander's mother now?' I asked, plucking up my courage, as Maddy began to clear away the plates.

'Jane? She remarried, she lives in New York.'

Ian stared across the room at his second wife, laughing and flirting with a smiling Peter, not looking at all serious at present as he reached for the wine bottle.

'Alex and I didn't really see each other, or have much of a relationship, when he was a little boy. I regret that now. I think he always feels that he's the least valued of my children. That's not really the case, but because we missed out on so many years together, it's hard to have the same intimacy with him as I have with Sam and Maudie.'

His face grew sad as he spoke, and I felt a quick twinge of sympathy.

'If it's any consolation, Olivia always accuses me of favouring her brother,' I told him. 'It isn't always easy to know what to do for the best.'

'And do you favour him?'

'I make every effort not to, but Olivia and I don't always see eye to eye. Nicholas is much more easy-going – and there's also the fact that he is all I have left of Nick.'

Again, I couldn't keep the emotion from my voice, and Ian glanced at me, hesitation in his eyes. Luckily, Maddy intervened over my shoulder.

'Eithne, be a dear, and come and help me with the puds. Elena is putting the children to bed now.'

I was glad of an excuse to end the conversation with Ian. In the chaotic kitchen, strewn with dishes, plates, papers and every conceivable make of toy lying underfoot, life took on a more everyday feeling again. I assisted with the turning out of the summer pudding, always a momentous task, and watched while Maddy put the finishing touches to an enormous trifle.

'Hand me that spatula, please,' she said. 'Aren't the Inglises lovely? She's stunning, and he is a real charmer. Did all the girls fall for him when you worked together?'

'Pretty much,' I said, ducking away from some greying underwear dangling from the drying rack over the Aga. I didn't want to be blinded by a bra strap.

'You too?' she teased.

'He was my boss,' I said, hoping this would do for an answer. I picked up the pudding plates, and carried them quickly back to the dining room. I wasn't keen on pursuing this line of talk.

Conversation became more general as the meal progressed, with laughter and joshing across the table as the cumulative effects of wine and good food kicked in. I was happy to sit and observe the company.

Peter was more looking animated than I had seen him for some time. He and Maddy were now arguing good naturedly about village politics, and I could tell that he had drunk enough to let down his usual guard. He even accepted a glass of port with cheese, an almost unprecedented event. I hoped it wouldn't push him from relaxed to confrontational mode. Although he was normally the most laid back and easy-going person, I had once or twice seen Peter lose his temper, and it wasn't an experience I wanted to repeat. It was as if a long-dormant volcano had suddenly sprung into cataclysmic eruption, and all those present had been stunned and cowed.

I was conscious that he had not really talked to Ian at all during the evening, and now felt it would be better to keep the two of them apart.

Coffee was served in the drawing room. Maddy and Judy devoted themselves to Ian, each sitting on one side of him on the big settee, and vying for his attention in a positively schoolgirlish way.

Somewhat to my surprise, Laura came to sit beside me. Peter, Rick and Alan were deep in conversation about the village cricket team, and no doubt she felt unable to contribute much to their discussion.

I noticed that her hands were long and beautifully manicured. She wore a platinum wedding band, and her engagement ring was a diamond flanked by emeralds. For a moment, I remembered the three massive diamonds Ian had given me, which had never sat quite easily on my finger.

She gave me a quick, meaningful look.

'My husband has told me of your little secret,' she murmured, looking across to where Ian sat with the other ladies. 'I suppose I should be grateful to you. If he hadn't made that rebound marriage to Jane, I probably wouldn't be Mrs Inglis now.'

What could I say to that? I muttered something in assent, aware that Laura was scrutinising me closely.

It must be strange to meet someone your husband once wished to marry. I remembered that, when the children were small, Peter's ex-wife Silvia had paid us a very unexpected visit, and I had been amazed that she and Peter could ever have thought they had enough in common to wed. She seemed utterly unsuited to the man I knew, because she was a noisy and frivolous butterfly of a person, incapable of sticking to anyone or anything. I could only suppose they had felt a powerful physical attraction to one another, which had waned as quickly as it had arisen.

He had not enjoyed the visit, which had never been repeated.

'Did you ever meet Jane? I didn't know her,' I said wildly, feeling at a loss to know where to turn the conversation.

'No. But she was quite wrong for Ian. He needs someone very strong, to keep him toeing the marital line. I expect you understand what I mean.'

I remembered Ian's remark about her looking the other way. Perhaps I really had a lucky escape when I went back to Nick. Anyway, the less said in public about such matters, the better, as far as I was concerned.

'Tell me about your children,' I said, desperately, for the second time that night. But Laura appeared not to hear me.

'I had a most interesting talk with your husband. My father was in the same line of business, and my brother has taken over the family firm. I was fascinated to learn about some of the new developments from Peter,' she said, gazing at me with clear brown eyes.

'I'm so pleased. I'm afraid I've never understood the least thing about it,' I confessed, finishing my coffee. She raised a well-shaped eyebrow to express her amazement at this admission.

'I've always made it my business to keep up with whatever Ian's been doing,' she explained, smoothing her skirt with a graceful gesture. 'I think it's so important for a wife to be able to support her husband in every way possible.'

'Well, I'd need a degree in engineering to keep up with Peter, and I'm afraid my interests lie elsewhere,' I retorted, hackles raised. 'Silly cow!' I thought to myself. But then, if Peter had the habits of the Lothario she was married to, I might have been more motivated to get involved with his working life.

An uneasy silence descended. I thought to myself after this exchange that Laura and I were unlikely to have anything much in common, and was relieved to hear the doorbell ring, announcing the arrival of Nicholas, come to take us home.

Alan answered the door, and he ushered Nicholas in to the drawing room, rather against the latter's will. However, I was pleased to see that Nicholas remembered his manners, and greeted everyone very politely, kissing Maddy and Judy, and shaking everyone else by the hand.

I saw Ian gazing across at him in a speculative way. He rose, abandoning his ladies, and went over to talk to Nicholas. I could hear him asking questions about Nicholas' car and his holiday activities, and felt unaccountably pleased that Ian was making an effort to draw him in.

'Your son?' Laura murmured to me. 'But he doesn't resemble either of you, with that very dark colouring.'

'Peter isn't his father. Ask Ian to explain,' I said, rising quickly from the sofa. I felt disinclined to go into details at such a late hour.

I walked across to Nicholas, and took his arm. 'Hello darling. Thank you for coming to pick us up,' I murmured. Ian smiled, and leaned over to brush my cheek with his.

'Goodnight, Eithne. I've just been saying to Nicholas that he and his sisters must come up for a swim tomorrow afternoon. It's forecast to be a very hot day, and our children and their friends will be enjoying the pool. Perhaps you'd like to join them?'

I thanked him, but made no promise regarding his offer. Others were getting up now. The dinner party was coming to its close, and we went through the usual farewell rituals. Peter and Ian shook hands again, but made no effort to sustain any conversation, for which I was grateful.

I sat in the back of Nicholas' little car, bowling through the country lanes, and was relieved that the evening had passed so pleasantly. Peter was unstinting in his praise of Laura Inglis, somewhat to my amusement. I listened in silence while he enthused about her interest in his company, and the extent of her knowledge.

'Laura was really nice. I can't understand how someone like Ian Inglis attracts such decent women,' he pronounced. This puzzled Nicholas.

'What do you mean, Dad? He seemed an okay guy to me, he was very friendly. And I know that he used to work with Mum.'

'Dad means that he has a reputation for being – well, rather ruthless and self-centred. That's a definite requirement if you want to get on in the advertising world,' I explained. My husband snorted, but made no further comment, and soon we were safely back at home. However, there was one final surprise to come.

As we undressed, Peter turned to me.

'You never told me that Ian Inglis was so good-looking,' he said, a note of accusation in his voice.

'Didn't I? Obviously, I felt it wasn't relevant,' I replied, pushing aside a sudden feeling of guilt.

'Nick ... and then Ian ... was it a difficult decision to marry someone who's somewhat less than an Adonis? Or did you feel you had no other choice at the time?'

This surprised and disconcerted me. Maybe it was the effect of alcohol, but I had never heard Peter express similar sentiments before, and it made me sad. I sat down next to him on the bed.

'I married you because I thought we could be happy together,' I said. 'And I think we have been happy. Isn't that the important thing?'

For a moment, he sat there, quiet and unresponsive. Then he put his arms round me, and drew me into an embrace, before pulling me down into the sheets and sinking his body into mine. I think he felt possessive for once.

# Chapter 4

The children needed little persuading to accept the invitation to swim at Delamere Court the next day. They piled into Nicholas' car after lunch, and we didn't see them again until quite late in the evening. The swim turned into a barbecue and sports in the new games room.

I chivvied both the girls into bed when they were back. Lou had school, and Olivia was due in for her final year assembly the next morning. Nicholas lingered in the kitchen, to tell me about the great time they'd had.

'There was a whole crowd of us, Mum. We knew most of the kids, and the Harveys came as well.'

'The Harveys! I am impressed,' I replied. Sarah and Bill Harvey were very much the local toffs, and we didn't rub shoulders with them very often.

'The pool was great, and then they insisted we stay on for the barbecue. Ian's got one of those gas ones, and it's really easy to use. He's an interesting man. We talked a lot about careers and stuff, and I'm going up again tomorrow.'

'Please don't wear out your welcome,' I said.

Peter pulled a face at me. I could tell he wasn't keen on his children becoming fixtures at Delamere Court, but I reasoned that the novelty would soon begin to pall.

Next morning, it seemed strange to see Olivia back in school uniform. This was her final official day of school, although Louisa would not break up for a week or so. Olivia affected a teenage nonchalance, but underneath it, I thought she was more than a little sentimental.

Peter's face was a picture as he watched her stroll into the kitchen. His little girl was growing up, and already the uniform looked out of place on her willowy body. I knew he minded much more than I did that she was rapidly becoming an adult, with her own very decided views on life, and I hoped he would begin to sympathise with my desire for her to start taking some adult decisions about her future.

'Where did the time go to?' he murmured in my ear, as he collected his briefcase and prepared to leave for the office. 'It seems only yesterday that she was pushing her dolls about in that little grey pram, and now she's leaving school. I worry she's not ready for what might come next.'

'That's one thing I don't worry about,' I reassured him. 'Olivia is a tough cookie. She will cope with anything life throws at her.'

Olivia returned from school with the news that her friend Poppy had issued an invitation to accompany her family on a trip to Scotland. It meant some negotiation with Terry at the pub, but she managed it with her customary efficiency, and Friday morning saw Olivia heading north with her suitcase and much excitement.

Peter was forlorn at her departure. I was irritated, because I had hoped she would be able to help me with some overdue tasks in the house and garden, but I probably got on more quickly without her.

Nicholas suddenly became very distant, spending time with Sam Inglis and the Harvey boys, and enjoying the superior amenities offered by their households. We hardly saw him, and this disturbed me. Peter worried that he was getting used to a style of living which we could not compete with.

After he twice asked me for money for petrol and going out, I began to feel rebellious.

'What about spending a week or two in the office with Dad?' I asked, doling out another twenty pound note with some reluctance. 'He said he can always find something for you to do, and it would pay enough to fund all these evening activities. It's all very well mixing with the Harveys and the Inglises, but they're much better off than we are.'

Nicholas looked guilty.

'I'm sorry Mum, but I've been having a really great time. I would take up Dad's offer, but I've been talking a lot with Ian, and he says he might be able to get me a work placement with Laine and Laine for a month. That's much more the sort of thing I'd like to do. You know I'm not a technical person.'

Laine and Laine was a Manchester based advertising agency. I supposed Ian must have a personal connection there, but I felt uneasy about being beholden to him for any sort of favour.

'That's very good of Ian, but it's asking rather a lot. If nothing happens by next week, you really must speak to Dad.'

'Ian and Laura were asking why you haven't been up for a swim,' Nicholas said, deftly turning the subject.

'I suppose because I'm from a generation which waits for a definite invitation.'

However, I made a mental note that I would need to make contact with them soon. Lou and Nicholas were almost living there at present, enjoying the pool and their new-found friends, and we would need to reciprocate in some way.

I was thinking about the Inglises, when the telephone rang. It was a pleasant surprise to find Rosine, Nick's sister, on the line.

'Rosine! How lovely to hear from you. Thank you so much for all your kindness to Nicholas in France. He seems to have had a wonderful time,' I said.

'Yes. It was fun.'

Her voice sounded somewhat distracted, unlike her normal relaxed tones. 'Eithne, could Andrew and I possibly come to see you later this week? Just overnight. Friday would suit us best. And if you don't mind, we'd like to bring an American acquaintance with us, a man called Luke Simons. He was friendly with Nick when Nick was working in New York, and would like to meet you.'

For a moment, I felt apprehensive. What could this unknown man want from me? I wasn't at all sure I wished to meet him. I had never been keen to learn the details of Nick's time in the States, when his life hadn't included me at all. We had been estranged for several years before he had returned to me in London.

'We can stay at the Three Feathers if it's easier,' Rosine continued, and I began to smell a rat.

'No – if it's just overnight, it won't be a problem. Olivia's away just now,' I said. 'But Rosine, I'm puzzled. Why on earth does this man want to talk to me?'

She was silent for a moment. Eventually, she said,

'Eithne, I can't go into it over the telephone. It's complicated. But there's nothing for you to worry about, please believe me.'

These words had the effect of making me worry more. I didn't believe her – but I felt unable to press her for more details. We agreed the arrangements for Friday, and the talk turned to family news. I had a surprise for her, too.

'Tell Andrew his old school chum, Ian Inglis, has moved to live near here. You can guess what a shock that was,' I said.

'Your ex-fiancé? My God, Eithne, how do you feel about that?'

'It's fine. We've buried the hatchet, and I hope we can all get along without any bad feelings,' I replied. 'Perhaps you would like me to ask him and his wife over when you are here?'

'Not this time, please, Eithne. But I'll tell Andrew. He will be pleased to hear that you and Ian are friends again.'

Peter and I discussed this puzzling conversation at some length. He tried to reassure me.

'You know how sociable Americans are. I expect he feels he would be doing something nice by sharing his memories with you. It's funny that he's waited so long, though.'

I was kept very busy with the preparations for the impending visit for the next few days. Unlike Maddy, I didn't have extra help in the house, and I had to press Nicholas and Louisa into assisting with the cooking and cleaning.

On Friday afternoon, Nicholas escaped for a quick swim at Delamere Court. Our visitors were expected any time after six o'clock, and I had given Nicholas strict instructions to be home before then. The clock ticked on, and I was just beginning to feel irritated at his absence, when a large grey Mercedes swept into the drive.

'That's the Inglises' car,' Louisa said, astonished.

'Oh bother. I don't need any more visitors at the moment.'

I removed my apron, and walked out to the front of the house. Nicholas, Ian, and a girl I did not recognise were getting out of the car.

'Hullo Ian. This is a surprise,' I said, not very graciously. Nicholas was looking sheepish, and I wondered what had happened.

'The Mini wouldn't start, Mum. Ian's kindly given me a lift home. I said that Dad and I would go up tomorrow and try to fix it,' he added.

'That's very kind of you, Ian. We could have come to collect him.'

'It's no bother.'

Ian's eyes flickered over me, and he smiled politely. 'Nicholas told me you were expecting visitors, so we thought we'd save you the trouble of coming out.'

I realised I had been remiss in not acknowledging the girl, and turned to greet her. She had chestnut hair falling to her shoulders, an attractive dusting of freckles across her nose, and her wide-apart brown eyes were fixed on my son with an expression I remembered only too well – the dreamy, doting gaze I had so often turned on Nick when we were teenagers together.

'Oh no. More complications,' I thought to myself.

'You must be Maudie,' I said aloud.

She gave me a shy smile.

'How do you do, Mrs Leigh?' she murmured, before transferring her attention back to Nicholas. Then Louisa appeared, and exclaimed in pleasure at the sight of her friend.

I felt that I ought to offer Ian a drink. His family had been more than hospitable to my children in the last week or so, and there was still time before our guests were due.

'Do you have time for a drink Ian, to say thank you for bringing Nicholas home?' I asked.

'We don't want to intrude if you're busy.'

'You're not intruding – and in any case, you know two of our visitors. Andrew and Rosine Maynard are staying overnight, with another friend of theirs.'

'Yes, Nicholas told me. I do hope that we can all get together the next time they come to Cheshire.'

'A drink, then?'

'Well, if you have a bottle open. Maudie!' he called, as the girls moved towards the house. 'We won't be staying long, so don't disappear on me.'

She nodded, and continued on her way with Louisa. I looked at Nicholas. His hands were filthy, presumably from rummaging in the Mini's inner workings, and a long smudge of grease ran down his shirt.

'Please go and wash, and change your clothes. You look disgraceful,' I told him firmly, as I led Ian to the kitchen, and Nicholas sloped off, evidently recognising he was out of favour with me at present.

I took a bottle of white wine from the fridge, and looked round for the corkscrew, but Ian took over as I started to wrestle with the foil.

'Please – allow me,' he murmured. He opened the bottle with a deft twist, and poured two glasses.

'Cheers,' I said brightly. 'Shall we sit in the conservatory?'

We settled ourselves in opposing chairs. Ian was in a good mood. He asked me for the recent news of Rosine and Andrew, and then said, in courteous tones,

'Nicholas is a nice boy. Does he look like his father?'

Nick and Ian had never met, although their paths had crossed so dramatically all those years ago.

'Not really. They have the same colouring, but Nick was quite devastatingly handsome, with the most knockout smile —'

I broke off, realising this was not very tactful of me. Ian gave me a pained glance.

'You needn't rub it in.'

'Don't tell me that it bothers you, Ian. You know you always had a queue of women falling at your feet.'

I couldn't help laughing, and a reluctant smile crossed his face too, as we remembered old days.

Nicholas appeared, looking presentable again. He didn't seem to be interested in Maudie, who was probably too young for him anyway, but I thought I might need to give him a hint later, to put him on his guard.

He began to talk with enthusiasm to Ian about marketing and career paths, and I had the feeling they had conversed in depth on the subject before. I didn't intend to interfere. I thought that Ian might conceivably be useful to Nicholas in helping him weigh up different options. My own experience told me that he would get little practical help from his university or college.

After ten minutes or so, Ian looked at his watch.

'We ought to be going. Please give my best regards to Andrew and Rosine, and I hope you have a great time. Would you mind fetching Maudie please, Nicholas?'

Nicholas went in search of the girls. Ian rose from his seat, and put his wine glass down. He seemed very tall as he stood over me, smiling as if there was something pleasant on his mind.

'You look very pretty today, Eithne. Sometimes I find it hard to believe that you have such grown up children. Thank you for the drink,' he said. Then he bent down swiftly, put a hand on my shoulder, and kissed me on the lips – a real kiss, gentle, lingering, with a hint of tongue. Taken by surprise, I felt a warm response flood through me, and it seemed an age before he released me and straightened up again.

'Ian – I'm not sure that was a good idea,' I muttered, conscious of the blood rising to my cheeks. He was looking like the cat who got the cream. He picked up my hand, and kissed that too.

'Don't you think you owe me a few, Eithne? I'm looking forward to collecting some more,' he said, with a provocative grin.

I was relieved to hear the children clattering through the kitchen, and stood up, smoothing back my hair. Perhaps this was Ian's idea of a little joke, in which case, I would have to make sure we were not alone together very often in future.

As he and Maudie were leaving, Maudie issued an invitation to my children to go up to the Court later on, to play table tennis.

'Thanks, Maudie, but we have company. Maybe tomorrow,' Lou said diplomatically.

What did Ian think he was playing at? I was puzzled, as I returned to the kitchen and the dinner preparations. It was inappropriate behaviour, and I should not have responded in the way I did. I was disappointed to think I might not be able to trust him – or myself – after all.

# Chapter 5

There was a flurry of activity almost as soon as Ian and Maudie left. Peter arrived home from work, and I explained why I had already started on the white wine. He turned to Nicholas, with ill-concealed irritation.

'Any idea what the problem is with the car?' he asked, putting another bottle in the refrigerator. 'What's the state of the battery these days?'

'It isn't the battery, Dad. Perhaps we can run up tomorrow and have a look at it. You usually manage to sort it out.'

Peter growled. He looked put out, and I hoped this would not spoil our evening. Before he could say anything else, Andrew, Rosine and their visitor drove up to the house, and we all assumed our best manners to welcome them.

Rosine and Andrew kissed me with a warmth which surprised and pleased me. I'd always been close to Rosine, especially since Nick's death, but living so far apart meant that we didn't manage to meet very often, which was a constant regret.

I surveyed Luke Simons closely as we were introduced. He was slim and of medium height, in his early fifties, and dressed in that inimitable preppy style favoured by wealthy Americans. He reminded me of my old friend and mentor John, from my university days.

Luke seemed to be especially interested in Nicholas, and I assumed that was because of his previous friendship with Nick. Over drinks in the conservatory, I heard the two of them chatting amicably, and hoped it was interesting for Nicholas to learn something about his father's life in the States.

Conversation flowed pleasantly over dinner, but I had an uneasy feeling that there was some sort of elephant in the room. No one had yet given any special reason for Luke's visit, and I had not had time to speak to him much myself, occupied as I was with domestic duties. I noticed that he ate sparingly of the casserole I had made, but he gave a greedy gasp when I brought in the trifle, decorated with almonds and sugared rose petals.

'This is exactly what I like, Eithne,' he said. 'Old fashioned English puds are my weakness. It's a good job my partner Ray isn't here. He's always making me count the calories, but in his absence, I propose to do justice to this creation.'

We laughed, but my suspicions were aroused. Partner ... obviously, Luke was gay. Could he and Nick have had an affair? But I immediately dismissed the thought, with an inward chuckle. In all my time with Nick, he had never been anything but enthusiastically heterosexual.

As I was clearing away, Peter asked Lou about her plans for the weekend.

'Not sure, Daddy,' she replied. 'Maudie asked us up tonight for table tennis, but I said we had visitors.'

Andrew looked up swiftly, as if sensing an opportunity.

'It seems a shame to keep the young ones in to listen to us oldies reminiscing,' he said, his voice carefully modulated. 'I haven't drunk very much. I could take them to the Inglises and collect them later. I understand it's not far.'

I was very surprised by this offer.

'Surely the children can give the Inglises a miss for once, when we have visitors?' I exclaimed.

Andrew sent Peter a meaningful glance. Something was going on which I did not understand. Peter said quickly,

'Are you happy for them to do that, Andrew? I can take them there, that might be easier.'

'Well, if that's all right with you, Peter ...'

After picking up on the cues I had been given, I turned to the children.

'Get ready quickly now, and you must be ready to come away when your father comes for you later on.'

They disappeared, fleet-footed, to collect their things, and I sent a quizzical glance in Andrew's direction. He came across, and whispered in my ear.

'Thanks, Eithne. You'll understand in a while,' he murmured.

'Let me give you a hand with the dishes,' interrupted Rosine. We chatted casually as we cleared away the meal, but my mind was agitated. I wondered why Andrew had been so keen to get rid of the children, and I was definitely worried now.

'Is everything all right, Rosine?' I asked, as I untied my apron. 'I have the distinct feeling that there's something going on, and I'd rather not be kept in the dark.'

'Can we talk over coffee? There is something we want to discuss with you, but it's complicated, and we'll need to take our time over it. I think Peter needs to be here, too.'

I couldn't begin to fathom out this mystery. I made coffee, and by the time I'd carried the tray into the conservatory, Peter had returned from dropping off the kids. He came in, smoothing back his cropped hair, and frowning.

'I can't believe the Inglis parents will want to put up with entertaining the local teenagers for much longer. It's like a bear garden up there,' he said. 'But it's been useful tonight.'

He sat beside me, and I poured coffee, with a hand which was a little tremulous. There was a sense of expectation in the room, and I waited anxiously for one of our visitors to break the silence. Luke glanced at Rosine and Andrew, and then he addressed me.

'Eithne, I expect you're wondering about the reason behind this visit. First, I want you to know that Nick and I became great buddies during his last months in New York. I was doing some freelance writing for *Sphere* at the same time, and I admired Nick and his work very much. Nick often visited for weekends with me and my family in the Hamptons, and we were all very sorry when he decided to go back to England – although now I've met you, I can understand his desire to return. We were devastated when we heard about his death.'

Luke bowed his head towards me, and I gave an awkward smile. Somehow, I didn't think that Luke had come all this way to fill me in about a long defunct social life.

Rosine shifted in her chair. He continued his narrative.

'I would also like to tell you about a young man called Josh, my cousin's son.'

He paused for a moment, and his face clouded. 'His mother, Kate, was a single parent. Josh was born in late 1974. Thing is, Kate never let on about who Josh's father was. All she told us was that the baby was the result of a one-night stand, and she was in no kind of relationship with the guy involved. She knew he wouldn't be interested in a baby.'

He paused to drink his coffee, and I wondered where this story was heading. I was aware of sudden tension in Peter, sitting beside me, and his hand sought mine.

'Ray and I had quite a hand in Josh's upbringing, because Kate died of breast cancer when Josh was only four. She asked us to take care of him after she died. Her own parents were elderly, and they disapproved of her lifestyle, and weren't really interested in Josh. But he grew up to be a great kid. He was doing really well at MIT, studying engineering like Peter here.'

Luke coughed, and took another sip of coffee.

'Never gave us a moment's worry – until a few months ago. He got in with a bad crowd, fell for some airhead who dumped him, started taking drugs. As a result, he dropped out, and he's back home with us, very miserable and depressed. He's off the drugs now, but we're worried he'll end up doing something silly.'

Although I felt very sorry for the young man, I couldn't see that this was any concern of ours.

'He's been seeing my shrink, at our insistence,' Luke continued. 'We think that part of Josh's trouble is rooted in his insecurity. He's never really known who he is. He hardly remembers Kate, and no one could tell him anything about his father. He's very sensitive about his lack of background and not knowing where or whom he belongs to. We've done what we can, but it's not enough.'

'What about his grandparents? Surely they must have wanted to help in some way?' I asked. Luke grimaced.

'Very little, I'm afraid. Anyway, Kate's father's been dead for years, and her mother suffered from dementia. They couldn't give him what he needed. But something happened recently which has thrown some light on Josh's antecedents.'

I felt a little prickle on the back of my neck. Something told me I was not going to like this. Why could that be?

'Kate never let on about the identity of his father. As I said, it was a one-night stand, and she knew there was no future for her and the man responsible. He'd left the country before she even realised she was pregnant. But she did leave a whole trunk of stuff with us before she died. It's been taking up space in the attic, and recently, Ray persuaded me that we had to throw it out.'

He coughed nervously again. 'Before I chucked it all away, I sorted through it, in case there was anything which might be of interest, or help, to Josh. And I found some old diaries.'

The twilight deepened around us, and Peter got up to switch on the table lamps. My interest was aroused now.

'Well?' I prompted.

'I read them. I think I know now who Josh's father is,' Luke said, his voice very quiet and low.

'Isn't that a good thing? Perhaps you can put them in touch, if you do it tactfully,' I said.

'I'm afraid not. The man concerned is dead.'

There was a significant silence. Luke couldn't meet my enquiring gaze. Slow wheels were turning in my head, and suddenly I understood what he was trying to tell me. My head spun, and I felt faint.

'*What?* Are you saying that Nick was Josh's father? That's simply ridiculous! Nick never mentioned anything about it. I can't believe you're trying to pin this on a dead man!' I cried.

'Eithne, he didn't know. They weren't in a relationship. Kate was very honest about that. But it's evident from the diaries that they slept together on at least one occasion, after a family wedding. The dates are right, too.'

Peter came across the room and put an arm round my shoulders. I stared at him in disbelief.

'This is all some fantasy made up by a stupid girl,' I exclaimed, with rising anger. 'It's all too much of a coincidence. I don't believe a word of it.'

'Strange things happen, Eithne. Life's full of unexpected turns,' Luke said, his eyes fixed intently upon me, as if he was willing me to believe.

This time, the silence was awkward and hostile. Tears started a slow course down my cheeks.

'I can't understand why you would want to come and upset me like this,' I accused Luke. He frowned, looking agonised himself.

'Eithne, I am very sorry if this has upset you. But I would do anything in my power to help Josh. I traced Rosine first, and we've discussed all this, but I thought that if there was some way of bringing you together ...'

'No!' I shrieked. I felt a deep sense of outrage and betrayal, and then another thought crossed my mind. 'If you think you can come here and do Nicholas out of any part of his grandparents' inheritance, you'll have a fight on your hands! Rosine and Andrew won't take kindly to some unknown boy putting in a claim either. Don't you realise that?'

Now Luke flushed, and he looked angry and disconcerted in his turn.

'I can assure you that's the last thing on my mind. Josh is well off in his own right now his grandmother has died, and I don't believe he'd be entitled to anything here anyway,' he retorted.

'Well what do you want then? Why did you have to come and stir things up, and sully poor Nick's memory like this?'

My voice sounded high and strange to me, and I was conscious of my heart pounding. Peter held me tighter, his face pale and anxious.

'My darling, this has nothing to do with you and Nick, or your life together,' he said, with urgency. 'If I understand this, Luke simply wants to be able to help Josh find out about his biological father. If he's right, you are one of the few people who can help him do that, let alone the fact that Nicholas may be his half-brother.'

The thought pierced me like a sword. No one was going to usurp the special place that my son held amongst his relatives, no matter how good his claim.

'It's all false!' I shouted, pushing him aside, and jumping from my chair. 'Rosine, I can't believe that you think a word of this is true. I won't hear any more about it.'

I fled to the safety of my bedroom – I would have locked myself in if it were possible. Sobbing, I collapsed upon the bed. All kind of nightmare scenarios raced through my head, and I felt as though I was trapped in a horrible dream. I hated Luke, and I almost hated Nick, for putting me through this unexpected ordeal. My heart raced, as I wondered what this news would do to Nicholas – if it turned out to be true.

After a while, I was conscious of Peter sitting next to me. I turned my face away, unwilling to make contact with anyone in my grief.

'Eithne, darling, you must calm down,' he said gently, stroking my hair. 'I know you didn't want to hear any of this. You'll feel better in the morning, and then we can talk some more with the others. Luke's in a terrible state. He didn't think you'd react in this way.'

'Did he think I'd be pleased to hear about another bastard child?' I hissed. 'Did he think I would welcome confirmation of Nick's wild times in the States? Tell him to go, Peter, I never want to see him again. Why on earth did Rosine and Andrew bring him here?'

He sat there for a while in silence, stroking my back. Eventually, he said, 'I suppose they think that what he's saying may be true. If that's the case, then we have to acknowledge that Nicholas has an older half-brother. I must go and pick up the children now. Put the light out and get into bed. I'll tell them you've got a migraine, because I don't want them to see you like this. Try to see that it isn't as bad as you think, even if it turns out to be genuine. It all happened before you and Nick came together again. Nothing has changed.'

'Everything's changed ...' I muttered sulkily. Peter rose to go.

'Please get into bed, darling. I don't want the children worried,' he said emphatically.

'I don't want to see anyone.'

'I know.'

He left the room, and I heard the Jaguar drive away. Gulping, I dragged myself up, and went to the bathroom to splash my eyes with cold water. The face of an old woman looked back at me from the mirror, swollen and bleary. I snapped off the light, and pulled off my clothes carelessly, before groping for my nightdress and falling into bed. My sobs had subsided now, and my brain was reacting more rationally, but I pushed aside any attempts at processing the information I had received, and lay in a welcome stupor caused by so much weeping.

Some while later, the car returned, and I heard whispered voices outside the door.

'Can't I just say goodnight to her?' Nicholas was saying.

'I expect she's asleep by now. Please leave it until the morning.'

Peter's tone was firm, and the voices moved away. By the time Peter came to bed, I was drifting off, thankful that the events of the evening were fast receding.

I was dreaming about Nick, as I still did so often. In the dream, we were sitting on the balcony of my flat in Wapping. He gave me his beautiful smile, pushing back his floppy dark hair with an expressive hand, and as ever, my heart contracted with love for him.

'Of course, you knew I wasn't a saint all that time I was away from you,' he was saying, taking a drag on his cigarette. 'You even went and got engaged to somebody else – but it didn't matter when I came back. Nothing else matters now we're together again. When I get home from Africa, we'll have fun. Must do things before the baby comes, because there's so much still to do.'

'You don't come home from Africa!' I cried, tormented. He stretched out his arms to me, and then the vision faded, and I awoke in my bed at the Old Rectory. Tears filled my eyes as I realised it was only a dream, and I lay there almost wishing I was dead too.

At length, I blew my nose, and told myself to get a grip on things. Peter was fast asleep, his face pale and drawn, as though he was going through an equal torment – and perhaps he was.

I still looked very blotchy, but my face was at least recognisable in the mirror. My throat was dry. I felt desperately in need of tea, and pulled on my dressing gown, silently padding down the stairs to the kitchen. While the kettle was boiling, I opened the back door, and the cat ran gratefully into the dewy garden. Sunlight spilled into the room, and my mood slowly began to lift. It was a soft, scented morning, and I felt better for breathing the summer air and hearing a blackbird singing in the bushes.

There was a brief noise behind me, and Luke stood there in pyjamas and dressing gown, looking rumpled and anxious. I realised that he had passed a bad night too.

'Eithne, I am so sorry,' he murmured. 'I feel I've handled this whole thing very badly. You must know I never meant to upset you so much – but I owe it to Josh to help him if I can. I want you to meet him, Eithne. I want you to know him and tell him about his father. Is that too much to ask?'

I struggled to find the right words.

'I don't know what to do for the best. But if you are sure about all this, Luke, if you are really sure, then I suppose the least I can do is meet him and talk to him. There is one thing, though – I don't want to have to tell Nicholas about this until I believe that Josh absolutely is Nick's son.'

'I can live with that.'

His face relaxed, and he sat at the table while I made the tea. We sat quietly with our steaming mugs. The tension between us had dissipated, and I was grateful.

'It was just a one-night stand,' Luke told me, eyes fixed on the table. 'Kate was quite honest about that. She thought the condom had split. It does happen. Anyway, she realised that Nick wouldn't want a baby, let alone any kind of relationship, and she made no attempt to get in touch with him once he'd left, or let him know the result of their night together.'

I winced. I didn't want to think too closely about the details.

'That doesn't surprise me. He hardly wanted to know about Nicholas at first,' I murmured. 'Does Josh look like Nicholas?'

'No, I can't say that he does. Maybe there's a slight resemblance around the eyes. But even full siblings can look dissimilar,' Luke replied.

I turned the matter over in my mind. Last night, I had been furiously, illogically jealous of this unknown girl who had shared Nick's body. Today it just seemed a sad story, part of a sorrowful legacy which never really went away. If Nick had lived ... but then so many things would have been different.

'When do you propose that I meet Josh?' I asked Luke, thinking I would need some time before I could contemplate doing so.

'Well, he's here in England now, staying with some friends of mine in London. I sort of hoped we could all get together before I have to go back next week ...' His voice tailed off, and he looked at me with hopeful eyes.

I gasped. It seemed far too soon to me.

'Don't you think we should arrange for DNA testing?' I asked.

This process was just becoming available to settle family issues, and I clung to the thought like some kind of lifeline.

'I think that Andrew wants to take that route. I guess it's understandable, in the circumstances,' Luke replied. 'I have no objections, but I'm hoping there will be something about Josh which persuades you of the truth of all this.'

'And what about Nick's parents? It would be a terrible shock to discover their son left another child behind.'

This thought worried me intensely. I knew that Nick's mother's health was not robust, and the upset might well be too much for her.

'I don't know, Eithne. I have to leave that to Rosine and you to decide.'

The situation was growing more and more complicated.

'Please don't let the children know,' I said. I wanted to shield them from the worst of the drama which might unfold, and I could not believe that Nicholas would welcome the prospect of a half-sibling who might encroach on his special territory. 'I don't want them involved until things are clearer. And if you really want me to meet Josh now, it will have to be in London. I can't have him here.'

'Yes, I understand.'

'Have you told Josh about all this?'

'No, not yet. I will do so, before you meet. It will be a huge shock for him, too.'

I heard footsteps in the corridor, and made a warning face at Luke. Nicholas breezed in, stopping short when he saw me.

'Jesus, Mum, are you all right? You look terrible.'

He came across and bent to kiss my cheek. I put my hand up to his face, feeling a great rush of love for him, unwilling to disturb his happy existence in any way. It looked as though we would be shaking his world to its foundations if this turned out to be true.

'I had a bad night, darling, but I'm okay now. Did you have fun at Delamere Court?'

'Well, not fun exactly. I had a long talk with Ian. He's had a very interesting life. It must have been great working with him.'

I was conscious that my everyday life had suddenly grown very complicated, full of secrets and surprises, and I wondered why on earth I had ever wished for change. The last time I had felt happy and carefree was during my trip to Chester with Olivia, and I realised with chagrin that I missed her brusque common sense. I felt she would deal with all this stuff about Josh much better than me.

Rosine and Andrew came in for breakfast, and the conversation became more general. Louisa appeared, and began to demolish a large plate of toast, prior to her riding lesson. I was just thinking of waking Peter, when he walked in, looking tired and strained. He glanced quickly in my direction, and seemed relieved that I was apparently back to my normal self, albeit rather puffy round the eyes.

'Is your head better, Eithne?' he asked, giving Lou a quick pat on the back as she finished her toast and rose from the table.

'Yes, loads, thanks. Things are getting back to normal,' I told him, messaging with my eyes that I was beginning to deal with the trauma of the evening before. His shoulders relaxed, and I felt a twinge of guilt for giving him a difficult time.

Nicholas looked across at him, biting his lower lip, a sign that he was feeling abashed.

'Dad – when would it be convenient for you to come and take a look at the Mini?' he asked, his manner somewhat more subdued than normal. Peter groaned.

'I'd forgotten the blasted car. I suppose it'll have to be this morning. Give me an hour or so, Nicholas, then we'll go across. I just hope it's something I can deal with.'

We lingered over breakfast, as if we were all unwilling to face the difficult situations awaiting us.

'What do you have planned? Do you mind if I go with Nicholas?' Peter asked me, as he rose to go. I looked at Luke.

'I think that Rosine and Eithne and I need to spend a little more time together,' he said quickly.

'Yes, I agree. But you go with Nicholas, Peter. I can cope with things today,' I said.

Peter sent me a resigned look as he left with Nicholas for Delamere Court. I smiled in sympathy, hoping he would be able to manage the combination of car and Inglises without too much stress. It wasn't turning out to be the best weekend for him, either.

After breakfast, Rosine, Luke and I wandered idly round the garden. Now the emotion of the previous night had subsided, I felt strangely calm, and could not understand why I had reacted so strongly to Luke's story – as Peter said, nothing had really changed for me. Nicholas was now my main concern, and I said as much to my companions.

'He may be delighted to find he has a half-brother,' Luke said. 'He seems to be a sensible and mature person, so why should he be threatened by Josh? And I know that Josh will be over the moon to find he has someone with whom he has a blood tie. It was such a shame that Kate's mom couldn't be persuaded to take an interest in him. Ray and I tried our hardest, but I think Josh has always been sad that he missed out on being part of a proper family unit.'

We sat on the bench under the cedar tree at the far end of the lawn, enjoying the scent of roses massed in a nearby flower bed.

'Nicholas has been lucky. He's always had a family, he's always been loved,' Luke continued. 'It's obvious that he thinks of Peter as his father. I don't see why this should hit him too hard.'

I was not convinced. Nicholas did regard Peter as his father, but he also enjoyed the special position he held amongst the DeLisles, as the only descendant of their adored, and much mourned Nick. I could not see him wanting to share that, and I was apprehensive on his behalf, although common sense dictated that the boy who had been cherished since babyhood, and whose mother had shared Nick's life, would always be the favoured one.

The sun was shining strongly now, and the air was alive with insects and busy birds. We relaxed on the seat, and I began to feel sleepy after the turmoil of the night before.

'What would Nick want me to do?' I asked myself. The question was impossible to answer. He had been reluctant to embrace fatherhood, and I thought he would have been appalled and then disinterested at the thought of anything resulting from a one-night stand. However, I didn't think that prevented me from being bothered in his stead.

Luke returned to the house, and Rosine and I were left alone. She put an arm round my shoulders, in a hesitant, apologetic way.

'I am so sorry that we've sprung this on you, Eithne, but we couldn't see what else to do. Andrew has really grilled Luke on the details of all this, and he thinks that his story may hold up. But we will insist that a DNA test is carried out before things go any further.'

I gave a huge sigh.

'I'm beginning to see that it could perhaps be true. But do you really think this young man needs our involvement in his life? I assume he isn't after any financial gain – whatever else I may feel about Luke, I can see he is a person of integrity. Would it really help Josh as much as Luke appears to think?'

'That I can't say. But, Eithne, if he is Nick's son, then Nicholas has a right to know, and the family must accept some responsibilities.'

We sat in the sun for a few moments, each occupied with our own thoughts. Eventually, Rosine said,

'Luke asked us to show him some photos of Nick, in case there is any marked resemblance to Josh. After all, it's over twenty years since Luke saw Nick, and memory can play one false. But for some reason, we hardly have any. In our wedding pictures, Nick's almost unrecognisable in that morning suit he wore. Do you have any photos we could see?'

Did I have any photos of Nick? Yes, secreted in a little folder, which I occasionally took out and wept a few tears over, when no one else was around. There were not nearly enough. For some reason, we had never taken or kept very many, but there were one or two excellent likenesses.

'Yes, I do have some. Come inside, and I'll fetch them.'

We walked back to the house, both deep in thought, and sharing a similar sorrow. I had lost my partner and my baby's father. Rosine had lost her only brother. Although years had gone by, the sadness was still raw at times like this.

Rosine went to find Luke and Andrew, to bring them into the conservatory. I went upstairs for the photographs.

I wasn't going to bring the entire folder down. That contained some precious letters and keepsakes as well as the photos, but I selected a couple of the clearer pictures. Sighing, I sat on the bed for a few minutes, studying the well-loved face. I could go for months on an even keel, keeping Nick's memory alive without too much pain, and then something would happen which would bring everything back to me in unbearable detail, and I would have a bad few days. Now I could feel grief welling up in me again.

As I returned downstairs, Peter walked into the hall. There was no sign of Nicholas, and I hoped this did not mean there were insuperable issues with the car, but Peter merely said to me,

'There was a problem with the fuel pump relay. Somehow, he'd got it wet, and it shorted out. Anyway, I managed to get a new part from Crosby's, and it's fixed now. Nicholas is staying there for lunch.'

I pulled a face.

'He does spend a lot of time with them. Was everything all right with Ian?'

Peter sent me a wry glance.

'Smooth sod, isn't he? Anyway, we were civil enough. Nicholas certainly seems to think he's the world's wonder at present.'

His tone was very dry. Was he hurt by Nicholas' interest in a man whom he had cause to distrust? I felt upset on Peter's behalf.

'It's just a passing phase,' I said, reaching out to give him a hug. 'He's a bit dazzled by Ian and his contacts, that's all. That doesn't compare to a dad who can fix cars.'

Peter grunted, but his face cleared, and he looked happier. I stood with my face against his shoulder, absorbing his familiar, comforting presence.

'Where are the others?' he asked.

'In the conservatory. They want to see some pictures of Nick.'

He looked anxiously at me.

'Are you okay with that, my love?'

'Yes. I can see we need to do it.'

He stroked a curl back from my face.

'I've been asking myself what Nick would have wanted us to do, but I really can't decide,' he said.

'Me neither,' I whispered.

We stood together for a moment, then went to join the others. As soon as Rosine saw the photos, she burst out crying, and that set me off, too.

'Darling Nick! It's so unfair, such a waste of a life,' she sobbed, looking to her husband for consolation. 'He didn't deserve to die so young.'

The men stood by awkwardly as we mopped up the tears. When she was in control of herself again, Rosine turned to Peter, touching him on the shoulder.

'Peter, I am sorry. I'm not denigrating you in any way. You know how grateful we are to you for being such a wonderful father to Nicholas.'

'Yes, I know. Please don't worry about it,' he murmured, looking embarrassed. It was a difficult situation for him, in a different way.

Andrew passed the pictures to Luke, who studied them with care. After a minute or so, he looked across to me.

'I'm not sure if these are much help,' he said, disappointment in his voice. 'Apart from the colouring, these photos don't look much like Nicholas, who we know is a direct descendant. Josh doesn't have dark hair or eyes, but there's something about the smile in this photo – I could swear there's a likeness there.'

Nick had a distinctive and devastating smile, once seen, never forgotten. A pang shot through me. I had always regretted that Nicholas had not inherited that feature from his father, and I would be most upset to find it in this American boy.

I began to harden my heart against Josh.

Luke was still studying the photos.

'I had forgotten how handsome Nick was,' he said quietly, laying the photos down and giving me a look which expressed understanding and concern. 'Both Nicholas and Josh are nice looking boys, but they can't compete with their father.'

Andrew had been fidgeting with a paperweight during this conversation. Now, he put it down, and looked hard at Luke.

'I assume you still want to pursue this,' he said. 'Don't you think you might make things worse for Josh if you raise his hopes, and then we find out he isn't related to the DeLisles? What if Kate had sex with someone else back then, and just didn't record the fact?'

Luke drew himself up, and took a deep breath.

'I believe that Josh needs to know about his parentage,' he stated. 'I am quite happy for you to do all the testing you want. I'm already convinced that he is Nick's son, and I want Josh to get some understanding of his father's life, and hopefully, to establish some sort of relationship with his blood relations. Eithne, too – she knew Nick better than anybody. Josh needs that knowledge to be able to find himself.'

There was a long silence, while we pondered on his words. I began to see that there was only one way to take this forward, and Andrew said what I was thinking.

'We must insist on DNA testing, Luke. We have to be sure,' he said.

'When the presumed father is dead, it gets more complicated,' Luke said. 'But if Nicholas and Rosine are prepared to give cell swabs, we ought to be able to determine the paternity one way or another.'

I looked unhappily at Peter.

'That means we will need to tell Nicholas,' I murmured. I had hoped we would not need to involve him until we knew the truth.

'But who will tell him?' Peter asked. He had been following the conversation intently, and I knew he wanted to protect Nicholas as much as possible.

We all looked at one another. After a while, Rosine said,

'I think Peter should tell him. Eithne will get too upset, and Peter is someone who Nicholas loves and trusts, and who has always been there for him. Would you do it, Peter?'

My husband looked surprised, but I thought he was pleased as well, to have this acknowledgement that the DeLisles appreciated his care for his stepson. I was pleased, too. I thought he deserved nothing less.

'I'll do it if you want,' he agreed. 'But I must tell Nicholas that nothing is certain at this stage. It's not ideal, but I can't think of any other way.'

This brought matters to some kind of close. We had a quick lunch at the Three Feathers, and our visitors took their leave. After some discussion, Rosine and I agreed to meet Luke and Josh in London for lunch on Wednesday. We stipulated that Josh should understand that the situation was unclear, and that tests would need to be carried out, to settle the question one way or another.

I didn't look forward to Wednesday at all.

After our guests had departed, we tried to resume our normal Saturday lives. I stripped the beds and put some washing on, and wandered through to where Peter was reading the papers. He looked up at me, his face sombre.

'It's a shame you can't just meet the boy, show him a few photos, and tell him 'your father was incredibly handsome and charming, but most of the time he was a totally selfish bastard,' and be done with it,' he said.

'Peter!'

I was furious. 'That's not very fair.'

He shrugged his shoulders.

'Nick never could keep it zipped up,' he stated, and my jaw dropped.

He glanced at my angry face, and became defensive. 'You do idealise Nick, you know. Sometimes I wish you would be able to accept that he was just as human as the rest of us – and capable of some less than perfect behaviour. But perhaps it's too late for that.'

He put down the paper, walked away, and I heard the door of his study bang. This was getting to him as much as it was to me. I wanted to go after him and demand a proper apology, but Louisa burst in full of excited chat about her morning, and the moment passed.

At teatime, Peter came in to the kitchen, still wearing a very long face. Louisa's presence meant he could not allude to our previous conversation, however, he came across and gave me a swift hug. I knew he would be feeling sorry for his uncharacteristically harsh words, but I was still sore.

He kissed me, and Louisa went out to the guinea pigs. When he was sure she was out of earshot, Peter turned to me.

'I'll speak to Nicholas as soon as he gets back from Delamere Court,' he murmured. 'If it has to be done, I'd rather get it over with.'

No sooner had he spoken, than Nicholas roared into the drive. The Mini had evidently recovered from its recent problems.

'No time like the present,' Peter said, looking a little grim, and he went outside.

Lou settled down with the TV in the snug. I started to prepare supper, worrying how Nicholas was going to react to this potentially life changing scenario. It was too much to hope that he would be pleased with the news, but he might perhaps be intrigued.

The minutes ticked by. I was on tenterhooks, and eventually, I couldn't stand the tension any longer. I found Nicholas and Peter in the drive, standing over the Mini. Its bonnet was raised, and they were inspecting its anatomy. Why wasn't Peter doing what he had promised?

They both looked up as I approached.

'Mum!'

Nicholas extended a dirty hand towards me, and I recoiled.

'Darling – you are *filthy*,' I exclaimed.

'Sorry, Mum. Dad's just been giving me the lowdown about Luke and this other boy, and then I wanted him to look at the relay again,' Nicholas explained, seemingly unperturbed by the bombshell which had struck the rest of us. Seeing my face, he went on hastily, 'It's a bit of a bummer, but I suppose it has to be sorted out. I'm sorry if you've been upset, Mum, but don't worry too much. If I had a dozen half-brothers, I don't see how it could affect me, so long as they're not after my grandparents' money. I'm not going to live in America, and I don't suppose this other chap will want to live here. Hopefully, it will all blow over once he's been able to meet you and Aunt Rosine.'

I was silent, digesting this. It appeared to me that Nicholas had not even begun to think about the full implications of the matter. Peter sent me an exasperated grimace from under the bonnet.

'Anyway, I have some good news,' my son continued, his face beaming. 'Ian's arranged for me to visit Laine and Laine on Monday, to see about getting some work experience. I'll go in with him. He wants to see Derek Laine anyway, so it all fits in very well.'

This was obviously more important than anything else in Nicholas's current universe. I didn't know whether to be pleased or annoyed.

'That's very good of Ian,' I murmured. I did not like to feel we were indebted to him, but this could be useful for Nicholas, and it was a welcome distraction in the current circumstances. Peter slammed the bonnet shut.

'It's fine now,' he told Nicholas. 'You had better go and make sure you have suitable clothes for this interview. Wash your hands first.'

Nicholas strolled away, humming to himself. I looked enquiringly at Peter, who shrugged his shoulders.

'He can't think about anything except bloody Ian Inglis and Laine and Laine,' he said, sighing. 'I thought at least that he might be interested in Josh, but he doesn't seem to realise what the acquisition of a half-sibling might mean. Perhaps it's for the best at the moment.'

'Why is Ian being so helpful? Do you think he has an ulterior motive?' I queried, unable to quell a niggle of suspicion.

'Like what? No, I think perhaps he's bored in the country, and this helps to keep him amused,' said sensible Peter.

Supper was a quiet meal. Peter and I were drained by the recent upheavals. Lou was tired from riding, and Nicholas was thinking about his forthcoming interview. Before we turned in for the night, I asked Nicholas to switch off the lights in the conservatory. He did so, returning with the photos of his father, which we had left there in the morning.

'Is that why you were looking at these?' he asked me, examining the pictures with interest. 'He was really good looking, wasn't he? I can see why you fell for him. Please don't be upset by this Josh stuff. Dad said it was before the two of you got back together, and Aunt Rosine always tells me how much he – my real dad – loved you. I wish I'd known him,' he added.

My heart throbbed painfully.

'Oh, darling. I wish you had, too,' I murmured.

When I went upstairs, Peter was reading in bed. He glanced across the room at me, and put down his book.

'I suppose it isn't rational, but I find it hard to forgive Nick for this upheaval,' he said, perhaps wanting to justify his earlier outburst. 'I don't want my family hurt as a result of some fling he had twenty-five years ago.'

I didn't know how to respond. It wasn't as if Nick had intended any of this to happen, after all.

'I worry about the children growing away from us,' he continued, as I slipped on my nightdress and got into bed. 'Nicholas is starting to spread his wings, and I can see that Olivia will be the next to go. Why should we allow Nicholas to be upset just to make some stranger feel better? Things are getting beyond our control.'

I grunted, and turned over to sleep. It would be some time before I forgave him for his totally unfair words about Nick.

# Chapter 6

We all got up late on Sunday, and I made us a cooked breakfast, as a treat. Nicholas was in excellent spirits, and chattered happily about all manner of things, except Josh, of course, as we didn't want Louisa or Olivia to be told about the matter at present.

'Sam and Ian were very impressed with the way you sorted the Mini out, Dad.'

Nicholas yawned, and stretched. He was still in his pyjamas, and his rumpled hair made him seem like a little boy again. I was very sad to think of the disruption which might be in store for him.

Peter looked across at us, his face reflective. I think he was also feeling sensitive on Nicholas's behalf.

'You seem to get on well with Ian and Sam,' he said carefully. 'What is it that attracts you so much? Apart from the lavish lifestyle, that is.'

Nicholas looked surprised, but he managed a laugh.

'It isn't so much that. Ian's got a lot of business experience which interests me. I wish I had a bent for engineering, Dad, but you know how bad I am at that sort of thing. It isn't feasible to think that I could come into the firm and take it on when you retire. I just couldn't do it. So I'll have to make a career elsewhere. Ian's helping me weigh up some of my options, but that's only because he's got the know-how.'

He paused. 'Sam is okay once he drops the self-important stuff, and Laura and Maudie are always very welcoming.'

'I think Maudie likes you,' I said, teasingly, recalling the sheep's eyes she had been making at him. Nicholas wrinkled his nose.

'She's a nice kid – but she's just a kid, Mum. She'll get over it soon enough.'

Poor Maudie. I hoped that it was only a passing crush.

Later on, Peter and I worked in the garden, both of us rather silent, as we tried to come to terms with the events of the weekend.

'I'm glad it's Monday tomorrow,' murmured Peter, as we lay in bed later on, too tired to move. 'Work is going to be a piece of cake after the weekend we've just spent.'

We now had a period of relative calm. I went into Chester on Monday, returning in the late afternoon to find Nicholas and Ian having a cup of tea in our kitchen. Nicholas was exultant, as he had made a good impression on Derek Laine, and he was going to start his work experience the following day.

'I'm getting paid, too. Not much, but it all helps. As for getting there, I thought I'd go in to the office with Dad, then get the tram in.'

He had it all worked out.

I looked at Ian, who was calmly eating a large piece of cherry cake. As ever, he was expensively suited and booted, and looked very much at home, as he sprawled in the rocker by the window.

'This has been extremely kind of you, Ian. Peter and I really do appreciate your help,' I said, hoping that Peter was right in his assessment of the situation.

'It's my pleasure.'

Ian studied the cake with interest. 'Did you make this, Eithne? It's very good. I seem to remember you could scarcely boil an egg in the old days.'

Nicholas laughed, interested in this picture of his mother's youthful prowess – or lack of it.

'What was Mum like when she worked for Mackerras Mackay?' he enquired, with a cheeky grin.

Ian smiled, and a reflective look came over his face.

'Well, very pretty, obviously, and she was efficient at her job. But she was not at all domestic. Luckily, I had a cleaner and a laundry service, and Harrods delivered to Chelsea, where my flat was.'

I gasped, taken aback by this revelation. Was it just a careless slip of the tongue? Nicholas' face was a study, as he took in the underlying meaning behind Ian's words, and he turned questioning, almost hostile, eyes on me. I had to think quickly.

'I don't think I could have even sewed a button on when I was at Oxford,' I said, laughing. 'But I'm sure I make up for that now.'

The conversation moved on to less dangerous ground. I told Ian I would be in touch with Laura to agree a date for them to come to dinner.

'I'll give her a ring later this week. I'm off to London on Wednesday, for the day.' I said.

Ian purred away in his Mercedes, and Nicholas accompanied me back to the kitchen. He seemed distracted, fiddling with a sliver of cake, and slopping the milk as he poured himself a glass. I knew what was coming, and braced myself.

'Mum – what did Ian mean about you not being domesticated?' he asked, after a pause. 'How could that have mattered at work? Did you go out with him or something?'

I considered what I ought to tell him. Although I had agreed to keep our past connection a secret, I felt that Ian himself had revealed too much for me to brush things under the carpet. Nicholas would have to know the truth, but I would ask him to keep silent about it. I leaned against the table, and looked him in the face.

'Yes, we had a relationship,' I told him. 'In fact, we were briefly engaged, but I broke it off when your father came back into my life, and I realised how much I still loved him. We agreed that we didn't want that generally known here. Dad and Laura are aware of it, but not the children. I can only think Ian wasn't concentrating and forgot himself today. Anyway, Nicholas, I am telling you this in confidence, so you must keep it to yourself.'

'You were *engaged!* '

Nicholas' tone was disbelieving, and this annoyed me.

'Yes. Why do you sound so amazed? Anyway, you should be glad we didn't marry. You wouldn't be here now if we had.'

'I know. But I would have thought Ian was a great catch,' said my irritating child. I sighed, knowing how difficult it was to explain my actions in those distant days.

'Materially and physically, I suppose so. However, he's a very controlling person, and I didn't love him like I loved your father. Can we leave it like that?'

He muttered, and slouched out of the room. Poor Nicholas. Life was springing surprises on him from all directions at present.

Later on, I told Peter what had happened. He was amused.

'Bit careless of Ian, really. Anyway, Nicholas is good at keeping secrets. I don't think it matters if he knows.'

Luke rang me on Monday, thanking us for our hospitality, and saying that he had spoken with Josh, who was thunderstruck by the revelations. Now, they were both looking forward to our meeting on Wednesday. Rosine and I agreed to have a coffee together at Euston first, in order to decide how we would handle the discussions, and to brace ourselves for what might turn out to be a very awkward meal.

I was uptight on Wednesday morning, and Peter tried to calm me.

'Just take things very slowly,' he advised. 'I don't really understand why Luke is so keen for you to meet each other at this stage, but you needn't commit yourself to anything. Having Rosine there will help. And don't forget that Olivia will be home tonight. That's something for you to look forward to.'

Was it? I wondered how long it would be before she winkled out the secret the rest of us were keeping.

I drove myself to Crewe, to catch a fast train at about nine thirty, after the rush hour was over. I stood on the platform, lost in thought, while contemplating the day ahead of me, and I jumped about a foot when a deep voice said in my ear,

'Good morning, Eithne. How very nice to see you.'

It was Ian, looking distinguished in a pale grey suit and lavender tie. He embraced me gravely, and over his shoulder, I saw Laura emerge from the shop and saunter towards us. She wore an elegant navy two piece, and her blonde bob brushed her shoulders. For a moment, I felt provincial and underdressed in my cotton summer frock and cardigan. It was annoying that Laura always looked as though she had stepped out of a fashion magazine, but I told myself stoutly that she could afford to dress in a way which was beyond my reach.

'Eithne, hullo. Are you catching the London train?' Laura enquired, smoothing her cuffs.

'Yes. I'm meeting Rosine for some family business,' I faltered.

'How nice. We can sit together,' Ian beamed.

'I'm travelling Second Class,' I began – I knew they wouldn't be – but Ian immediately replied,

'Then it will be my pleasure to upgrade your ticket.'

Before I could object, the train whistled in to the platform. Ian took my elbow, and led me firmly towards the First Class compartments, as ever, sparsely populated with travellers. We sat at a table, the two of them facing me in calm contemplation, and I wished I didn't feel so much like a mouse, about to be tormented by a couple of sleek cats.

'This is a much more comfortable way to travel,' he told me. I supposed it was, if money was no object.

There was a banging of doors, whistles blew, and the train began to pull away.

'Are you going to London for business or pleasure?' I murmured, wondering how I would manage to keep up a conversation for the hour and a half ahead of us.

'For both.'

Laura gave a tinkly laugh. 'Ian has a boring meeting, and I'm seeing a girlfriend for lunch and shopping in Peter Jones.'

The train manager appeared, and there was a slight skirmish as I tried, and failed, to pay for my upgraded ticket.

'It's very kind of you, Ian.'

I was unwilling to feel myself under yet another obligation, but it was not worth the fuss of objecting further. With an effort, I turned to Laura.

'Peter and I are very grateful to Ian for all the help he's been giving Nicholas with work experience. He really enjoyed his first day with Laine and Laine,' I said. She nodded, but did not appear to be surprised.

'I'm pleased for him. It's useful, having good contacts,' she replied.

Ian added smoothly,

'I hope your husband doesn't mind, Eithne. Obviously, he's in a different line of business, and it's more difficult for him to point Nicholas in the right direction. I understand that Nicholas isn't a technical person, and his skills are more suited to marketing or advertising.'

'Ian says that Nicholas reminds him of himself, when he was young,' Laura told me with another annoying little giggle.

'Really?'

I hoped I sounded amused rather than appalled. 'In what way, exactly?'

'Bright, ambitious, curious about things.'

Ian's tone was decisive. 'Our daughter certainly thinks he's the bee's knees.'

'Oh dear. I don't think Nicholas is really up for romantic entanglements,' I said. 'I hope it's just an adolescent crush.'

The train was travelling at speed now. I gazed out of the window at fields and cows, searching for conversational inspiration, and asked them about their plans for Delamere Court (extensive and expensive), and the children, (education their main priority), but eventually, I ran out of ideas. It was Laura's turn.

'How did you come to marry Peter? I know now that he isn't Nicholas's real father,' she asked, betraying signs of interest.

'Well, I'd known Peter for as long as I'd known Nick. They were school friends, and somehow, Peter was always supportive when Nick and I weren't together,' I replied. 'He was very good to me after Nick died, and he'd been through a difficult divorce himself. In the end, it seemed a natural progression.'

'How nice. That's really rather romantic!' she exclaimed, surprising me. I had never thought of things in that light before; the arrangement had seemed to be practical as much as romantic at the time. However, I felt pleased by this view of our marriage, which seemed to offer a new confirmation that I had made the right decisions in the past.

There was silence for a while. Ian got up to go to the lavatory, and during his absence, Laura said, with an extreme lack of tact, which amazed me,

'I can't really envisage you with Ian. I don't think you would have been strong enough to deal with him, Eithne.'

I gaped at her, wondering where on earth the conversation was headed, but she seemed to find it amusing.

'You may be right,' I murmured, very unwilling to pursue this any further.

'Has it been difficult, seeing him again?' she continued, perfect eyebrows lifted in enquiry. 'Is there some little part of you that wishes you were still together? It's a strange situation in some ways, you must admit.'

I felt myself blushing under this cross examination, although I would have given anything not to do so.

'Well, it was all a long time ago. It's nice that we can be friends now.'

This conversation was veering into territory which I would prefer to leave unexplored. My cheeks grew even warmer, as I recalled the kiss Ian had given me in the conservatory and my enjoyment of the physical contact between us.

Laura gave a little, crinkly smile.

'I'm quite used to women wanting my husband, but that doesn't mean I let him out to play.'

What did she think she was doing? Warning me off? I had no intention of enticing Ian out to play, as she phrased it, despite his attempts to engage me in a little light flirtation.

I was extremely relieved to see Ian return to his seat. We chatted about Rosine and Andrew, and I told them of Flora's engagement. They knew her fiancé's family, and both agreed it was a good match. Then the buffet trolley clanked in, and we all accepted coffee.

Laura got up to use the facilities. I hoped fervently that Ian would not give me any conversational shocks in her absence, but he merely smiled at me, and said

'This reminds me of old times. I like that apricot colour you're wearing. It complements your complexion.'

'And you look very smart – but then, you always did have the most beautiful suits. Do you still go to the same tailor?'

'Yes, I do. I can't get away from Savile Row. They're always reliable.'

I suddenly remembered something I needed to say to him.

'By the way, Ian, you really let the cat out of the bag the other day, when you were talking about my lack of domestic skills. I'm afraid Nicholas put two and two together,' I said rapidly. He grinned.

'I did realise afterwards what I'd done. I wasn't thinking. Was he very surprised?'

'I think he wonders why I let you get away.'

Perhaps that wasn't the most sensible thing to say. I bit my lip. He gave me a quick, searching glance.

'Ah, yes. We all wonder that.'

Laura returned, and sat down again. I registered with a jolt that I had not thought at all about Josh and the forthcoming meeting during the journey. At least, sparring with the Inglises had saved me from a lot of introspection.

It was a relief to see the grimy suburbs of North London slide past the carriage window. However, as we glided into Euston, I began to feel apprehensive about what awaited me. We alighted, and walked to the barrier, where Rosine was waiting for me. She looked very chic, in a shift dress with chunky jewellery.

She exclaimed when she saw Ian and Laura, and there was more embracing and explanations. Ian turned to kiss me goodbye.

'Goodbye, Eithne. Have a nice day,' he murmured into my hair, holding me a fraction too long and too close. I resisted the urge to give him a sharp pinch, to let him know that two could play at this game.

Rosine and I made our way to a coffee shop, where we could sit and talk.

'I've been thinking,' she said, as we sipped our coffees, which were a much better brew than I had partaken of on the train. 'We all need to be very straightforward today. No hidden agendas. No trying to catch anyone out. It may be true, in which case, we owe it to Nick to be fair to the boy.'

'I agree.'

I gazed at the throng of busy people packing the station concourse, and wondered how many of them were facing a difficult interview. These days, London seemed unfriendly and remote. I could hardly imagine life in Wapping, where I had lived in my parents' flat and spent those few, blissful years with Nick. It was another world away.

'Eithne!'

My attention had wandered, and Rosine recalled me to the present. 'Let's take a cab. I know it's early, but I'd like to get to the restaurant first.'

We had arranged to meet at an Italian restaurant in Kensington, which was always very busy, and where we felt we would be of little interest to other diners. Although we were early, Luke and Josh were already seated at a table when we arrived. They rose politely as we approached, and Luke made some swift introductions.

I no longer felt any animosity towards Josh's mother. Now the first shock was past, I accepted that Nick's life in the USA was something on which I had no claim. However, I couldn't repress a little tremor of apprehension as I shook hands with Josh. We observed each other very closely. I managed a smile, but his face was serious. As I sat down, I took a long and hard look at this unknown boy.

I was looking more for a resemblance to Nicholas rather than to Nick, but I was disappointed in both respects. He appeared to be roughly the same height and build as my son, but his colouring was much lighter, and his hair had a tinge of auburn. Was he like Nick? His face in repose was more like Luke, I thought, but there was something about his mouth and jaw which seemed familiar.

The waiter hovered, to take our order. I was almost indifferent to what I ate or drank, but finally plumped for veal, which I hardly ever saw at home.

Josh's attention was focussed on Rosine – was this smart lady his aunt? As they exchanged hesitant pleasantries, Luke sent me an anxious smile across the table.

'Are you okay, Eithne? You seem fine today,' he murmured.

'Yes, I am. I've got my head round things,' I told him. The worst was over. I began to relax, and sat back in my chair, enjoying the friendly bustle around us and the delicious smells coming from the kitchen.

'Josh, this must be as difficult for you as it is for us,' Rosine said frankly, as we sipped our wine. He was drinking Coke, and had ordered pizza, and I thought he was rather young for his age.

Josh looked embarrassed, and nodded his head.

'It was a shock. I guess it was for you ladies, too. I'm very happy for you to do whatever tests you need to. It isn't that I'm looking for a whole lot of your input into my life, but it would be good to know about my roots,' he explained.

He had an attractive voice, low and husky, and he coloured slightly as he spoke.

'It's just that we all ought to be sure of where we stand,' Rosine told him. 'That's particularly important for someone like Nicholas, as well.'

Josh looked across the table at me. His eyes were a watery green colour, long lashed and limpid, and there was something forlorn in his expression, which caught unexpectedly at my heart.

'Nicholas is your son – yours and Nick DeLisle's?' he asked. 'Are we at all alike?'

'No, I don't think so.'

I felt it was best to be truthful. 'But even if you are related, you would only be half-siblings. Nicholas doesn't look anything like the children I have with my husband.'

'Tell us about yourself, Josh,' Rosine broke in. 'What have you been doing in London?'

'I've been staying with friends of Luke and Ray,' he replied. 'It's my first time in England, and they've been showing me around. I've had a great time. But I sure wasn't expecting anything like this.'

Slim-hipped waiters bustled up with plates of food. My veal looked appetising and delicious, and I suddenly realised I was ravenous, no doubt the result of so many pent-up emotions.

We all tucked in. The mood lightened, and Luke and Rosine began to discuss the next steps for arranging DNA testing. I listened with half an ear, intent on my lunch.

Josh was merely toying with his pizza, and I wondered whether he was nervous or just not hungry. He looked as though he could do with putting on weight, and there was something insubstantial about his slight frame. He glanced at my choice with interest.

'That smells good, Mrs. Leigh. What is it?' he asked politely.

'It's veal. Would you like to try a piece?'

I cut off a chunk, and forked it on to his plate. Although this seemed to surprise him, he ate it, and expressed approval.

'It's great. I must try that sometime. Will you tell me about your family?' he asked, evidently not wanting to join in the DNA discussion.

I told him about the children, where we lived, and about Peter and the family business. His ears pricked up, and he asked questions about the company which I couldn't answer.

'I'm afraid I don't really understand about Peter's work,' I explained.

'It's a wide field. I was studying it myself until – until recently,' he replied, that miserable look coming into his eyes again.

Whatever his parentage, I found myself feeling very sorry for Josh. There was a sad air of hesitancy, a lack of confidence about him, which I couldn't help contrasting with the bumptious cheerfulness of my children. How serious was the breakdown he had suffered? In a funny way, I almost began to hope that he was Nick's child, and that we could help him in the future.

'Eithne.'

Luke recalled me to the main conversation. 'Andrew is going to contact a company he's found about the testing so we can sort it out as soon as possible. Business is calling me back to Washington, but we'll find a hotel for Josh to put up in, until the swabs can be taken. Unfortunately, our friends are going away, so he can't stay on with them.'

Josh nodded, but I thought that his face fell at the prospect, and he looked even more bereft.

It made me do something very rash.

'Josh – would you like to spend some time with us in Cheshire?' I asked impulsively. 'I don't like to think of you stuck in a hotel on your own, and I think you'd enjoy talking with Peter and meeting the children.'

Luke gaped across the table, and Rosine gave a little gasp. As for Josh, his face lit up, and split into an unexpected grin, and I suddenly felt faint. His face was transformed by a wonderfully attractive smile, similar to one which I had seen many times before.

'Christ!' muttered Rosine, and clutched my hand under the table. I think we both knew the truth at that instant.

'Are you sure, Mrs Leigh? I'd like that.'

Josh didn't seem to notice the paralysing effect he had on Rosine and myself.

Luke did, though. He immediately opened his mouth, then closed it again, looking puzzled and thwarted. Josh turned to him, more animated than I'd seen him before.

'I'm not being too forward, am I?' he demanded.

'I know Eithne wouldn't ask you if she wasn't sure about it,' Luke responded slowly.

The waiters intervened to clear our plates. No one wanted dessert, but coffee was ordered. The atmosphere had become sparky and electric. Luke said something indecipherable in Josh's ear, and he immediately rose from his seat.

'Excuse me, ladies.'

He set off for the bathroom. When he was out of earshot, Luke leaned forward.

'Would you like to tell me what's going on?' he asked, quietly but forcefully.

Rosine's eyes met mine. There was a curious mixture of alarm and resignation on her face. Nothing had changed, but the ground had shifted under us.

'It's Josh – when he smiles like that – it's very like the way Nick smiled,' I said, when it became clear Rosine wasn't going to respond.

'But he doesn't look like Nick,' Rosine pointed out eagerly.

'No. But the smile ... it really is uncanny,' I said, my heart sad within me. I would so much have liked my son to have inherited that wonderful feature.

Luke's face relaxed. I think he thought we had made up our minds the other way.

'I hoped there would be something,' he murmured.

'We still need the DNA test to be sure,' Rosine said sharply. 'And, Eithne, is it a good idea to invite Josh to visit you? What are you hoping to achieve by it?'

'I don't know; but he looked so sad before. I thought he might like a change from London, and some company.'

Now I began to think of the problems it might cause, but it was too late to retract the invitation.

'I think it would be wonderful for him, Eithne. It's incredibly generous of you.'

Luke smiled his approval across the table. I nodded, and uttered a quick prayer that I would not regret my impulsive gesture.

Josh stayed tactfully away from the table for ten minutes or so. I think Luke had asked him to leave us for a while. When he rejoined us, we all sat quietly over coffee. The die had been cast. This issue was now going to roll on until we knew the truth – or, at least, the truth as far as it related to Nick.

Luke called for the bill.

'This is on me,' he said, as Rosine and I began to open our handbags. 'Eithne, much as we appreciate you asking Josh to visit, do you think you should maybe discuss it with your husband first? We don't want to make things any more complicated.'

I considered his words. Nicholas was already in the picture, but there would be no need to tell the girls the whole truth at present. I thought we could probably manage events smoothly, and I wanted very much to see Josh looking happy. His shoulders had drooped again as Luke spoke.

'I'll discuss it with Peter as soon as I get back, but I don't think there's likely to be any real problem,' I replied. 'If you can give me a number where I can reach Josh, I'll ring to confirm the arrangements tomorrow.'

Outside on the street, we exchanged somewhat stilted goodbyes. I wondered what the next weeks would bring, and whether we would be getting to know one another better, or drawing a line under the episode and consigning it to history.

Luke took my hand in both of his, and gave me an unexpected kiss.

'Thank you so much for wanting to help my boy,' he muttered into my ear. 'It's very good of you to ask him to visit, and I'll feel happier about him, knowing he's with friends. He's a great guy, and he's had a tough few months.'

Then he turned to Rosine, and embraced her as well. While they conversed, I smiled at Josh, who was standing awkwardly on the edge of the pavement.

'I hope I'll see you soon, then, Josh,' I said.

'That will be great, Mrs Leigh.'

He gave me that sudden, brilliant smile again, and I felt rocky. We said goodbye, and Rosine and I watched them walk away.

'I must grab a cab,' she said. 'Eithne, I hope you know what you're doing. Just because he has a similar smile doesn't make him Nick's child. And Nicholas may not be very pleased to have Josh sprung on him in the short term.'

'Nicholas can only think about the Inglises at present,' I said. 'There's such a lot going on in his life, and he won't have time to worry about Josh. Anyway, I feel sorry for the boy, whatever the truth is, and I think he'd enjoy himself with us. He doesn't seem to pose any sort of threat to me.'

I hoped that Peter would agree, and would understand why I had acted in the way I had.

Back at Euston, I was relieved that there was no sign of either Inglis, as I caught my train home. The second class coaches were busy, but I dozed off for a while, tired with the stresses of the day. I stumbled off at Crewe, found the car, and was back home in time for supper.

Peter had ordered takeaway Chinese as a treat, and the children were delighted. Nicholas and Olivia, now returned from her trip, were vying with each other in their accounts of their recent exploits, and no one else got a word in. It was nice to see them both so enthusiastic about life, and I hoped this ebullient mood would cover up my own pensive state.

Eventually, they clattered off to their respective rooms, and Peter and I were left with the debris.

'Nice of them to help,' he said, frowning. 'Just because we didn't cook, it doesn't mean there's nothing to do now we've finished.'

'A black sack will soon sort it out,' I said soothingly, and gathered everything up to take out to the bin. Peter was making coffee when I came back into the kitchen.

'So how did you get on? Tell me about the famous Josh,' he said, over the cafetière. This was the first chance we had to discuss my day. 'Do you think Nick might be his father now that you've met him?'

I reflected on that sudden shock I'd had in the restaurant.

'Well – I think he could be,' I replied. 'He has a very similar smile. Do you remember how Nick had that really wonderful beam, and how disappointed I was that Nicholas doesn't have it? When Josh smiles, I get the feeling I've seen it before.'

There was a pause, while Peter considered this information. I knew he would not be convinced until the scientific testing could be done.

'I feel really sorry for the boy,' I continued. 'He seems very lost somehow, and unsure of himself. I hope you don't mind, but I've asked him to come and spend some time with us here, until the test can be carried out. He was so cast down at the prospect of staying on his own, in a hotel. Have I done the right thing?'

My voice tailed off, quavery with uncertainty.

Peter looked across at me, amazed.

'I don't understand you, Eithne!' he exclaimed. 'A few nights ago, you were in the most terrible state about the boy, and now you want him to be part of the family. And how do you think Nicholas will react? Does this mean we have to tell the girls as well?'

I hung my head. As I travelled home, I had pondered on my offer, and been afraid of this response.

'Oh, Peter. It's difficult to explain,' I murmured. 'I just felt so sorry for him. Our children have such a happy, secure existence. Josh seems to be lacking any sort of self-confidence compared to Nicholas or Olivia, and I felt he looked lost and very solitary. Will it be such a problem to offer him some hospitality for a short time? The girls needn't know. They can think he's a friend of Rosine and Andrew. Nicholas may be a bit more difficult, but he's hardly here now with this Laine and Laine stuff going on. Whatever the truth turns out to be, I feel a responsibility for Josh somehow.'

Peter shook his head, but the expression in his eyes was resigned.

'You always did have a soft spot for the underdog – and I love you for that.'

He smiled reluctantly. 'I can see that whatever happens, we're going to have to get to know this boy. Just don't expect Nicholas to welcome him with open arms. You'd better speak to him tonight about this.'

He poured me a coffee, and took one for himself. 'This whole thing is like a runaway train,' he complained. 'And I'm surprised to see you clambering aboard.'

That reminded me of my uncomfortable morning's journey.

'By the way, I met Laura and Ian at Crewe station,' I said. 'We travelled down to London together. Laura did say some odd things,' I added, with a grin, hoping to lighten the conversation. 'But I get the feeling she approves of you. It must be the way you chatted her up at the dinner party.'

Peter contented himself with giving me an exasperated glance. This sort of teasing was not to his taste. Nicholas came back into the kitchen, and he regarded us suspiciously.

'Secrets again?' he asked.

I wanted to tell him about Josh's impending visit there and then, but the girls were coming down the hallway. Later on, I managed to get him alone in his room.

I hadn't thought that he would mind too much – after all, his initial reaction to the news had been fairly unemotional – but to my chagrin, he was both angry and upset.

'Why must he come here now? Suppose he turns out not to be related to me?'

His face was dark and scowling, a sight I wasn't used to, and it made me anxious. 'We'll have gone to all this trouble for nothing, and it's unbelievably awkward. I wish you hadn't asked him, Mum.'

'I can put him off, but I really don't want to,' I said, feeling guilty as I spoke. I sat down on the bed. Nicholas was flicking moodily through a car magazine as he perched on a stool by the window, as if unwilling to hear any more.

Perhaps I had been wrong. However, the memory of Josh's downcast face came into my mind, and I tried again.

'Honestly, Nicholas, I almost don't care whether or not he's your half-brother. As far as I'm concerned, he's a rather sad young man who has missed out on the sort of happy family life you and your sisters have always enjoyed. I feel sorry for him,' I said. 'There's no need for us to tell the girls anything at this stage. Aren't you the faintest bit curious to meet him? You might get on with one another.'

'I doubt it.'

Nicholas chucked the magazine to the floor, looking mutinous. 'Thank God I can be out of the house most of the time. Have you thought how you'll manage with him? He'll be bored stiff here in a day or two.'

'Well, he seemed quite interested in Dad's work. He was studying engineering in America.'

Too late, I realised this was entirely the wrong thing to say. Nicholas gave me a furious glare.

'Great. He'll soon be well in with everyone then,' he said, in an icy tone.

There was a long, uneasy silence. I got up from the bed, feeling tired and sad.

'I'll ring him tomorrow and put him off,' I said, as Nicholas muttered, and turned away.

Later, I was sitting at my dressing table, brushing my hair, wondering how I would deal with the problems facing me the next day, when I heard voices, and Peter and Nicholas walked in to the room. Nicholas came across and rubbed his cheek against mine.

'Mum, I'm sorry I was such a bear just now. I wasn't expecting anything like that, and if I'm honest, I suppose I do feel threatened by things. I don't know how I'm expected to behave with him, for a start.'

I turned round to give him a hug. Perhaps I was expecting too much of Nicholas. He was poised on that difficult cusp between boyhood and manhood, and his normal air of maturity masked a whole host of uncertainties underneath. I sometimes forgot how very young he was.

'Just be yourself. No one's expecting you to fall on his neck. Treat him like any other boy – man – you're meeting for the first time. It will be a lot harder for him,' I said.

'I've explained to your mother that I think she's gone out on a limb here,' Peter told him, throwing his sweater down on a chair. 'But I think we can deal with it. As far as everyone else is concerned, he's simply a visitor from the States. Just get on with your own life, Nicholas. Make the most of this time with the agency, and leave the rest to us.'

'Yes. Thanks, Dad.'

Nicholas left the room, and I turned to Peter to say something, but stopped when I saw the expression on his face.

'What's the matter?' I asked.

'I wish sometimes that you'd think before you speak. Perhaps hinting that Josh's engineering background might be of interest to us wasn't your smartest move,' he said. 'You are lucky that I was able to smooth things down.'

I was chastened – but I also felt a tiny hint of irritation brewing within me. Family politics seemed to be a full time business at present, and I was finding it harder to ignore a little voice which urged me to rebel.

## Chapter 7

The next day, I spoke to Josh, and we arranged that he would come to us after the following weekend. This gave him time to round off his visit to Luke's friends, and me time to prepare the ground before his visit to Fenwich.

But before he arrived, we received an impromptu invitation to a pool party at Delamere Court on Saturday lunchtime.

Olivia was pleased, because she would not be working, and Alexander would be at the party. Louisa was pleased, because she liked swimming and being with Maudie. Nicholas was pleased, because he could also spend time with his friends, and talk to Ian about his experiences at Laine and Laine.

I was apprehensive about appearing in a bathing costume before the assembled company, so I decided not to swim. This year, I had not had time to get a tan in the back garden, as I usually did.

Peter didn't want to go.

'Please, darling. We needn't stay long,' I cajoled. 'It will look very pointed if you aren't there. You don't have to swim, and you can chat with the lovely Laura.'

He gave me a sarky look.

'It's no good, Eithne. I don't want to make small talk with Ian Inglis.'

'But lots of our other friends will be there. You can't duck out of everything involving Ian, or we'll end up without any social life at all.'

This prospect probably appealed to Peter, but I was not about to let him go in that direction. 'Please. For me. And I'm sure you'll be interested to see the house and grounds.'

'Well, I'm not staying very long. I'm planning to drive to Beresford on Sunday, with Nicholas. I want to see my mother, and Nicholas is overdue a visit to his grandparents.'

Peter's widowed mother now suffered from Alzheimer's, but she was very comfortable in a nursing home in Beresford. My parents still lived in the house where I had been brought up, and enjoyed reasonable health for a couple in their seventies. But Nick's parents were now in their eighties, and Mrs DeLisle was very frail. They thought the world of Nicholas, and he was very good about going to see them. I had tried hard to temper the charm he had inherited from his father with concern for the feelings of others, and he was a much less selfish person than Nick had been at his age.

I told the girls about Josh's impending visit, but they didn't seem very interested.

'You'll have to entertain him, Mum. We're too busy,' Olivia warned me.

'Yes – running up my phone bill.'

Since her return from Scotland, Olivia seemed to spend hours on the telephone, mainly talking to Alex Inglis as far as I could tell. She shrugged her shoulders, and stalked away. Both she and Nicholas had their eyes firmly fixed on the Inglis constellation at present.

'You'd be interested to meet Josh, wouldn't you?' I asked Louisa, feeling hopeful that she would be more welcoming.

'Does he like animals?'

I crossed my fingers that they would be more friendly when he was with us in person.

Saturday dawned hot and cloudless, and the children were exultant. We set off for Delamere Court shortly after midday, taking two cars, so Peter could make an early getaway if he found it all too much for him.

I was wearing a sundress which I was very fond of, but which didn't often see the light of day, owing to the vagaries of the English climate. It was in red and white gingham cotton, with a halter-neck and full skirt, and had a vaguely fifties look about it. I made Peter anoint my back with sun cream, as I didn't want my fair skin to burn.

Although I was loath to admit it, I was curious to see Delamere Court for myself. The drive wound uphill through thick greenery and rhododendron bushes, before reaching a large gravelled courtyard. The house was of no special architectural merit, but it was large and rambling, and I wondered how much help Laura required to run it. She didn't seem the type to do her own housework.

However, I definitely envied them the pool and the gardens. Sparkling and blue, the swimming pool lay on a large terraced area, enclosed by white walls which were smothered by climbing roses and scented shrubs. There were proper changing rooms, and a hospitality area at one end. A stretch of very green grass at the other was decked out with tables, chairs and umbrellas. Mature and leafy trees trembled in the breeze outside the walls, and the place was a real suntrap.

I could tell that Peter was admiring it too, whatever his feelings about the owners. The ground was already lively with teens and adults, laughing, drinking and swimming, and the atmosphere was summery and festive.

Laura advanced to greet us. She was wearing a mini, flared sundress in a vivid lime green, and I saw Peter blink slightly at the bright colour and her long, tanned limbs. Her skin was enviably brown all over, and I wondered whether this was due to the sun or the beauty salon. I suspected it was the latter.

'At last. We wondered when you would pay us a visit,' she exclaimed.

A waiter (a waiter!) approached with a tray of drinks. Peter accepted a beer, and I took a glass of fruit punch, enticingly capped with strawberries and mint. I scanned the faces around, and was relieved to see several that I knew.

Laura took Peter's arm in a chummy way.

'There's someone I'd like you to meet,' she purred, and led him away towards the tables, where Ian and several men I did not know were deep in conversation.

I wondered who she had in mind – and also why she had, almost pointedly, left me on my own. For a moment, I recalled the crushing sense of abandonment which used to assail me at teenage parties, when Nick was off smoking dope and socialising with his mates. Even when one was grown up, such incidents could wound.

The children had already disappeared into the changing rooms, eager to join their friends in the water. I sipped at my drink, which had an unexpected kick to it, and moved tentatively towards a group of people where I recognised a few friends. Luckily, Maddy Potter saw me coming, and waved a greeting.

'Eithne, come and join us. I must say I envy Ian and Laura with their lovely pool on a day like this. Alan and I were wondering if we could fit one into the garden at home.'

I became absorbed into the group, and stood there, nodding and smiling. Introductions were made to fellow guests I did not know, and the conversation grew noisy with laughter as the drinks began to take effect. Peter was still talking to the group of men with Ian, while Laura hovered, and I thought with some annoyance that he was probably having a more interesting time than I was. I hadn't realised the party would be so large. My preference was for smaller gatherings, with people I knew well.

Now the waiters were moving amongst us with trays of delicious finger foods. Alexander materialised at my shoulder with a plate.

'Hullo, Mrs Leigh. Come and sit down. You can't manage to eat and drink properly standing up.'

With some relief, I followed him over to a table. 'Just a minute,' he said, and went off again, bringing back a platter heaped with dainties, before taking a seat next to me. I felt grateful for his attention.

'Where's Livvy?' I asked, a little surprised they were not together.

'She's swimming. I'm not that bothered about the water, and I'm hungry,' he explained.

So was I. We nibbled appreciatively at the savoury morsels, and I was very impressed by the variety which was on offer. Little patties, mini smorgasbord, baby skewers of prawns and marinated meat – it certainly made a nice change from sausage rolls and quiches, the usual Fenwich buffet fare.

'Surely your mother – I mean Laura – didn't make all these?' I enquired. Alex gave a snort of laughter at the idea.

'No. She uses a firm from Chester. This stuff is nice, but it's just a mouthful. I prefer it when my father barbecues, but there are too many here today for that.'

'Ian and Laura are very social animals,' I observed. 'I can't understand why they are happy to have all the local teens here almost every evening, but it doesn't seem to bother them.'

'The house and outbuildings are so big, that there's a ton of room for everyone to do their own thing,' he explained.

Alexander seemed relaxed and friendly today, and it encouraged me to try to get him to open out a little. If Livvy was going to get serious about him, I would like to know him better.

'How often do you see your mother, Alex? I believe she lives in America,' I asked.

A faint cloud passed across his face, and he put down the confit chicken wing he had been nibbling.

'Not as often as I'd like. She doesn't have any sort of contact with my father now. I expect you know they had a difficult divorce, and she had full custody of me for quite a while when I was young. She prefers to be in America, with my stepfather. I try to get across to see them a couple of times a year, but it's not always easy.'

'Wouldn't you like to live there?'

'I like Britain. Plus, I want to see my father, now we've established a relationship again.'

I pondered on what he was saying. Even though they were estranged in earlier days, at least Alex had always known who his father was, unlike poor Josh. I was glad to think that Alex and Ian were now on good terms with one another. It was evidently what they both needed.

There was a flash of blue, and Olivia joined us, slim in a T-shirt and shorts, with her hair curling damply around her shoulders. Alex gazed at her, his eyes full of admiration and a happy anticipation, which made me recall my own youth and the exciting pangs of early love. I felt sad all of a sudden, to think those days were behind me.

'How was the water?' he asked, as Olivia sat down next to him.

'It was lovely. I can't think why you didn't come in.'

'I have to be around to help. My father might need me to do stuff.'

A very wet Nicholas wandered up, and dripped in another chair.

'What a beautiful day,' he exclaimed, grabbing a tiny savoury tart from my plate. 'But I imagine the weather usually does what Ian and Laura want it to.'

I could see Alex was amused at his words, but I knew exactly what he meant. Life would accommodate their wishes very smoothly – apart from the odd disruptive element, such as the one I had provided all those years ago.

After we had eaten, the party became more fluid. I sat at the edge of the pool, and dangled my feet in the water. It was too good to resist, and I almost wished I had been brave enough to join in the fun, especially when Laura and one or two other ladies emerged from the changing rooms and joined the younger ones as they splashed and shrieked. I noticed that Laura wore a rubber bathing hat covered with water lilies to protect her sleek hairstyle. It was difficult to imagine her ever having a hair out of place.

Peter was sitting in the shade of an umbrella, talking intently to Rick Ryan, his long legs stretched out before him. He looked comfortable, and I felt pleased. We were definitely beholden to the Inglis family in various ways, and we needed to be able to get on with them as neighbours now.

A shadow fell over me, and I looked up to see Ian standing there. He was relaxed and smart in a navy polo shirt and shorts, although his dark glasses meant that it was impossible to read his expression.

'Hullo, Eithne. Are you having a good time?' he enquired.

I swung my legs round, and shook the water from my feet, before putting my sandals back on.

'Yes thank you, I should think that everyone is.'

I stood up, swaying slightly, and he put out a hand to steady me.

'Come and have a drink with me,' he said, and steered me to a table by the roses.

We sat down, and someone brought us more glasses of fruit punch.

'You seemed to be having a long talk with Peter earlier on,' I said. 'Do you still think Peter is a serious person?'

The implication of my tone was that serious equalled boring, as he had hinted at the dinner party. He smiled, but didn't rise to the bait.

'Did I say that? How very rude. I hope you'll forgive me. No, I can see that he's a very knowledgeable chap, especially once you get him on to his particular field. That was Laura's brother we were talking to. He's in the same line as your husband, and they know each other professionally.'

We were interrupted by a gurgling laugh, and a figure swayed up to the table, glass in hand. I recognised Sarah Harvey, who I didn't really know, although Nicholas was friendly with her sons. I thought she had maybe had a drink or so too many, judging by her flushed cheeks and unsteady gait.

Ian stood up politely, and she bumped down into a chair. He seemed a little irritated by her interruption.

'I'm Sarah. Who are you again?' she demanded, giving me what my mother would have called an old fashioned look.

'I'm Eithne Leigh,' I murmured. Ian looked surprised. I suppose he thought we would know one another.

'Oh yes, I vaguely remember you from somewhere,' Sarah said, in a patronising way. 'I like your dress. My grandmother used to have a tablecloth in that material – in the servants' kitchen.' She laughed again, and I felt my cheeks tingle. There was no mistaking the deliberate rudeness, and I wondered why she felt it necessary to be unpleasant to me. Perhaps she wanted to embarrass me before our host.

'I think Bill wants you,' Ian said tightly. He rose, and took her firmly by the arm, leading her up to where her husband was standing with a small knot of people. He said something to Bill, left Sarah with him, and rejoined me at the table.

'I'm sorry, Eithne,' he said, giving me an apologetic glance. 'Pay no attention to her. I think you look charming, but then you always do.'

'It's all right, Ian, you don't have to pat me on the head. I don't give a damn for her opinions,' I replied, feeling nettled, despite my words.

'I can't say I care for either of the Harveys, but Laura seems to like them.'

We sat in silence for a few minutes, watching the swimmers. Ian reached over and touched me on the shoulder.

'You must be careful, Eithne, your back is looking pink. Aren't you wearing sun cream?'

His hand travelled lightly over my shoulder blades and across my back. For a moment, I remembered caresses of old, and a little tingle ran through me. The hand stayed on my back, just above the dress.

'You still have the most beautiful skin,' he murmured in my ear.

'Ian! Stop teasing.'

I looked at him directly. 'You must stop this behaviour, especially when we're in public. I can't work out what you want. Are you trying to make me feel uncomfortable? If so, you're succeeding.'

His mouth twitched, as if he was trying not to laugh, and he continued to stroke my back. I couldn't remove his hand without wriggling round, and making it even more obvious that something was going on.

There were two reasons why I wasn't comfortable about these little displays of affection. Firstly, I couldn't work out his motivation. I hoped we were on our way to being friends, and I didn't want him to spoil that. But more importantly, it brought back memories of our previous physical relationship, and these were becoming increasingly troubling and exciting. I needed to stop him.

'Do you think Laura or Peter would be pleased to see you stroking me?' I asked.

'I like to think you might be enjoying it. I certainly am.'

He was impossible. However, he removed his hand, and I was relieved about that, as I saw Peter coming across to where we sat. To my surprise, Peter joined us at the table. He was smiling, and he seemed to have dropped the wary expression he usually wore when confronted with Ian, in thought or in person.

'You have a very nice place here,' he said to Ian, looking round at the pool and its surroundings. 'The views from the house across the plain must be wonderful.'

'They are, especially in the evening, when the sun sets behind the Welsh hills,' Ian told him. 'It almost makes up for being away from city life.'

I remembered Peter's remark about Ian being bored in the country. Ian had certainly never seemed to be a lover of rural pursuits in the past, and I didn't think he was a golfer. I guessed he was busy with his plans for the house at present, but I was sure he would soon need something else to occupy him.

Anyway, I was grateful to Peter for dropping his animosity. He glanced at my back, and ran his hand over it, just as Ian had done.

'Darling, your skin looks a little pink,' he said. Ian gave me a tiny wink. 'Perhaps we should be going home now.'

Ian demurred at this, but Peter told him firmly that we had other commitments over the weekend which required our attention, and we all got up.

'Is it okay if the children stay on for a while?' I asked. 'I'm sure they're having too good a time to want to leave.'

'That's fine.'

Peter walked ahead of us, looking for his hostess, and Ian put an arm round my waist.

'Are you sure you have to go?' he asked me softly. 'The fun's only just beginning.'

Perhaps it was – but I thought that we might have different views on what constituted a fun afternoon at this party. Something made me look towards the pool, and I saw my son and daughter in the water, eyes fixed upon me and the embracing arm. Nicholas looked amused, Olivia's face expressed disgust and disapproval. Hastily, I wriggled away.

Peter was whistling to himself as we drove home, a sign that he was feeling comfortable with life. I asked him about his conversation with Laura's brother, but he would only say that they had run across each other at a recent conference, and had many business contacts in common.

'I suppose they aren't so bad,' he said, referring to the Inglises as a family. 'Anyway, we can forget about them for a while now. We have other fish to fry next week.'

# Chapter 8

Josh arrived.

I had arranged to meet him at Crewe, and waited with some anxiety on the platform as the London train drew in. At first, I could not see him amongst the throng of people heading for the stairs, but then I caught sight of a slight figure with a suitcase and a back pack, looking very lost in the crowd.

'Josh!'

He lifted his head, and his solemn face brightened as he saw me. Fleetingly, I wondered whether I should kiss him, but decided to hold out my hand instead.

'Hi there, Mrs. Leigh.'

'Please say Eithne,' I said, giving his arm a little squeeze. We made our way out towards the car park, and he looked around with interest.

'Crewe. Is this a big place?' he asked, eyeing the dingy buildings and drab surroundings as we waited to cross the road.

'No, not at all. It's an old railway town, but it's definitely seen better days, I'm afraid.'

There was a tense look about his shoulders, but he began to relax as we left the town behind and drove on into the countryside.

'It's all very green,' he observed. 'I guess this is what you call good farming country.'

'Yes. Cows do well round here. Lots of horses, too. My younger daughter is a keen rider,' I told him. We chatted casually about his life in America, but he grew serious again as we approached Fenwich.

'Do all your family know about my history?' he asked, a nervous little tic twitching in one cheek.

'No. Only my husband and Nicholas. We thought it best not to tell the girls or anyone else until we have a definite answer from the

DNA test. Livvy and Lou simply think that you're here as a friend of the Maynards visiting the country,' I explained. 'I hope that's okay.'

'Sure. I still feel this is very kind of you – Eithne,' he said, twisting the cuff of his sweatshirt with nervous fingers.

'Well, I hope you won't be bored,' I said frankly. 'Nicholas is out all week doing a holiday job at an agency in Manchester, and the girls are a bit young for you. But I'm around if there's anywhere special you'd like to visit, and I'm sure that Peter would be delighted to show you his office if you're interested.'

'I'd be more than happy to help out if there's anything that needs doing.'

He coughed. 'I don't quite know how I'm feeling about meeting Nicholas. Perhaps he may not be too pleased to see me.'

His voice held a question, and I considered his words, wondering how best to respond.

'It's a difficult situation for you both.'

By now, we had reached Fenwich, and I turned the car into the driveway, wheels ploughing up the gravel. I glanced across at him. His face looked shuttered and pale. 'Don't expect Nicholas to be too effusive. Treat him like anyone else you are meeting today. If you do turn out to be related, there will be plenty of time to think about developing a relationship later on.'

For a moment, I thought he wanted to stay in the car. Then he took a deep breath, as if he had to face up to something hard, and he climbed out, looking with interest at the house and grounds.

'This place must be pretty old,' he said, sounding surprised.

'It was built around 1840, but it's had a lot done to it since then,' I told him.

The hall felt dim and cool after the sunshine outside. Josh put his things down on the tiled floor, and jumped as the grandfather clock struck a sonorous chime to mark the half hour. I thought that it must feel very different to the stark, modern architecture of Luke's house in Washington. Luke had insisted on showing us some pictures of his home, perhaps to prove that they did indeed come from a moneyed background. As well as coping with a complex situation, poor Josh was having to adapt to a very different environment as well.

'Come through to the kitchen,' I said, hoping the hub of family life would seem more welcoming.

He sat awkwardly at the table, while I filled the kettle. I wondered whether he was one of those Americans who only drink coffee, but he accepted tea, and his posture grew less rigid as I chatted away, hoping to put him at his ease.

Footsteps clattered down the passage, and Olivia strode in. Josh got to his feet, a little clumsily, and proffered a hand. Olivia looked surprised, but took the hand briefly in her own.

'Oh, hi. You must be Josh. I'm Olivia,' she said, shaking back her curls. Somewhat to my surprise, she was wearing her waitressing gear.

'You're not working tonight, are you?' I asked, feeling disappointed that she would not be there at dinner. I was relying on her usual flow of chat to cover up any difficult moments.

'I've swapped a shift with Marnie. Alex and I are going to a gig in Manchester on Saturday,' she said.

Josh was gazing at her with fascination. She sat on a corner of the kitchen table, swinging a leg, and gathering her hair into a ponytail, the picture of confidence, and proceeded to give Josh all the details of her working life at the Three Feathers, while he listened intently. I had the feeling that he'd never come across a girl like this before.

'Can you run me down to the pub, Mum?'

It was the usual request. I started to say that I did not want to leave Josh on his own, but Louisa walked in at the back door, and Livvy seized her chance.

'Lou can entertain Josh for five minutes,' she said triumphantly.

Josh had risen to his feet again, but Louisa was equal to the occasion.

'Hello, Josh. How are you with guinea pigs?' she demanded.

'Er – okay, I guess.'

He looked slightly stunned.

'Good. You can come and give me a hand.'

She bore him off to the stables with a proprietorial air, and Olivia gave me an amused glance.

'He seems nice,' she said, slamming the car door shut. 'Shouldn't be too much of a pain for you having him here. How long's he staying?'

'I don't know.'

As I spoke, I realised that we had not agreed an end date for this visit, but we were due to spend the last weeks of August in Wales, so there would be a natural limitation.

When I returned from the pub, Louisa was in full control, giving Josh an exhaustive tour of the gardens and house, and showing him to the small guest room I had allocated for his use. However, he seemed to be enjoying it, and I recognised that it had been a good idea for Lou to take charge of him and break the ice with her cheerful common sense. She was too young to be an object of romantic interest for him, and she was helping him to feel at home.

However, both Josh and I were apprehensive about the first meeting with Nicholas. We were sitting in the conservatory, me with a glass of wine, Josh with a Coke, when we heard Peter and Nicholas returning from Manchester. Josh looked at me, and his face assumed that closed off expression again.

'It will be all right,' I found myself saying, and then Peter walked in, with Nicholas following a few steps behind.

I was grateful to Peter for giving Josh a smiling welcome and a hearty handshake. Nicholas hovered with a casual air, which did not deceive me for an instant. I knew that he was as nervous as Josh.

Nicholas was looking very smart. Agency ways had rubbed off on him quickly, and he enjoyed being dapper in a suit and tie for a change. I think this made Josh very conscious of his sweatshirt and jeans, and there was a muted formality in their greeting. We chatted artificially for a while, Peter leading the way with questions for Josh about America and his studies at MIT. Nicholas lounged against the wall, covertly eyeing this interesting stranger.

Now that I had the chance to examine Nicholas and Josh in proximity, I began to search for signs of similarity. Nicholas was much darker than Josh, and his eyes were brown, while Josh's were the strange, watery green which had struck me in the restaurant. They both had the same physical build, slim and of medium height, but you would not have immediately categorised them as brothers, and I had not discovered any new resemblance to my darling Nick.

I don't know whether Nicholas had been expecting a bratty, loud type of American, but he seemed reassured by Josh's quiet demeanour. Conversation flowed more easily during supper, although for once, I was sorry for Olivia's absence. Lou's artless prattle kept us all amused, and she seemed to have assumed the main responsibility for our visitor. After supper, she dragged him out to the stables again, this time with a tape measure and paper and pencil. Apparently, Josh had suggested an extension as an improvement to the guinea pigs' current living quarters, and she was determined to take him up on it.

'I apologise on behalf of my daughter,' Peter told him later, as we prepared to go to bed. 'Please don't let her monopolise your time.'

'It's no problem. I'm having fun,' he assured us. 'I suppose this is what it's like to have a little sister.'

His face split suddenly into the grin I had seen before, and I felt Peter grow very still beside me. Was he seeing the same resemblance to Nick that I had?

Nick was fully aware of his devastating smile, and had employed it with conscious effect, enslaving young ladies, charming older ones, and startling and disarming his contemporaries. By contrast, I didn't even know if Josh realised how attractive his grin could be. It seemed to be visible only on rare occasions when he dropped his customary guard, and admitted you into a close, private world, and you felt almost privileged as a result.

Peter followed me into the kitchen as I locked up and gave the cat a late night snack.

'That was quite unsettling,' he said, sitting heavily on a stool. 'I see what you mean now. All evening, I've been thinking that Josh is nothing like Nick or Nicholas, and now I'm not so sure. Maybe he really is Nick's child.'

'Whatever he is, he's a nice boy, isn't he? He's been very good with Lou. Apparently we've got to go to B & Q tomorrow, to get the materials he needs to extend the pen,' I said, smiling at the thought. 'We just need him to make friends with the other two now.'

Improving life for the guinea pigs proved to be the best possible way of involving Josh in life at the Old Rectory. He had come up with a very intriguing idea for extending their run, and even Nicholas became interested and helped with the construction when he got back from work. Louisa supervised them with a benignant eye. It provided a useful way of masking awkward tensions and shyness, and we christened the finished product with champagne after several days' graft. (We drank the champagne, the guinea pigs stuck to water.)

I think Josh had really enjoyed himself, and Peter was impressed with the skills he had shown. It was a relief for me to feel his visit to us was passing so smoothly.

'He's okay,' Nicholas told me later in the evening after the champagne launch. 'But I don't feel any real connection with him, Mum. I'll be extremely surprised if he turns out to have the same father as me.'

Rosine rang me the next day, and was pleased with what I had to tell her. The DNA swab kits were due to arrive any day, and I was beginning to think with satisfaction that whatever the outcome, Josh would remain a family friend. It was good to be able to tell Luke this, when he telephoned from the States a little later on.

Josh was beginning to open up now he was getting used to us. The girls had both taken him under a wing, in different ways – Lou with the guinea pig plan, and Olivia with her continual caustic commentary on all aspects of life in Fenwich and the surrounding area. She took him to the Three Feathers one lunchtime, where he was forced to admit that he had no taste for English bitter, much preferring the lighter lagers on offer. Terry and the regular customers made him welcome, and I think he enjoyed the curious questioning about life in America.

There was still a distinct barrier between him and Nicholas. I would have loved more opportunities to throw the two of them together, but agreed with Peter that it would be unwise to force matters. On Saturday, Josh accompanied Nicholas and Louisa to play table tennis at Delamere Court, and I was glad to feel they were including him in their social life. Nicholas introduced him to Ian and Laura, and told me later that Ian spent some time talking to Josh about his years working in America, which pleased me too.

But the next day, Josh declined to go swimming in the afternoon, saying he would like to spend time with Peter and myself. It happened that Peter had a report to write, so Josh and I set out for a walk across the fields.

The day was cloudy, and uncomfortably humid. We had to swat biting insects away, and cows turned curious eyes on us as we crossed the meadows, but were too indolent to follow us, greatly to my relief. Josh helped me over the stiles in a very gentlemanly way, which touched me.

'Are you enjoying yourself with us, Josh?' I asked him, as we sprawled on a bench out in the lane leading back to Fenwich. I was hot, and didn't particularly relish the prospect of the walk back home.

He turned those distinctive green eyes on me.

'Yes, I am. I'm very grateful for the way you've made me so welcome. It would be good to feel that Nicholas was more comfortable with me, but I can see it's difficult for him,' he said, shredding a piece of grass as he spoke.

I was considering how to respond, when he suddenly burst out,

'I'm jealous of Nicholas, I think. When I see the happy, normal life he has here, it makes me realise what I missed out on. Luke and Ray have been wonderful to me, but sometimes it was hard growing up with two 'uncles' instead of a family. I wonder whether I'll ever be able to make proper relationships for myself.'

My heart contracted with pity for him. I wished I knew what to say. All I could think was that I had better choose my words with care.

'Josh, of course you will be able to do that,' I said, more heartily than I felt. 'And don't forget that you have one thing in common with Nicholas, whatever the outcome of this test. You've both had to grow up without knowing your real father. I'm sure that despite the good relationship he has with Peter, Nicholas has insecurities which stem from that fact. Don't ever think you're alone.'

I was conscious of him gazing at me very intently, with a hungry appeal in his eyes. He shifted along the bench towards me, and for a moment, I thought he was about to reach out and take my hand, but then there was a swirl of dust, and a big grey car halted before us.

It was Ian in his Mercedes. The top was down, and he looked windblown and cool.

'Good afternoon, Mrs Leigh,' he said, with an air of formality. 'You look very hot sitting there. I'd be happy to give you a lift home.'

I got up and walked over to the car.

'We're just out for a walk,' I explained. 'It's very kind of you, but—'

'Get in, Eithne,' he responded. 'Your young friend can jump in the back. I want to talk to you. You've been ignoring us for days.'

It had been just over a week since I had seen him, but I didn't want to start an argument. I looked at Josh, and he reluctantly got to his feet, murmuring a greeting, before getting into the back seat. I climbed in next to Ian, wishing I wasn't quite so flushed and dusty, and he accelerated away with a squeal of tyres.

I thought he was going to take us home, but he took the turning to Delamere Court instead. Once there, he directed a reluctant Josh towards the pool and the younger ones, before shepherding me into the house.

I had not been inside before, and was impressed to see how spacious it was. The hallway was large and square, with rooms and passages leading off in all directions, and a weighty wooden staircase embellished with an elaborate balustrade led to the upper storey. Sunlight spilled across the floor from huge windows on the landing above.

'Come into the kitchen, and I'll get you a drink,' Ian said, leading the way. 'How are you getting on with your American visitor?'

I watched while he fetched a jug of some fruit concoction from the fridge, and added ice cubes to our glasses.

'He's a very nice boy. We all like him a lot,' I replied, conscious I must keep our current secret.

'Mm,' Ian said, handing me a glass. 'I suppose you realise he has a ferocious crush on you? He blushes when your name crops up — I noticed that when he was here yesterday – and it was very sweet seeing you getting chummy on that bench together, but perhaps it was as well that I came along.'

I was horrified. This was the last thing I had expected to hear. I stood as if paralysed, hastily reviewing the time I had spent with Josh over the previous days, trying to decide if Ian might be right. He was amused at my confusion.

'You are such an innocent, Eithne.'

I remembered how he had once made a similar accusation in the past. It stung.

'But that's nonsense. I'm old enough to be his mother,' I said, unbelieving. Ian walked round the worktop, and put an arm round my shoulders.

'Just giving you a little hint, darling,' he said into my hair. 'That may be true, but you are still a very attractive woman. We don't want any trouble at the Old Rectory, do we?'

He kissed my neck, and I turned my head sharply.

'Ian – don't.'

I moved away from him. 'Where's Laura?'

'Down at the pool, I expect. Come and give me a proper kiss.'

'What have you got in this drink? It seems to be affecting your judgement,' I said, putting my glass down with a thud. This was a mistake. He put his down too, and caught me by the waist. He looked deeply into my eyes, and I felt the same pang I had experienced in the Italian restaurant. Memories of the intense physical relationship we had once enjoyed came flooding back, and it was intoxicating to feel I was desirable again.

He bent his face towards me, and kissed me passionately. I tried to pull away, but he was too strong, and then I was kissing him back. I wanted to kiss him. Pleasant little tremors ran down my spine and across my stomach, and I felt my whole body glowing.

After a minute or so he released me, and we stood there, panting and flushed. I was about to reprimand him, when I heard voices, and took a hasty step backwards, grabbing at my drink. Hopefully, no one had seen us embracing.

The voices grew more distinct, and Laura came in to the kitchen, accompanied by Alex, Olivia and Josh. Laura was wearing a towelling wrap over her bathing costume, and a hostile expression.

'Hullo, Eithne. How are you?' she asked, giving her husband a little slap on the behind as she passed him. 'Isn't it a hot day for walking? You are welcome to a swim. I can find you a costume somewhere I expect.'

The implication was that I wouldn't fit into any of hers, which was probably true. My cheeks still felt tingly from the kiss, and this made them grow even warmer.

'Thanks, but this delicious drink is cooling me down,' I replied. I looked over towards the children. Alex had a casual arm round Olivia's shoulders, but poor Josh stood by himself, his drooping posture reminding me of the forlorn boy I had met in London. Perhaps Ian was right, in which case Josh would need careful handling. I decided it might be a good idea to ask Peter to take him in to his office for a few days.

Laura definitely had a prickly air about her, and I hoped she had not seen her husband kissing me. I started to think wildly of ways in which we could laugh it off.

'Don't forget we're out to dinner,' she said to Ian, on her way to the sink, where she rinsed a glass with a fierce jet of water. It was definitely a hint for me to leave.

'Go and tell Nicholas and Lou to dry off. We should be going,' I told Olivia, but she made no move to do so.

'Alex and I are going out in Chester this evening,' she informed me.

'I can run Eithne back. After all, I brought her here,' Ian said. Laura made no comment, and I began to feel even more awkward.

'If it's no bother ...' I murmured. I glanced across at Josh, still standing solemn faced at the far end of the room. 'Will you come too, Josh?'

'Yes.'

I finished my drink, and waited for Ian to pick up his car keys. He didn't appear to be in any hurry.

'Where were you thinking of eating in Chester?' he asked his son. They proceeded to discuss a number of options, while Laura fidgeted at the sink, and Josh and I stood, feeling superfluous to requirements.

'You're keeping Eithne waiting, darling,' Laura said in a tight voice, when there was a pause.

'So I am. I do apologise.'

This time, he did reach for his keys. We said a quick goodbye, and walked back outside. It was a relief to be out of the frosty atmosphere, because I didn't quite understand what was going on. Ian stopped before he unlocked the car.

'Josh, would you mind running down to the pool to tell Nicholas his mother is on her way home? I expect you'd like him back soon, Eithne?'

'Yes. Would you mind asking him to get his skates on please, Josh?'

He sloped off towards the pool area. Ian turned quickly to me.

'Sorry about that. Laura and I had a row earlier, and she's still sulking.'

I was relieved there was an explanation for her behaviour, but wished I had not had to witness it.

'Will you lunch with me on Tuesday, Eithne?' he continued. 'I'm on my own for a few days. Laura's going to Scotland to visit some friends, and I'm at a loose end.'

I was going to say no, but then I thought it might be an opportunity to speak seriously to him about stopping the kissing, and explain to him why it was not compatible with trying to be friends. Josh would probably be with Peter, but if not, he could fend for himself for once.

'I will, but only if we go to the Three Feathers.'

I knew Olivia would be working there on Tuesday, a reason why Ian would not be able to misbehave any further with me. He looked surprised.

'Really? I was going to suggest Chester.'

'No. If you want to see me, it will have to be in Fenwich,' I told him.

'Very well. I'll pick you up at one.'

When we got home, Josh disappeared to his room, and I found Peter making tea in the kitchen.

'Will you take Josh with you to the office for a day or two?' I asked him. 'I think he needs a change of scene. I'm sure you can find something he'll be interested in.'

He glanced at me as he stirred his tea.

'Have you fallen out? I wondered why you were so long.'

I told him in brief detail about our meeting with Ian and visit to Delamere Court, omitting Ian's words about the crush – and the kiss.

'Ian and Laura were rowing. That was rather unfortunate. But I would like a couple of days to myself.'

'Yes, of course. I was thinking of suggesting it anyway.'

Perhaps the bad feeling between Ian and Laura had made its way down the hill, because there was a tense and disjointed quality to the evening. Josh accepted Peter's invitation to go to the office, sending me a querying look which I ignored. Lou and Nicholas bickered over some triviality, the atmosphere was uneasy, and everyone went to bed early as a result.

Before Olivia came home, I returned to the kitchen and sat at the table for a while, wanting to be alone to think. Surely Ian was wrong about Josh? But I would make myself a little less available and sympathetic for a while, just in case. As for Ian, I felt confused. It was wrong of him to be so smoochy with me, yet at the same time, I was guilty too, because I had enjoyed kissing him. The strange thing was, I didn't know whether I would be betraying Peter or Nick or myself when, despite all my common sense could tell me, I really wanted him to do it again.

# Chapter 9

Monday passed without incident. Josh was in better spirits, having found his day with Peter very busy and interesting, and in the evening, I made sure I was not alone with him for any length of time. I still couldn't make my mind up about Ian's comments, but I didn't want to take any chances.

The DNA swabs arrived, were taken, and duly dispatched, and we tried to forget about them for the time being.

On Tuesday morning, I told Peter of my lunch date with Ian. He was surprised we were going to the Three Feathers.

'That will set tongues wagging,' he said, with a wry smile.

'Surely the reverse? If we were planning an intimate meal, wouldn't we go somewhere further afield?'

I couldn't quite look at him. I did, however, warn Olivia that I would be seeing her at lunchtime. She was not enthused, as she didn't seem to care for Ian.

'He was really horrible to Alex's mother,' she said, eyes flashing with indignation. 'Some of the stuff Alex has told me, you wouldn't believe it. Why on earth do you want to spend time with his dad?'

'We go back a long way,' I said. It was one of those irritating phrases people used that couldn't really be argued with, and it silenced my daughter, who huffed away to her room. Satisfied, I made a mental note of its effect on her. It might be useful on other occasions.

Ian collected me as promised, and we drove to the pub. It was less humid today, and we decided to sit in the garden, under the shade of an umbrella.

Olivia flounced out to us with menus. We ordered drinks, and she went to the bar to get them. Ian stared after her, a faint smile on his lips.

'I get the feeling your daughter doesn't like me very much,' he commented.

'She doesn't like me very much, either,' I told him. 'In your case, I think that Alex has spoken to her about your divorce from his mother, and she naturally takes his side. As far as I'm concerned, she's very much her father's girl.'

'She strikes me as a determined character. I like that,' Ian said. 'Actually, I think she's very good for Alexander. He needs an emotional focus of his own, now he's grown accustomed to being part of my second family.'

I hadn't really considered things in that light, but I was strangely pleased to hear it.

I asked Olivia for her recommendation regarding the food available. She tried in vain to impose her vegetarian preferences on us, and I ordered a chicken and avocado salad. Ian asked for a rump steak baguette.

'With chips,' he told her. 'I hope that your mother can be persuaded to share them with me.'

It was wonderful to be away from my kitchen. I had given careful thought to what I should wear, and had decided on navy capri pants, with a flattering new striped top. This was neither too casual nor too formal, and I was pleased with the result. Ian, smart as ever, was dressed in chinos and a crisp cotton shirt. He gave me a cheeky glance over the table.

'Is it my imagination, or are your boobs bigger these days?' he asked me.

'Bigger,' I confirmed. 'That's what happens after having children. Which reminds me —'

I told him quickly but forcibly that I wanted him to stop surprising me with the kissing and intimate caresses. After a momentary start, he listened without comment, his gaze wandering away across the pub garden.

'It isn't appropriate behaviour for friends, which is what I thought we agreed to be,' I lectured him. 'We're married to other people. I enjoy your company, Ian, but I don't want to feel I can't trust you when we're alone. Do you understand what I mean?'

He reached out, and just stroked my arm.

'I could have sworn you were up for it the other day,' he said softly. I tried to repress a blush.

'That isn't the point. Friends wouldn't do that smoochy stuff, it's potentially dangerous,' I told him. 'Surely you, of all people, can appreciate that?'

Olivia strode across the lawn with our food. Ian waited until she had gone, before responding.

'I do understand, Eithne, and I apologise if I've upset you. The problem is, I remember how things used to be between us, and sometimes it's difficult to get away from that. Be honest – don't you agree that, despite everything that's happened, there is still a very strong attraction between us?'

He gave me a mischievous glance, and I looked away, biting my lip, because I knew he was right. However, I wasn't going to admit it. He sighed.

'Okay, if that's the way it has to be, I promise that from today, I'll try to be the perfect gent. I don't want to call time on our friendship now.'

He looked down at his plate, and then grasped my hand.

'I'd really like to go to bed with you again. I don't suppose that's likely to happen, but I just thought I'd mention it.'

'Ian ... It's not going to happen.'

My voice was firm, but I couldn't repress a little shiver. I really couldn't let myself think about that.

'Now, let's change the subject and enjoy our food,' I said.

Over lunch, we chatted more comfortably about uncontroversial times, and family matters of the present day. Ian was excellent company, and our laughter attracted interested glances from other customers. Olivia watched us as she served them, a disapproving expression on her pretty face.

'I don't think parents are supposed to have any fun, or enjoy themselves,' I said to Ian after she had cleared our plates.

'No. But we won't let her into our little secret – we can have even more fun than the young ones do.'

We lingered on over coffee, and I remembered another subject I needed to raise with Ian.

'Please tell me you weren't serious when you said Josh had a crush on me,' I pleaded. 'You've made me feel very awkward – so much so that I've sent him in to the office with Peter for a few days.'

Ian stirred his coffee, looking pensive.

'I'm sorry, Eithne, but I think I'm right. The way he looks at you ... I know the signs. He'll get over it, don't worry. It's a shame Olivia isn't available as a distraction, but I'm afraid Alexander's pipped him to the post there.'

He looked pleased at the thought. Olivia came to join us at the table, having finished her shift.

'Can I cadge a lift home, please?' she asked Ian. 'I expect you're just going.'

Ian ignored the pointed hint, and offered her a drink, which she refused. Her presence chilled the warm atmosphere between us, and I felt annoyed with her.

'And what are planning to do with your life, now you've left school, Olivia?'

Ian's tone was deceptively emollient. 'I assume you won't want to work at the Three Feathers for ever. You're a bright girl. Perhaps Alex can help you find something more challenging in Manchester.'

Olivia opened her mouth to retort, but then changed her mind.

'Yes. Why didn't I think of that?' she said sweetly. 'Or perhaps you could, Ian. After all, you seem to have taken Nicholas under your wing. Why don't you find something to keep Mum occupied while you're at it? Apart from taking her out to lunch, of course.'

'Olivia!'

I was very embarrassed, and wished now that I had not insisted on the Three Feathers for my lunch with Ian. 'How can you be so rude? Apologise at once, unless you want to walk home.'

Olivia and Ian surveyed each other across the table while I held my breath. Then he began to laugh.

'It's all right, Eithne. Olivia's entitled to her own opinion. You really are a little firebrand, Olivia, and I hope that some of your chutzpah rubs off on my son. He might find it helpful.'

Olivia got up, scarlet in the face now.

'I'll wait in the car park.'

She strode away, slinging her bag across one shoulder, while we watched her retreating back – me with chagrin, Ian with apparent amusement.

'I am sorry, Ian. She is a little bitch at times,' I apologised, feeling ashamed at this demonstration of my inadequate parenting skills. Ian reached for his wallet.

'Well, I should apologise too, I was being provocative. It's a fault of mine, I know. Anyhow, we mustn't let this spoil things. Thank you for your company, Eithne, I've enjoyed myself very much. Let's do it again soon.'

This time, I insisted on paying my share of the bill. As we waited for Terry to deal with us at the bar, I nodded to one or two acquaintances from the village at a distant table, who regarded my companion with curiosity.

'Oh dear. Peter said that tongues would wag if we went here for lunch,' I said to Ian in a low voice. 'I'll just have to brazen it out.'

Terry detained us for a few minutes in chatter, and as we left, Ian said loudly,

'My darling, I've had a lovely time. We must come again very soon.'

I knew this was for the benefit of the other customers, and gave him a little shove.

'Do you want to ruin my reputation? I thought you were going to behave from now on.'

'Sorry. I wanted to see their faces. Don't forget that village life is new to me, and I like to think we've brightened their boring day.'

I hoped at least that I might have brightened his boring day. He had certainly brightened mine. Olivia was leaning against Ian's car, looking sulky, and I sent her a glance to say 'enough'. She got the message.

'I'm sorry if I was rude,' she muttered at Ian. 'I get really fed up with Mum going on at me. It's too much when other people start.'

'I expect your mother is only trying to help,' Ian told her, unlocking the car and pushing the front seat forward for her to climb in. 'You have too much going for you to be satisfied with staying in Fenwich. I'm sure you understand that too.'

We drove the short distance home in silence. When we arrived at the Old Rectory, Ian got out, but made no move to kiss me goodbye.

'Let's do lunch again soon,' he said, patting me on the arm. 'We're going to Italy in a week or so, but I'll try and see if I have a free day before then.'

Why did I feel dissatisfied as he drove away? Was it down to envy of the prospect of the Inglises enjoying unlimited sunshine in Europe? Much as we liked Wales, there was no guarantee of good weather, although we always hoped for the best. Or was I disappointed at the lack of a friendly embrace? After all, I had been the one to request a cessation of physical contact. It seemed that I couldn't manage to get things right on that front.

The rest of the day passed uneventfully. For once, we had a full house at suppertime. Olivia was quiet, but Nicholas and Josh talked about a recent film they had both seen, and I was pleased to see them in apparent harmony. Peter told me that he thought Josh was enjoying his days at Leigh and Co.

'His understanding of hydraulics is really excellent, and much more up to date than mine,' he told me as we cleared away. 'We're tendering for a big project in Germany at the moment, and he made some very helpful suggestions. I want him to come in again tomorrow.'

'Don't enthuse too much in front of Nicholas, then.'

Later on, Josh came to sit with me in the conservatory. He seemed more relaxed again, and I began to hope that Ian was wrong.

'Eithne, I've been thinking,' he said, fixing me with his pellucid gaze. 'Now the swabs have gone back to the DNA lab, there's no need for me to stay in England any longer. If it's okay with you, I'll book a flight back home next week. I know the results won't be back for some time, and even then, I don't really know what should happen if I do turn out to be related to you all. It's becoming clear to me that I need to start living my old life again, else I won't know where I am – let alone who I am.'

I didn't know whether to be pleased or sorry. Whatever the truth, I had grown fond of Josh, and provided we could keep things straight between us, I was in no hurry to curtail his visit.

'Oh, Josh. Don't feel you have to go on our account,' I told him. 'We're away in Wales in two weeks, but if you'd like to come too, we can probably squeeze you in. There's lots of good walking and beaching, providing the weather's kind to us.'

He cleared his throat, drumming on the arms of the chair with nervous fingers, and gazing into the dusky distance.

'That's very kind – but I guess I'll go back home. I'd like to spend another day or two in the office with Peter, though. This project he has on hand is right up my street.'

I nodded. It was not for me to force the pace one way or another. As Josh said, there was no point in making any decisions about what he wanted until the test results were known. Only then would we be able to decide whether Josh would remain a family friend, or become something closer.

And so, Josh's visit came to a natural conclusion. He flew back to America the following Monday, and there were no awkward personal moments before he left. I think we were all sorry to see him go, and the huge bouquet which arrived for me later in the week made me feel quite sentimental.

'I bet he wishes you were his mother,' Nicholas said to me privately, as I arranged the flowers. He had said nothing more about his real feelings for Josh, and this statement surprised me.

He put an arm around my shoulders. 'It's made me realise that I've been lucky. Even if my real father died, I've always had a mum and dad in my life. It must have been hard for Josh, growing up without either.'

I returned his embrace, thinking that it was important for Nicholas to recognise this. It might help him to feel more positively about forging a relationship with Josh in the future.

'I'm glad you see it that way,' I said, picking up a carnation and trimming the stem. 'I am sure he's appreciated getting to know us, and I hope we can help him, whatever the outcome of the tests. At least, the next time we meet, we'll know where we stand.'

The Inglises went to Italy. Having Josh to stay meant I had not been able to return their hospitality, and I felt slightly guilty about this, especially when Nicholas finished his month with Laine and Laine, and came away with the offer of a permanent job when he had finished his studies at Oxford. He was delighted, even if I suspected he really wanted to work in a bigger, London agency. Time would tell if he could achieve this ambition, but it was good to know he had an opportunity waiting for him.

Then it was time for our trip to Wales. We had rented a cottage on Anglesey, and despite a couple of half-hearted protests from the older children – Nicholas, because his friends were holidaying in more glamorous locations, and Olivia, because she would not see Alexander Inglis for a time – we had a good fortnight. For once, the weather was reasonable, and the children quickly reverted to the habits of younger days, spending hours splashing and shrieking in the chilly surf, and enjoying long walks along the cliff paths and the scrubby interior of the island. Everyone ate enormously, and I was kept busy producing huge quantities of food, although I insisted that we had a few pub meals to give me a break.

Peter always seemed younger on holidays. Absence from the office and his usual cares was a tonic for him. He was affectionate towards me, and told me how much he was enjoying this family time.

'This may be the last holiday we have all together,' he said, his face and voice regretful. 'Livvy and Nicholas will probably be doing their own thing next year. It's sad to think these occasions are coming to an end.'

'Well, they haven't ended yet, so don't be too down,' I replied. Privately, I was looking forward to more adult vacations, involving less cooking and more time to myself.

Towards the end of our stay at the cottage, the telephone rang unexpectedly. It only took incoming calls, and we tended to forget it was there.

It was Rosine's husband, Andrew, with the news that the DNA test revealed that there was a 98% certainty that Nick was indeed Josh's father.

Peter took the call. The rest of us were sitting over the remains of a barbecue in a rather midgy dusk, and when he came back outside, one look at his face told me that something serious had happened.

'Peter – your mother?' I queried. It was the first thing which sprang to my mind, but he shook his head. I could see him deliberating, and then he sat down and proceeded to speak very formally to the children about the real history of our recent visitor, culminating with the news that it was now certain that Josh and Nicholas were related.

I looked anxiously at my son, who was pale and quiet. Olivia burst out into a storm of protest, firstly that we had kept her in the dark beforehand, and now saying that she felt upset on Nicholas' behalf.

'Nick DeLisle must have been a horrible person,' she exclaimed, giving her brother a rare hug. 'As far as I can see, he caused nothing but trouble for everyone. Does this mean that Josh will be adopted by the DeLisles, and take Nicholas' place with them?'

'No, it doesn't, Livvy, and please watch your tongue. You don't know the background of how this came about.'

It was unlike Peter to speak sharply to her, and she subsided, muttering, still keeping her arm round Nicholas' shoulders. He gave me a rueful grimace, but I think he was pleased by this unexpected sisterly affection.

'It has been difficult for both Mum and Nicholas, but we've all met Josh, and I thought everyone liked him,' Peter continued. 'None of this is his fault. What is important for him is to get to know about his blood relations, Livvy. I think you ought to be able to understand that.'

We sat round the dying embers in silence. I thought about what Olivia had said concerning Nick, and felt very regretful. For the first time, I understood that the children were being asked to deal with events outside the normal humdrum pattern of family life, and it would not be easy, but would challenge them in many ways. Feelings of doubt and suspicion hung in the air, but then Louisa spoke up stoutly.

'Well, I like Josh a lot, and as Dad says, this isn't his fault. I think we should welcome him into our family – didn't we already do that, anyway? Of course, Nicholas will always come first, but surely we have enough love left over for another person too.'

Peter and I exchanged glances, and I felt a lump come into my throat. Nicholas and Olivia were such dominant personalities that we had a tendency to assume our youngest child was still very much a child, but she seemed to have developed a maturity all her own, and I think that her siblings were astonished, and possibly ashamed, by her ready acceptance of the situation.

'Well said, Lou,' Peter exclaimed, a smile lighting up his face. 'I think you are exactly right. The best way to deal with this is to seek out the positives. That's a good life lesson to learn, in any case.'

Nicholas gently removed Olivia's arm and went indoors. She made as if to follow him, but Peter restrained her.

'This affects Nicholas more than anyone, Olivia. Let him have some time to think,' he said.

'Come on Dad, we'll do the dishes,' said Lou, getting to her feet. She and Peter gathered up the plates, and could be heard clattering in the kitchen. Olivia stayed sitting with me in the deepening twilight.

'Mum – this must have been horrible for you,' she said, after a long pause, during which she pulled the petals off a daisy with deliberate care.

It was very unlike her to consider my feelings.

'I was upset at first,' I told her. 'But when I'd had time to think – it happened as a result of a one-night stand at a time when Nicholas' father and I hadn't seen each other for two years. Nick never knew about the pregnancy or the baby, and it's only by a series of very unlikely coincidences that Josh has been enabled to find out the truth. I don't feel that it affects the time that Nick and I spent together, or lessens the feelings that we shared.'

'Josh and Nicholas aren't very alike though, are they?'

Olivia continued to pick at random grass stems, frowning, thinking things through.

'Do you mean physically or as individuals?' I asked her.

'Both, I suppose.'

She wriggled in her chair.

'Well, they've had completely different upbringings, in different countries. Physically, I agree, they aren't alike, but don't forget they're only half-brothers. Nicholas doesn't look like you girls, either.'

'Does Josh look like Nick, then?'

'No, except for when he gives you that unexpected grin. He doesn't do it very often. You might not have seen it.'

A bat began to flutter amongst the fruit trees at the end of the garden, and a little breeze chilled my shoulders. Night was fast falling, and I wanted to go inside, but I sensed that Olivia needed to talk. We didn't often communicate so deeply, and I would let her have her say.

'What was he really like, Mum? Nick, that is, we never speak about him. In my mind, he's some sort of devilish, unreliable figure, who always got his own way and made you unhappy. I'm so grateful he wasn't my father. Why ever did you get involved with him?'

I was chilly and uncomfortable in a garden chair, and I really didn't want to delve into old memories, but I didn't have much choice.

'He was a very handsome and charismatic person, and I fell in love with him,' I said simply. 'I was younger than you are now when I met him, and I couldn't escape it. He took my heart, and that was that.'

A disbelieving expression passed across her face. I knew this emotion would not be in accord with Olivia's own practical – and inexperienced – views on life and relationships.

'You evidently like Alex a lot, Livvy, but I don't believe you are in love with him,' I continued. 'If you were, you would have some understanding of what I'm saying. Real love isn't something which can be controlled, or turned on and off.'

Her face was in deep shadow now, but I thought she was reflecting on what I had said, and applying the sentiment to her own feelings – with what result, I could not be sure.

'And did you ever think you'd made a mistake in loving him?' she asked, after a long silence.

'Yes, I suppose so, at times, but it was too late by then.'

She snorted.

'You're such a pushover, Mum. Thank God Dad came along when he did.'

'Don't forget your father also made a mistake, when he married Silvia. I hardly think your experiences have qualified you to comment on other people's lives.'

By now, I was definitely cold, and rose to go inside. Olivia gazed intently at the last glowing charcoals, as if she could somehow find answers to the things that puzzled her there.

'I think Alex may be falling in love with me,' she said, reluctantly getting to her feet. 'I do like him better than anyone else I've been out with. He's kind, and he looks out for me. We can say anything to one another, and I really look forward to being with him. But I don't know if I love him, not in the way you seem to mean.'

'Everyone's different, darling. Just wait and see what happens.'

To my surprise, she gave me a brief squeeze, something almost unprecedented in recent years.

'Thanks, Mum. And now let's go and make sure Nicholas is okay.'

'Who is looking out for Josh?' I wondered. I would have liked to let him know that I was pleased about the test result. But perhaps it would be better to wait until we all had a chance to assimilate the news.

# Chapter 10

Mrs DeLisle died.

It happened very suddenly, the week after we returned from Wales. Her health had been poor for some time, and she was in her eighties, so it was not entirely unexpected, but Nicholas took it very badly.

He had been extremely uncommunicative and terse with us ever since we received the news about Josh. This was only the second death in the family that he had known, and he had a much closer relationship with his grandmother than with Peter's father, who had passed away a few years previously. The shock made him even more withdrawn, and I was worried about him.

By unfortunate coincidence, the date of her funeral was almost the same as the day that Nick had been buried, and I was in an agitated state as we went into the church in Beresford. Tormenting memories revived in me, and my tears flowed, though whether they were for Nick or his mother, I could not tell. Nicholas sat apart with his cousins, stern-faced in black.

After the ceremony, we repaired to the churchyard, where Mrs DeLisle would be buried next to her son. I hung back, with Peter keeping a tight hold on my arm. I never wanted to visit Nick's grave, always wishing to remember him in as he was in life rather than in death, and I didn't want to see it now.

Luckily, there was a large press of mourners, who covered up my recalcitrance. Nick's parents were long term residents of Beresford, and had many friends. Afterwards, we went back to the DeLisles' house for drinks and refreshments, and I tried hard not to remember the exciting days I had spent there with Nick in my youth.

Rosine, red-eyed, but elegant in a black suit, caught my hand as we stood in the kitchen later on.

'Poor Mummy – but she's with Nick now,' she said, brushing away a tear. 'Wasn't it ghastly in the church? So many awful memories ... but at least I don't have to worry over whether she ought to be told about Josh. Andrew thinks that it might be a good distraction for Daddy to know about it, but I can't face it just yet.'

'Have you told Charlie and Flora?' I asked.

'Yes. They don't seem very interested really, as he's only a cousin. It's much harder for Nicholas, but he seems to be very grown up about it.'

I wondered whether this was really true. He had faced a few difficult weeks, and I was relieved to think he would soon be going back to Oxford, where he could settle into a more normal life again.

'Do we let it be known more widely – about Josh, I mean?' I asked her. 'Or perhaps it's better if it's something which gradually gets round, without a lot of fanfare. I think I'd prefer that.'

Rosine looked anxious. It was a situation without precedent, and there was no way of knowing the best way to proceed.

'Andrew has spoken to Luke. I think they are both undecided at present, and I don't want a lot of gossip until I've had a chance to tell Daddy. I don't think Josh has any plans to come back to the UK just yet, so hopefully, it won't arise for a while.'

'But isn't it important for Josh to find out more about his father?'

'He's waited a long time. He can wait a bit longer,' she said with decision. 'I'm sure he understands that things are difficult for us here at the moment.'

Even Olivia was quiet, as we returned home from Beresford. The girls had not seen a great deal of Mrs DeLisle in her lifetime, but they understood her importance to Nicholas, and were aware of how upsetting the day had been for him.

'Luke and Josh sent flowers,' Peter told me later. 'But there was no special message. That was sensible of them, I think.'

Nicholas went straight to his room after supper. I pottered around downstairs for a while, then went and tapped at his door. He was lying on the bed, ostensibly reading a magazine, but I didn't think he was taking very much in.

He turned solemn eyes on me, as I sat on the edge of his bed.

'This has been a funny summer vac,' he said slowly, as I patted his hand. 'Some of it was great. I loved working at Laine and Laine, and getting to know Ian and Laura. But the rest of it, I'd like to forget. I wish I could go back to where I was at the start, when I went to France with Aunt Rosine and Uncle Andrew. I was really happy then.'

What could I say to him? It was futile to expect that life would be cloudless skies and sunshine. Dark clouds could appear on the horizon when least expected, and one didn't always have an umbrella to hand.

'I think you have grown up a good deal, Nicholas,' I told him, stroking his dark head. 'You have coped very well with two difficult situations, and that will stand you in good stead in the future. Don't be too unhappy about your grandmother. She had a long life, and she is at peace now. And I think that time will enable you to accept Josh, and hopefully, become closer. Remember all the good things you had this summer as well.'

He rolled over on his back, and lay staring at the ceiling.

'I was thinking of writing to Josh, and telling him about the funeral,' he said. 'He didn't know Grandma, but he is – was – her grandson too. Do you think that's a good idea?'

'Yes, a very good idea, darling. I think Josh would appreciate that very much.'

It seemed to me a positive first step in establishing a more personal relationship between the two of them. I did hope that in time they could become friends, perhaps more than friends, although that wouldn't happen overnight. He sat up, looking more animated.

'Would you let me go back to Oxford a little earlier, before term starts? We've got the flat from next week, and I think Julian is planning to move in then. I feel as though I'd like to get back to my university life again, and be on familiar territory. I've still got some money from my summer job, so it wouldn't cost you and Dad anything.'

I would be sorry to see him go, but understood his reasoning, and thought that it was probably the best thing for him in the current circumstances. As it was his final year, he would be living out of college and sharing a flat in North Oxford with two close friends. Julian was a steady, sensible sort of person, and I thought his company would be good for Nicholas.

'Well, I shall miss you, darling, but if that's what you want to do, then I will understand.'

'Good. I'll just want to see Ian before I leave, to say a proper thank you for all his help this summer. When are they back from Italy?'

'I think they are back. School started at the end of last week, and Maudie would need to be home for that. Why don't you go up tomorrow? Take a bottle of wine of something. I think Ian would appreciate the gesture.'

'Okay.'

He got up, and went to his desk. 'But I'll write to Josh tonight, while it's all still fresh in my head.'

The next day, I received a letter from Luke.

'I'm sorry you have had such a traumatic summer, Eithne,' he wrote, in a distinctive, flowing hand. 'We were all very sorry to hear about Nick's mother. Perhaps it was as well that she never knew about Josh; who can tell?

'Josh has been pretty quiet about the test results. We asked him if he wanted to go back to England, because now I hope you and Rosine will be prepared to speak to him about Nick, and maybe Mr DeLisle would receive him too. But he seems reluctant, for some reason. Did something happen to upset him when he was with you?

'At least his visit has revived his interest in finishing his course. He's back at MIT, and I guess we have Peter to thank for that.'

I showed the letter to Peter afterwards, and he was surprised.

'I don't think we upset him, did we? I know Nicholas wasn't very forthcoming, but they rubbed along okay. I think the boy just needs time to come to terms with it all.'

Peter had evidently not noticed anything inappropriate, and I decided to leave things as they were. Josh would be welcome to visit us again, but only when he was ready.

Life settled down to its usual routine. Lou was now in the Sixth Form at school, and was taking her academic life very seriously after good GCSE results. Nicholas started to prepare for his return to Oxford, and then Livvy announced her intention of spending some days each week in Manchester, staying with Alexander Inglis in his flat. She pointed out that it gave her opportunities to look for a more challenging line of work, especially as her A level results were better than expected, but Peter was most unhappy about it.

I didn't exactly gloat, but I wondered whether he felt that he should have been firmer with her in the past.

'Alexander is a very nice boy. Livvy is nearly nineteen, and we have to accept that she will be forming adult relationships now,' I told him. 'Far better for her to be with Alex than any of her other boyfriends. And maybe she will find something she really wants to do.'

'I suppose you'll be glad to see the back of her,' he retorted sharply, and I stalked away. There were some subjects on which we could never see eye to eye, and this was definitely one of them.

I found myself complaining to Ian about Peter's attitude when I had lunch with him again, just after Nicholas left for Oxford. This time, I had agreed to go further afield, and we were dining in an upmarket French restaurant in Chester, which I had wanted to visit for a long time. I felt slightly smug as we sat there. It was some weeks since I had seen Ian, and it was nice to have a treat.

'Doesn't Laura mind us going out together?' I asked him, as I sipped at a delicate white wine, and took a covert glance at the other diners, all very smart and prosperous-looking.

Ian was amused.

'Not in the least. She has a very active social life, and she knows we're old friends. Does Peter object, then? He might well prefer to keep his women tied to the home.'

'He's a bit cross about Livvy staying with Alex. I've told him not to be such a dinosaur, but it's difficult for fathers where daughters are concerned. Wait until Maudie starts going out with boys in a serious way. You might feel the same.'

Ian was very tanned after his Italian holiday, and looked fit and well. I noticed several women giving him appraising looks, and was glad I had dressed in my new blue frock for the occasion. He considered what I had said, his fingers curled round the stem of his wineglass.

'I think it will be good for both Alex and Olivia. If you remember, I gave Olivia a hint about finding a job in Manchester when we last met. She could go a long way if she puts her mind to it. Alex is very keen on her, and he won't let her down.'

This was reassuring.

'I'm not concerned,' I agreed. 'Not that she listens to me, but I'd like her to have more of a definite direction. They are both adults, in any case, and we have to let them live their own lives.'

'It's funny, really, to think of our children being involved romantically,' Ian said, giving me a very deep look. 'Even if things didn't work out for us, there's a certain symmetry in the two of them being happy together.'

For some reason, this brought tears to my eyes. I blinked hard, and stared away over Ian's shoulder, trying to concentrate on the bright chatter and superficial glamour of the dining room.

'Eithne? What's the matter?'

Alarmed, Ian reached over and took my hand, and I forced a watery smile.

'Sorry. I'd never considered it in that way before, and I think it's sweet of you to put it like that. I'm so pleased that we're friends again.'

It was an emotional moment, and we sat in silence for a minute. He squeezed my hand very gently.

'My darling, I'm pleased too. Don't be sad, think of all the time to come when we can enjoy each other's company – just like today.'

We proceeded to enjoy ourselves very much indeed. The food was well presented and tasted divine, and the wine seemed to have gone straight to my head. And the best thing of all was that Ian made me feel attractive and amusing, not a boring wife and mother, and for this, I was more than grateful.

As we waited for coffee, I felt a hand on my shoulder, and jumped.

'Fancy seeing you two!'

Rick Ryan bent his head, and kissed my cheek, before extending a hand over the table to Ian. His eyes wandered over us in a speculative way.

'Of course, you're old colleagues, aren't you? I expect you ate at all the best places in London during your working days,' he continued, smirking.

'Well, Ian certainly did. He was a director with an expense account, but I was much further down the entertainment scale,' I said smoothly. Rick was a gossip, and I didn't want him spoiling my day. Ian gave Rick a cool look from beneath arched eyebrows.

'Rick, hallo. I thought you and Judy were in Paraguay,' he said.

'Just back, and catching up with work again. But it's not so bad when it involves a nice lunch. I'm here with Simon Greenfield of Maddox and Co. I expect you know them,' he returned, holding on to the back of my chair. He seemed reluctant to tear himself away.

He made detailed enquiries about both our families, before he finally wandered back to his table at the far end of the restaurant. Ian and I looked at one another, and burst out laughing.

'I get the feeling that he'd have liked to join us,' Ian said. 'Actually, I quite like Rick, although he can be an old woman at times.'

'He's a terrible blabbermouth. I expect I'll have Judy on the phone when I get home, avid for all the details. She'll probably insist that you entertain her next. I think they are especially interested in other people's affairs because they have no family of their own,' I hypothesised.

Ian looked dubious.

'Well, I suppose I could take her out, but with no very high expectations of pleasure. I think I'm going to need to be busy for a while.'

This time, I let Ian pay for lunch. I didn't think Peter would approve of such an expensive outing, and I knew Ian wouldn't mind. He was always very generous, and that was something I had liked about him from the first. As we were strolling back to his car, he said,

'Has Olivia told you about this holiday abroad yet?'

'Holiday? No, nothing at all.'

'She and Alex are planning a week away in France next month, to celebrate her birthday. I've recommended a few places to them, and I think they've decided on Brittany. You might want to prepare the ground for Peter.'

'Yes. Thanks for the warning.'

I digested this information as we drove back to Fenwich, and my spirits sank. It had been so lovely to feel free of my normal life for a few hours, and now the swamps of domesticity and family politics were about to pull me under again. I could see a fair bit of argument ahead when the topic of Livvy's holiday was broached, and I didn't look forward to it.

Ian stopped in the drive at the Old Rectory, but he made no move towards me, and I felt disappointed. We had been intimate and close in the restaurant, and now I didn't want the mood to go away.

I climbed out of the car, and went round to his side, and he lowered the window.

'Ian, thank you for a simply wonderful lunch. I have really enjoyed myself,' I said, putting on a suitably happy face.

He looked at me, with eyes slightly narrowed.

'Have you? You've been very quiet all the way home.'

'Sometimes it's hard going back to the domestic grind, that's all. I feel different when we're out together. We have fun.'

I sounded like a petulant child, and immediately wished I had kept my mouth shut. Ian switched off his engine, and was about to get out of the car, when there was a scrunching sound and Peter drove up behind us, narrowly missing Ian's Merc – I suppose he had not expected to find anything else in the drive. He slammed his door as he got out, looking annoyed and tense.

'Why are you all dressed up?' he demanded, eyeing me suspiciously. He looked over and nodded to Ian in an unfriendly way, and I hurried to explain matters.

'I told you we were going out for lunch, remember? Why are you back so early?'

'I have to catch a flight to Hamburg this evening. Is my blue suit back from the cleaners?'

'No. I didn't realise you needed it done so quickly.'

Now Peter thumped the boot lid down, looking even more furious.

'Thank you for entertaining *my wife*,' he threw over his shoulder, as he stomped off into the house. I was rooted to the spot, hot with embarrassment.

'Ian – I am sorry.'

'Don't worry. I can see he has more important matters on his mind. I'll speak to you soon.'

Ian started his car again, and began to reverse out of the drive. I felt quite wretched, and it must have shown on my face. He glanced at me, swore, got out and hugged me hard, climbed back in and revved away without looking back.

I didn't care if Peter had seen us.

Everything felt jangly, and out of place. I went slowly into the house, wondering what to expect. Peter didn't often get into moods, and I hoped this one was down to work related stresses rather than anything I had done. He was opening and shutting drawers in our bedroom, and I hurried to join him, anxious to help.

'Tell me what needs doing,' I asked, as he brushed past me impatiently. 'I'm sorry about your suit, but you didn't tell me it was urgent.' Then, seeing that he was ignoring me, a little demon inside prompted me to add 'You were rather rude and abrupt with Ian.'

'Fuck Ian.'

His face was red with exertion and annoyance.

'It's fine for him, swanning about with all his millions and other people's wives. Some of us still have to earn a living.'

He was throwing socks and underwear into a case, and I automatically bent to straighten them, but he pushed me away.

'Don't bother. I can do it.'

It was difficult not to interfere, but I held back. He looked at me with hostile eyes.

'You never dress up like that for me.'

This was really unfair and untrue, and I was moved to protest.

'Well, we hardly ever go out anywhere where dressing up is required. Don't fight with me when you're going away, Peter. I haven't done anything to deserve this.'

He went into the bathroom to pack his toiletries, and I sat down on the bed, feeling forlorn. My lovely day had turned into a domestic nightmare. Eventually, he came out, looking a little calmer, and began to rearrange the case more methodically. I hoped the crisis had passed.

'How long will you be away?' I asked, making my voice sound as normal as I could.

'Two – three nights, I don't know.'

'Is it to do with this big project?'

'Yes.' He zipped up the case, and looked over at me with a stony face. 'You'll be able to spend hours with Ian if you want to.'

'Peter! Today was the first time I have seen him for weeks. You must stop this. I don't like it when you are so irrational.'

The word stung him, and he looked away, frowning. I began to feel more in control again, and took a deep breath.

'Let's both calm down, and I'll make a cup of tea, if you've got time. When do you need to leave for the airport?'

'Dave's picking me up at four-thirty.'

He meant Dave Hill, his project manager. It was almost four, but I thought that a quiet half hour in the kitchen would benefit us both.

'I'll make the tea, then. Come down when you're ready.'

I busied myself in the kitchen, brewing a pot that was strong, the way he liked it. There was half a fruitcake left in the tin, and I cut some slices, and arranged them neatly on a pretty china plate which his mother had given me. After ten minutes or so, he came in, looking calmer and more like the everyday Peter.

I poured him a mug, and pushed the cake towards him.

'Thanks.'

He didn't sit down, but stood with the mug cupped in his hands, gazing into the garden. I was about to ask him why he had been so cross with me, when the back door opened, and Louisa came in from school. She looked rosy and tousled, and he brightened at the sight of her.

'Hullo, Daddy. You're home early.'

'Got to go abroad for a day or two, love.'

He reached out and stroked her cheek.

'Anywhere nice?'

'Hamburg. I suppose it could be worse.'

She grabbed a slice of cake, cramming it into her mouth very inelegantly. Even at her age, she was always starving when she got back from school. Silently, I poured her some tea, and she took the mug without comment. The doorbell rang.

'That'll be Dave. Finish your tea, I'll go,' I said.

Dave gave me a cheerful grin as I opened the door. He was a pleasant chap in his late thirties, with a joky demeanour which masked a high level of competence at his work. Peter liked and trusted him, and I was glad to think he would have an upbeat companion for his journey.

'Hi, Mrs Leigh. You look very smart today. Is the boss all set?'

'Almost,' I said. 'He's just finishing a cuppa. Would you like one?'

'No thanks, I'm fine.'

Peter appeared behind me, case in hand.

'Dave – chuck that in the boot for me. I just need to look out my passport.'

He strode towards his study. Dave and I walked out to his car, and I seized the chance to give him a hint.

'Peter's a bit uptight. See if you can get him to relax,' I said swiftly. 'Nothing major, but he's not his normal self. I'm glad you're going with him.'

'No probs. I expect it'll blow over, whatever it is.'

Dave looked surprised, but I knew I could rely on him. Peter came back outside, with Louisa hanging affectionately on his arm. He gave her a kiss.

'Don't get into mischief, darling. I'll see you soon.'

Ignoring me, he walked round the car and got into the passenger seat. I felt my cheeks flaming, because he wasn't even going to say goodbye to me. Dave's face creased with embarrassment.

'Bye, then, Mrs Leigh.'

He reversed hastily, and the car swept away, leaving us standing there. Lou didn't seem to have noticed that there was anything amiss.

Back in the kitchen, I sat down at the table, and looked around me. I was stunned that Peter had acted so coldly; we had hardly ever fallen out during our years together. This morning, I had tidied and finished my chores with a pleasurable anticipation before my outing at lunchtime, but now, a gloomy pall seemed to hang over the familiar surroundings.

And then I was cross. Peter had over reacted in the most childish way. Perversely, I felt pleased that he would be away from home for a while. Absence would surely make him realise how silly he had been.

I changed out of my frock, and forced myself to start the supper preparations. With only two of us at home at present, there wasn't a great deal to do. About six o' clock, the phone rang, and Louisa answered it. I wondered whether it was Peter, ringing from the airport to apologise.

She put her head round the door.

'Mum, it's for you – Ian Inglis.'

I went into the hall and picked up the phone. Sunbeams danced across the tiled floor, and made intricate patterns on the rug, and I felt a pleasant sense of anticipation.

'Ian?'

'Eithne. I hope your husband has left by now. I'm sorry if I caused you any problems.'

'It wasn't your fault,' I told him, tracing a pattern with one finger on the dusty table top. 'I think he was uptight about work.'

'How long is he away for?'

'A couple of days.'

There was a short silence.

'Well, you'll be at a loose end. How about going out somewhere on Thursday? Laura always visits her parents then. I'd appreciate some company, and I know you like to escape the domestic routine.'

He chuckled throatily. I couldn't help smiling.

'I suppose I should say no, but I'm not going to. Thursday it is. Where shall we go?'

We had a silly, giggly conversation, while Ian made a number of increasingly ludicrous suggestions. In the end, we agreed he would collect me about ten o' clock, and we would walk somewhere before grabbing a pub lunch.

I was smiling again as I put down the phone. Ian had restored me to good humour, although I had to repress a little, warning niggle that I was getting to like these diversions rather too much. Before I could move away, the phone rang again. This time it would be Peter. I picked up the receiver, determined to be sweetness and light, but a female voice accosted me.

'Eithne? It's Judy. I hear you had a fabulous lunch today. I want to hear all about it ...'

# Chapter 11

Peter did not telephone me, but the next day, I received a message from his secretary to say that he and Dave had arrived safely, and I must understand that they were so very busy, that it might be difficult for him to ring.

Fine. I didn't intend to be home much to take a call, anyway.

On Wednesday, I went to a charity tea with Maddy and one or two other friends. Olivia was in Manchester, and Louisa at school, so I was a free agent, and I liked it.

Thursday dawned bright but cool, and I cleaned my walking boots and searched for a padded gilet to protect me from penetrating breezes. I had no idea where we would be walking, but I needed to be prepared. Ian was prompt, and got out of his car to greet me, sensibly attired in cord trousers and a Barbour jacket. I couldn't help laughing.

'What's so funny?' he asked.

'It's just that you look so very much the country gent. All you need is a collie dog at your heels, and a gnarled old walking stick. I'm so much more used to seeing you in a suit and tie,' I told him.

He grimaced.

'I feel like a gnarled old stick myself at times, I can tell you. I'm not sure I'll ever really settle into country life. There are times when I miss London very much.'

He seemed downbeat today, and it subdued me. I seated myself next to him, wondering how I could cheer him up.

'Where shall we go?' I asked.

'Beeston Castle? It's a steep climb, but I'm told the view is worth it.'

He was not very talkative during the drive there. After a while, he roused himself.

'Sorry. I'm not great company today. Laura has been bending my ear about my reluctance to put our initial plans for the Court into action. Originally, we intended to gut the place, but now I'm doubting my commitment to staying there. I don't want to pour a lot of money into it if that's the case.'

This dismayed me. We had all found the Inglises to be a welcome addition to the neighbourhood, and my heart sank as I realised how much I would miss Ian's company.

'That would be a shame,' I said cautiously. 'You haven't been here very long, after all, and Maudie seems well settled into school from what Lou tells me. Please don't give it up just yet.'

Ian sighed.

'Laura talked me into buying the house. She remembered the place from when she was a little girl, and it was a kind of dream of hers to live there. Personally, I've been happiest in my flat in Chelsea. Do you remember it?'

'Of course.'

I also remembered the time I had spent there with him, not all of it happy for me. 'But that was at a different stage of your life, Ian. You can't expect things to be the same now.'

He remained morose, and I wondered regretfully whether he would stay in a bad mood all day. However, they say that exercise promotes positive feelings, and he cheered up as we laboured up the steep hillside to the castle ruins. When we reached the top, we could see for miles in all directions, and it was worth having aching legs for this alone. The trees were beginning to turn colour, and a vibrant tapestry of autumn tints stretched tantalisingly before us. Miniature cows grazed in patchwork fields, tiny farmhouses dotted the plain, and blue hills rose in mysterious shadow in the far distance. I remembered standing here with the children when they were small, and they insisted that we could see 'the whole of the world.'

A sharp breeze was blowing, and I felt glad of my gilet. Ian stood behind me, and put his arms round my waist. He was smiling now.

'Thank you for making me feel better,' he said in my ear. 'I suppose the country does have some delights.'

As I turned my head, he kissed me gently, and I didn't have the heart to reprimand him. I wanted him to be happy. A teenage girl climbing past us over the rocks gave me a quick, amused glance, as if it was funny to see two middle-aged people sharing an affectionate moment. I didn't find it funny. It was a lovely feeling, although I knew it was dangerous, too.

We climbed back down, hand in hand. Ian found a very superior pub for lunch, and once there, we talked happily of old days, relaxed and content in one another's company. Despite the coolness between my husband and myself, I had not felt so buoyant for a long time, and I pushed away any intrusive thoughts of everyday life.

Afterwards, he drove me home, and this time, he got out of the car and really kissed me goodbye. Neither of us spoke. I don't think we knew what to say.

He stared into my eyes for a long moment.

'I'll give you a call soon. We're away for the weekend.'

I nodded. He got back in, and drove away. I pictured him going back home to Laura, and was suddenly pained by the thought.

I was jealous. My house, normally so dear to me, seemed dull and unappealing, as I stood pensively on the gravel, wondering why I was allowing myself to be so stupidly self-indulgent. Then the gravel scrunched, and Olivia walked round the corner. She must have got off the Manchester bus at the crossroads.

If she had been a minute earlier, she would have seen us in each other's arms. Thank heaven for small mercies.

She eyed me in her usual irritated way.

'What was Ian Inglis doing here?' she asked, her tone disapproving.

'We had a walk and lunch together.'

She brought me back to reality with a thump. I turned and began to walk towards the house, while she followed behind more slowly. Inside, I went into the kitchen, and began to take off my boots. Olivia lolled against the doorpost.

'You're very chummy these days.'

'Yes, we are. It's kind of him to take me out. Your father's in Germany.'

My boots were muddy, and I looked for some old newspaper to protect the kitchen floor. The ham I had eaten for lunch had made me thirsty, and I poured myself a glass of water, while Olivia fidgeted about.

'I suppose you don't care if it upsets Dad – all this time you spend with Ian Inglis, I mean.'

She scowled at me over the table, and I felt myself growing defensive.

'It doesn't upset him half as much as the fact that you don't appear to consider his parental feelings any more,' I said. 'Exactly when were you going to tell him about your holiday in France? After you'd booked the ferry crossing, I assume, when it would be difficult to cancel. Your own actions aren't entirely above reproach, you know.'

Olivia's scowl deepened, and she flushed.

'Bloody Ian, I suppose. I'm an adult now, I don't have to consult you about every little thing I want to do.'

'That's true. But while you are still living under our roof – even if that's not all the time – it would be polite to keep us informed of your plans. As it happens, I don't have any problem with you going away with Alex. I approve of him very much, but Dad may need a bit more persuading.'

Eventually, she grudgingly told me that she and Alex planned to spend the second week of October in northern Brittany, touring the region, and ending up in Saint-Malo, before catching a ferry back. It sounded like fun.

'I assume that Alex is shouldering most of the cost,' I said. I knew that Olivia's wages from the Three Feathers didn't go very far.

'Yes. If you and Dad could give me some cash for a birthday present, that would help,' she said. She would turn nineteen earlier in the month.

'I don't think that's a problem. But I advise you to tell him about the trip as soon as he gets back,' I said.

Peter's secretary called me on Friday morning, to say that he would be returning from Germany early on Friday evening. I decided that I would let bygones be bygones, and made sure that supper was one of his favourite dishes. I also made an effort with my clothes and make up. There would be no cause for complaint if I could help it.

He walked through the door about six o'clock, looking tired and a little dishevelled from the journey.

'Hello, darling. How was your trip?' I asked brightly. He didn't reply, but walked swiftly round the kitchen table, and gathered me into his arms.

'Eithne, I am so sorry about the other day. I was distracted about the business, and I'm afraid that, stupidly, I resent the fact that you have time to spend with Ian. I felt really wretched when I was away. Don't quarrel with me again.'

With an heroic effort, I forbore to mention that I hadn't been the one doing the quarrelling.

'Your blue suit will be ready tomorrow,' I murmured, as he hugged me.

'To hell with the blue suit. Give me a real kiss.'

It was a shame that Olivia was working. I thought she would have been delighted to see her parents in an affectionate clinch, and it would quell her impulse to niggle at me.

After this, we passed a happy evening. Peter told me that his firm had won the German contract, which would be an important boost for them after a very slack period.

'The only downside is that I will have to be away a lot before Christmas. Can you put up with that?' he asked, giving me an apologetic grin.

Why did that make my heart gave a little jump? Surely not because I would be free to please myself about what I did – and whom I saw – when he was away. I assured him that I was prepared to cope with his absence, and that we would plan some time for ourselves when he was less busy.

As I had predicted, Peter was not entirely happy when Olivia told him about her French trip, but there was nothing he could do about it. Alex came over on Sunday, and spent a long time with us, going through the details of their itinerary, and this helped to mollify Peter. It was very evident to me that Alex was serious about Livvy, and I hoped that she was beginning to return his feelings in the same way. He was such a pleasant boy, and with luck, the influence of his extra years would begin to smooth out some of Livvy's more childish traits.

It had been an emotional week. As if to balance things out, the next ten days or so were very flat and boring. I was disappointed not to hear from Ian, but when I met Laura at a local cancer fundraising coffee morning, she told me that he was unexpectedly busy in London, advising on a potential takeover bid for one of the businesses with which he was involved. I was still trying to ask the Inglises to dinner, but their very complex social life meant that Saturday nights were ruled out for weeks to come. In the end, we agreed that they would come for a family dinner on the Sunday when Alex and Livvy were ending their holiday in France.

In the midst of all this, we had not forgotten Josh. Nicholas rang from Oxford one weekend, and told me that he had received a warm, if slightly disjointed response to the letter he had sent after his grandmother's death, and I hoped this was a first step to the boys establishing a genuine regard for one another. I thought about Josh, and worried about him more than a little, when I remembered the emotions which had been unresolved during his visit to us. In the end, I wrote to him, and told him simply that I was glad to know he was Nick's child.

'Your father was the person I loved most in the world. I look forward now to being able to tell you about him,' I wrote. 'Please don't leave it too long before you return to England. I think that Nicholas would like to see you, too.'

I sent a similar message to Luke. Now the ball was in their court again.

The day of the Inglises' visit rolled around. It would just be the six of us – Peter and me, Ian and Laura, Louisa and Maudie – and so I decided to keep things informal. We dined in the conservatory, which I had decorated with the last of the summer flowers and some berry laden branches, and the menu was simple, but I made a big effort with the cooking and used the best possible ingredients, and I think everyone enjoyed their food, judging by the empty plates.

After dinner, we relaxed with coffee and some wonderful chocolates which Laura had brought. The girls disappeared to Louisa's room. Ian and Peter conversed affably about business matters, and even Laura seemed to make herself at home. She shed her normal polished manner for something more human and approachable, and I was pleased that the evening was going so well.

The telephone rang, and Peter went to answer it. I heard his voice rise, and after a minute or so, he came back into the room, his face pale and lined with worry.

'Do either of you speak good French? I'm having some difficulty,' he said to our guests. 'I think that the children have been in some kind of accident.'

Ian was on his feet in an instant.

'Where's the telephone?'

The two men left the room, and I stared at Laura, paralysed with horror. She came quickly to my side.

'Don't worry, darling. I expect it's something quite minor; you know what foreign police are like. Ian will sort it out,' she said, patting my arm.

I nodded, unable to voice my fears, although a terrifying scenario of mangled machinery and bodies was playing itself out in my head. My heart was thumping, and it felt difficult to breathe. It seemed an eternity until the men returned, Ian looking very grim and businesslike. He stood, looming over me.

'Eithne. It's all right. They have been involved in an accident, and they are in hospital in Saint-Malo, but neither of them have life-threatening injuries. By all accounts, it was a head on collision, and they both have pretty severe concussion and cuts and bruises. The hospital wants to keep them in for a couple of days for observation, especially as they aren't local. I think that I'll fly out there tomorrow, to be on hand. I know Alex's French isn't up to much, and I expect Olivia's isn't either.'

He hesitated. 'Do you want to come too? Olivia may be glad to see you, and I know it's difficult for Peter to get away.'

'Not just difficult, impossible. The Germans are coming on Tuesday to tie up the final details for their contract, and that's going to take a few days.'

Peter clenched his hands, looking anguished. Laura stepped in to add her voice to the discussion.

'Louisa can stay with us, if it makes life easier. I think it's a good idea for Eithne to go. Olivia will want her mother.'

'She would prefer her father,' I thought wryly, but that wasn't an option.

Everyone began to talk at once. Ian asked to use the phone again, and was gone for a long time. Lou and Maudie joined us, looking scared, as they realised the seriousness of the situation, and my attempts to calm Louisa enabled me to resume some control over myself, although my legs felt like jelly, and my heart was racing. Peter went out to see if Ian needed any assistance.

'We were having such a nice evening. What a shame it's ended like this.'

Laura sounded genuinely sad. I felt myself warming towards her in a way which I had not expected, and I was touched by the concern with which she urged Louisa to stay with them in my absence.

'What about Daddy?' Lou asked in a small voice.

'I expect he'll stay in Manchester if he has a client to look after,' I said. There was a small flat attached to his office for this very purpose.

Ian returned, with Peter at his heels.

'We're booked on a flight from Stansted to Dinard tomorrow morning, and we'll pick up a hire car at Dinard airport. Then we can go straight to the hospital. Visiting hours are from one until eight in the evening.'

He glanced at Laura. 'I'll try to call Jane tonight when we get home, but I don't expect she'll feel it necessary to come across. My intention is to reserve rooms in a hotel I know in Dinard, as it's quieter than Saint-Malo and almost equally convenient for the hospital. Can you drive us to the airport tomorrow?'

'No, I can do that,' Peter interrupted, anxious to assist in some way. 'I don't need to be in the office until tomorrow afternoon, and I'd like to help where I can.'

I knew he was feeling bad that he could not do more, but Ian had everything well under control. Laura agreed to bring Lou down to the house every day, to feed the animals. Peter would stay at the office flat at least until Thursday, unless we returned from France before then.

'I imagine the car's a write off, so we'll probably all fly home together, Ian said. 'Luckily it's out of season, and there appears to be plenty of room on the flights.'

He gave me a small, reassuring smile.

'Don't worry, Eithne. I'll try to speak to the hospital when I get home, but the very helpful gendarme who was on the line assures me that the children are in no real danger. All you need to do is pack a case and find your passport. Leave the rest to Peter and me.'

As I hastily washed up the remains of our dinner a little later on, I remembered with a jolt that I had flown to France with Ian on our very first date. My stomach lurched as I recalled the nights of passion that had ensued, then I put the memories firmly out of my mind. This trip was going to be very different.

# Chapter 12

I was up early and busy the following morning. Lou needed help with her clothes, and then I quickly packed two cases with the things which Peter and I would need for our respective days away. He was most upset that he was unable to come to France.

'Peter, the children are not in any danger now. I'm afraid your duty is to the firm,' I told him. 'I will keep you fully updated, and I think that Laura is right in this instance. Livvy needs her mother.'

'Don't get cross with her.'

'Of course I won't. I don't suppose any of this is her fault.'

We left Louisa with Maudie and Laura when we went to Delamere Court very early the next morning, to collect Ian. Laura fussed over him on the steps. He embraced her quickly, and climbed in next to Peter.

'I managed to find out a little more when I got home last night,' Ian informed us as we drove back down to the main road. 'Alex wasn't to blame. Another driver shot a red light, and is facing prosecution. They were just in the wrong place at the wrong time.'

I shuddered slightly, relieved that the outcome had not been more serious. Peter also seemed pleased to hear this. I suspected he had been reproving himself for allowing Olivia to go off with Alex in the first place, although he could not really have prevented her.

We were all quiet during the drive to the airport. Ian asked Peter a few polite questions about the German contract and the negotiations, but our minds were fixed on France and the children. Peter hugged me very tightly when he dropped us off. His eyes were misty, and his voice sounded choked.

'Look after yourself, my darling, and give Olivia my very dearest love. Tell her I would have come, only ...' His words tailed away, and he blew his nose.

'Don't worry, she will understand. We'll be back before you know it, and it will be as if all this never happened.'

I couldn't have been more wrong, but I didn't know that at the time.

The plane was very small, and propeller powered. I gasped when I saw it – I was always a nervous flyer – and Ian had to help me up the steps. I slithered unhappily into my seat, and he grasped my hand.

'Don't worry. These little aircraft are very reliable. It's a quick journey anyway, and we'll be there before you know it.'

The morning was calm and sunny, and I felt better once we were airborne, and I realised the plane was able to cope with the conditions. Ian still had my hand in his and I left it there, because it was reassuring. Drinks were served, and I gazed out at the coastline far below. The Channel lay blue and sparkling beneath us, and tiny waves frothed over the surface of the sea.

'I expect we'll get a good view of the Channel Islands today. The weather's remarkably calm for October,' Ian said.

I found that I was so entranced by the panorama of land and ocean, that I almost forgot my nerves, although I didn't enjoy the turbulence as we came through a cloud bank on our descent to France. Dinard airport was very small, and for a moment I wondered if we were in the right place.

Ian proceeded to tear a strip off the car hire company. He had requested an automatic, as he said it was difficult to change gears with the wrong hand, and there was some argument over availability, but he eventually got his way, and we loaded our cases into a smart saloon. I was very impressed with his command of the language, and complimented him as we set off again.

'My Italian's better, really.'

How nice to be so talented. He swung out into the traffic on the road heading to Saint-Malo.

'The hospital is on the outskirts of the town. I suggest we stop at a cafe and grab a quick bite before we go to the hospital. We might not be able to eat there.'

I wasn't very hungry, but once we were sitting in a small bar with an omelette and frites before us, I was glad of the food. If the circumstances had been different, I would have been enjoying myself, and I was so grateful that I had not had to make the trip on my own. There was something very reassuring about the efficient way Ian took control, and I was more than happy to be told what to do.

We ate quickly, then headed for the hospital.

I had to leave the talking to Ian when we got there. Everything seemed very calm and quiet, and there was none of the anxious bustle which seemed to characterise British hospitals. After speaking to the reception staff for a few minutes, Ian turned to me.

'I'll come with you to find Olivia, then I'll go to Alex. They are on different floors, and we'll want to make sure they have everything they need, so I may have to float between the two of them. Do you speak any French at all?'

I hastily reviewed my schoolgirl lessons.

'Only a little I'm afraid, but I probably understand more than I speak. Sorry.'

We began to walk down a wide, white corridor. After a turn or two, we came to the ward, and I scanned the faces with worried eyes and an anxiously beating heart.

Olivia was lying in a bed at the far end, by a window. She turned as we approached, and her face lit up.

'Oh, Mum!'

We hugged each other, incapable of speech for a moment or two. She had a huge bruise above one eye, her head was partially bandaged, and there were several dressings on her exposed arms, but she looked and sounded pretty much like the Olivia I knew, and I was reassured. She smiled at Ian, as he stood at the end of her bed.

'Ian, thank you for bringing Mum to me,' she said, with genuine warmth in her tone. 'Tell me about Alex. It's been really difficult, because hardly anyone speaks English, and my French is terrible. I'm so glad you're both here.'

Ian pulled up chairs and we sat down. He explained briefly what we knew about Alex's condition, and then rose to go.

'Sorry, Olivia, but I'm anxious to see him,' he explained. 'I'll be back later to update you. Just enjoy your mum's company now, and let us know what you might need. Have they said anything about discharging you yet?'

She shook her head, wincing slightly, her fingers exploring a sore place beneath her curls. We watched Ian stride back down the ward, and the curious eyes of patients and visitors followed his tall figure with interest.

Olivia turned back to me.

'It wasn't Alex's fault, Mum. Some stupid Frog ran a red light, and Alex couldn't do anything. It was awful when it happened, and I was knocked unconscious. They've been good to me here, but I wish I'd been able to understand or speak more of the language.'

Her eyes filled with tears, a sight we hardly ever saw.

'One of the doctors speaks English, and he told me Alex wasn't badly hurt, but I haven't seen him since. Do you think we could go and find Alex too? I really want to see him, and I am allowed to walk to the bathroom and things.'

I patted the hand lying on the coverlet.

'We'll see, later on. Can you tell me anything about your concussion?'

But she was very vague about her condition. Whether this was due to lack of information, or the injury, I couldn't tell.

'Dad and Lou sent their best love,' I told her. 'Dad was ever so sorry he couldn't come, but he's got a really important contract negotiation on at home. We'll ring him later to tell him how you are.'

'You won't leave me here and go back to England?'

Her face was woebegone at the thought.

'No, of course not. I think Ian is hoping we'll all be able to travel together in a day or two.'

She relaxed a little at that. I made a list of things which she needed, assuming she was going to spend a few more days on the ward, and she explained hospital routines to me, sounding more like her usual self.

'The food is amazing, Mum. It's like a restaurant. I couldn't eat yesterday, but I really enjoyed my lunch today – three courses, and it all tastes so good.'

The afternoon wore on. Ian reappeared, and after some negotiation with the matron, accompanied by a good deal of gallant flirting on his part, we were allowed to take Olivia in a wheelchair to visit the injured Alex.

He was in a men's ward, and looked a great deal paler and more fragile than Olivia. She leapt out of the chair to embrace him as soon as she could.

'Alex darling!'

Ian and I tactfully looked at each other and smiled as our children held one another in a loving hug. I was amazed by the emotion in Olivia's voice, as I wasn't used to her being so open and affectionate with anyone, apart from her father. Perhaps her feelings for Alex were really becoming true and deep. I had no doubt that he felt that way about her.

When they finally released each other, I went across to the bed and kissed Alex too.

'Eithne, I am so sorry. I feel so bad about Olivia,' he murmured, giving me an agonised glance. I smoothed back his hair, remembering his mother was very far away, and wishing he didn't look quite so wan and weak.

'Alex, it wasn't your fault. These things happen. We just want you to get well now as quickly as possible,' I said.

A doctor appeared, looking very surprised to find so many people by the bed. He and Ian conversed at some length, with much Gallic shrugging and hand waving on the doctor's part. When he had gone, Ian told us that they would not be willing to discharge either of the children for another day or so. Both of them had been rendered unconscious by the crash, and the hospital wanted to ensure that the concussion was not going to result in complications.

'Sorry, old lad. With any luck, it will only be few days, and we'll stay until we can get you home,' Ian told him.

This made my legs wobbly again, but it was stressed this was very much a precautionary measure, and their good recovery so far meant that all was likely to be well.

We finally got away just before the end of visiting hours, laden with requests, and both of us feeling very tired. Then we drove to our hotel in Dinard, desperate for dinner and a hefty drink.

The hotel looked old fashioned from the outside, but was delightfully modernised within. We had been given adjoining rooms on the first floor, and I gaped appreciatively at the sea view. It was partially obscured by darkness, but the twinkling lights of boats dotted the water below us. I washed and tidied myself rapidly, before joining Ian in the restaurant.

We were hungry, and for once, I drank my full share of the bottle of wine. I didn't object when Ian ordered brandies with our coffee, either. The alcohol was helping me to relax and assimilate the stresses of the day.

Ian told me that he would ring Laura after dinner, and she would then pass on the relevant information to Peter in Manchester. It was easier for us all to have a single point of contact at this stage.

'I haven't been able to reach Jane. She and her husband must be away. But I don't think it's a problem. I would have been very surprised if she wanted to drop everything and get over here,' he said, lazily swilling his brandy around his glass.

We sat in companiable silence for a while longer. The dining room was now emptying fast, and waiters began to clear round us with increasingly meaningful glances in our direction.

'Come on. You look worn out,' Ian said, helping me from my chair.

The lift whooshed us to the first floor. I fumbled with my key, and Ian had to help me unlock the door. He walked into the room before me, and the door swung closed behind us.

'Better just check there's no one under the bed,' he said, smiling, as he drew the curtains to shut out the night.

A car hooted angrily in the street below, and I could hear the faint mewing of sea birds. Suddenly, I felt very far from home.

A confusing tide of emotions surged through me as I stood there. Relief that the children were going to be okay, gratitude – something much more than gratitude towards Ian for being there, and handling everything with such grace and efficiency, and an unexpected sense of relaxation and well-being after the wine and the intimate dinner. I shrugged off my jacket, but two tears rolled down my cheeks as I did so.

Ian looked across the room and saw the tears.

'Eithne, darling, whatever is it?'

He came swiftly to my side, and put his hands on my shoulders. 'Don't cry. The children will be fine. I know it's been a shock, but it's going to be all right.'

He stroked my hair, then kissed me gently, as if I were a wayward child. His touch galvanised me, and I caught his face in my hands, kissing him back, eagerly and with desire.

'Ian ... '

The kissing intensified, became questioning and arousing.

After a few minutes, he raised his head and looked into my eyes. Realisation dawned on his face.

'Eithne... is this really what you want?' he muttered, his body hardening against me.

'Yes,' I whispered.

He pulled me down on to the bed with him. Our clothes came off any old how, and then we were under the sheets, locked together in a tight embrace. He moved across my breast, and eased himself into me, and my body responded eagerly to his passionate invasion.

During our recent times together, I had found it difficult to suppress vivid little memories of being in bed with him. There was a rough edge to his lovemaking which I found very arousing after my gentle husband, and I was shaken by an orgasm which left me gasping with its intensity.

When it was over, he lay by my side, and we began to come to our senses. I was unbelievably happy. At this time, I had no thought of what might result from our actions, no regrets for having stepped outside the boundaries of my marriage. It simply felt the right thing to do.

He kissed me, and then sat up, and began to dress.

'Where are you going?'

I was alarmed – surely he wasn't just going to get up and walk away?

'I need to unpack, and I have to call Laura to tell her about the children.'

We exchanged a guilty glance. He obviously wasn't going to be telling her about this part of the day's activity. 'But then, I'd like to come back, and spend the night with you.'

'Take the key with you then.'

I lay there in a contented daze for a while, then got up to perform my usual nightly rituals. I straightened the tumbled sheets, and slipped on my nightdress. By now, the fatigue of the day was beginning to overwhelm the excitement of the previous hour, and I got back into bed, still feeling little pulses throb inside from the passionate sex we had shared.

Then I sat up, thinking with shock that we had not used any form of protection during intercourse. But I remembered almost immediately that I had heard Laura extolling the virtues of vasectomies, so there would be nothing to worry about on that score.

I heard the door open, and Ian slipped in, wearing his pyjamas and a bathrobe. He slid in next to me, and drew me to him.

'What is it with you and French hotels?' he murmured, smiling, and we both fell asleep without another word.

We made love again when we awoke early the following morning, and it was tender and beautiful. Ian left to shower and dress, and I did the same, eventually making my way down to the restaurant for breakfast. We had hardly spoken two words to one another, but I hoped that our actions said everything that was needed.

He was sitting at a table, reading *Ouest France,* and nursing a large cup of black coffee. As I joined him, I realised I was ravenous, and tore into a large glazed brioche roll, which I spread thickly with a gooey greengage conserve. This was followed by a delicious, buttery croissant. He looked on, amused at my appetite.

'Why don't croissants taste like this in England?' I demanded, licking a flaky finger.

'It's a mystery. No one has ever been able to fathom it,' Ian said. He laid the paper aside, and cleared his throat.

'It's a lovely day,' he said. 'I suggest we take a walk. There's a delightful path along the sea by the yacht club and beyond, and we might as well enjoy the scenery while we're here. Then we can go to the nearest shopping centre to pick up the stuff Alex and Olivia have asked for, and have a quick lunch before going on to the hospital.'

'That sounds good.'

I brushed aside the last crumbs of croissant, deciding reluctantly that it would be piggy to take another one. We returned to our rooms to collect our coats – although the day was bright, there was an October freshness in the air – and then stepped out into the street, blinking in the sunshine. Ian took my arm, and guided me down some steep steps to the waterside below.

It was a beautiful scene. The stone walls of the ancient seaport of Saint-Malo glowed serenely in the sunshine across the estuary of the river Rance, and a high tide lapped along the sea wall at our feet. Elegant houses with terraced gardens graced the cliff behind us, and the path was bordered with beautifully planted flowerbeds, still bright and attractive despite the late season.

'Do you know this place well, Ian?' I asked, gazing, enraptured, at the sights around me.

'Fairly well. It's some years since I've been here, though.'

We walked along by the sea, with careful steps. Just past the yacht club, Ian dropped my arm, and leaned on a railing, looking at me with a searching, almost an accusing gaze.

'Are we going to talk about last night?' he asked, very quietly.

My eyes dropped.

'I don't know what to say,' I confessed, after a long silence.

He waited for me to continue, and I began to feel a little niggle of worry. 'Do you wish it hadn't happened?' I asked, after another pause.

'No – Christ, no, it was amazing.'

He put an arm round my shoulders, and I felt better. 'But I'm not sure what you're expecting now. Was it planned, or did it just happen? What do you want, Eithne? You'd better tell me before things go any further.'

What did I want? I wasn't sure if I knew. I wanted the excitement and passion of being with him, but was it possible to have that without disrupting two families and setting off a bomb in a number of lives? Did I want a full-blown affair, or was this going to be a few nights of lust for old times' sake?

Ian seemed concerned at my silence. I really did not know what to say to him. After a while, he spoke gently to me, turning me to face him as he stood framed against the sea.

'However tempting it may be to walk away from a marriage and start again, it can't be done on the spur of the moment. It's a huge decision, with endless complications. Take it from me, I know. I've done it once already.'

'Ian, I'm not thinking about anything like that.'

My voice trembled. The implications of the previous night were only just filtering through to me. 'I suppose I feel that because we're away from home, we're somehow in a different life. It's as if we can do what we want and it won't count afterwards. Does that make any sense?'

'You mean, three or four days of great sex, and then it's back to being neighbours? I'm not sure if it works like that, Eithne.'

He took my hand firmly, and we continued down the path. There was a seat set into a rocky part of the gardens, and we sat there, neither of us quite able to look the other in the eye.

He sighed.

'I have to confess that I haven't always been faithful to Laura – sexually I mean, not necessarily emotionally. But I bet you've never strayed before, and I can't see Peter being the type to turn a blind eye to any peccadilloes. If you want, we can simply draw a line under it now, and pretend it never happened. No one else need ever know. Don't you think that might be best?'

He stroked my cheek very gently, and I caught his hand, and kissed it.

'Ian, I don't want it to stop. I can't stop now. I want you to make love to me again. Is that really awful of me?'

A tiny smile played over his lips as he considered this proposition.

'Well, it might be difficult to say no to you. But, Eithne, I want you to be aware of what you are doing. I can't make any promises to you, and despite our past history, I would hate you to get hurt.'

The gulls screamed overhead, fighting for fish and scraps as a fishing boat chugged past. Couples strolled along, many with tiny dogs in tow, and a few heads turned curiously towards us as we sat pensively in the hazy October sun.

There was no easy way out. I thought about Peter and my family, and I knew my loyalty was to them. But I wanted Ian, too. Surely we could have these few days together without hurting anyone else, if we were careful?

I was in too deep to consider whether either of us might be hurt.

'Let's be together, properly, for the time we are in France,' I said to him. 'I mean at the hotel – obviously we are not going to carry on in front of Alex or Olivia. That might be enough.'

'Enough for what? And what if it isn't enough?'

'Ian, I don't know. But unless you say you want it to end now, I would like to share this special time with you.'

I put my head on his shoulder, and he sighed again.

'I never envisaged this happening, and I'm afraid that there's a trap waiting for one – or both of us. Above all, we have to keep this to ourselves,' he said. 'Is that understood?'

'Yes, of course.'

We must have looked like any other middle aged couple out for a walk that day, but our respectable exterior veiled a churning mix of excitement, fear and longing. We walked on, taking coffee at a cafe whose tables overlooked the main beach, and then left for the shopping centre. Nothing more was said about what had happened between us, and we pulled on the cloak of parenthood again.

# Chapter 13

I could tell that Olivia was getting better, because she was more than a little grumpy about one or two of the items of clothing I had bought for her, despite my protestations that my choice had been limited.

Ian had discovered that the children's luggage and personal effects had been recovered from the car and were being safely stored, and we would need to collect them at some point. The car was indeed a write-off, and it was miraculous that they had not been more seriously injured.

We were now hoping that they would be released from hospital on Thursday, but there was an added complication. The Friday flight to England had been cancelled, owing to a sudden strike by French airport staff.

'We'll take the ferry back from Saint-Malo on Friday morning. It won't be a problem at this time of year, and I can arrange for a car to take us back from Portsmouth in the evening,' Ian told me.

'But Peter will be available then, and he'll want to help. I'm sure he could collect us,' I replied.

'Perhaps he can. We don't need to decide either way until tomorrow.'

We were dining in a fish restaurant, set above a picturesque little inlet. I hadn't felt up to the demands of a seafood platter, as I didn't like oysters, cockles or whelks, but my langoustines and crab salad tasted as if they had been caught only minutes before.

Ian calmly worked his way through a huge pile of assorted seafood. I shuddered slightly as he demolished the innards of a big, rubbery looking whelk, smothered in mayonnaise, and tipped yet another oyster down his throat.

'Delicious,' he said, giving me a dark look across the table. 'You don't know what you're missing.'

I should have been happy, but I was uncomfortable instead. Since we had returned from the hospital, I was conscious of a definite constraint between us, as though there was a looming subject which we couldn't talk about. After the morning's frank exchange, this disappointed me, and I wondered painfully whether Ian was having second thoughts about the direction our relationship had taken.

A long silence when we had finished eating threatened to become ominous.

'Ian, despite what we said this morning, if you want to draw a line under what happened, I will understand,' I said, a feeling of sadness stealing over me. He looked up, surprised, his face solemn and pensive.

'I apologise if I'm quiet tonight,' he said. 'I think the events of the last few days have caught up with me. And there's the feeling that I could get used to this. It worries me rather.'

Used to the two of us together? My heart thumped, as I allowed myself to consider the possibility, but my common sense quashed it immediately.

I hated seeing him look so concerned.

'I'm not expecting you to change anything about your life,' I murmured, conscious as I spoke that this wasn't entirely true. I hoped very much that we could keep some degree of intimacy between us in future. 'As I said this morning, let's seize these few days and make them ours. It isn't for very long.'

He still looked grave. He said,

'This has brought back memories I hoped I'd buried for good. It's made me think about what I missed out on. I looked at you as you were sleeping this morning, and thought 'this could have been us every day'. If only...'

If only I hadn't made the choice I had done all those years ago. Tears gathered, and I blinked them back. I didn't regret that decision, but perversely, I wanted to feel that Ian and I could have a special relationship again.

'I hoped that this was a kind of healing experience for us,' I pleaded. 'Because I've realised that I do care for you. I can't undo the past, but I'd like to think I could make some small amends.'

'With a couple of nights of adulterous sex? I don't think so.'

I gasped, feeling as if he'd hit me. It was as well that the waitress chose that moment to begin clearing our plates. She made some laughing comment to Ian about the meal, to which he responded, and they exchanged a few minutes of banter, all of which was lost on me. I sat with a fixed smile on my face, feeling as though time had flown backwards and deposited me in the Italian restaurant in Chester.

'Do you want anything else to eat?' Ian asked. I shook my head, knowing that if I spoke, I would cry. 'Fine. *Deux cafés, s'il vous plaît, mademoiselle.*'

The waitress shimmied away, her attention turning to the next table. Ian regarded me unsmilingly.

'I'm wondering if this is my fault. I have enjoyed every moment, but I'm afraid I was playing a little game with you, with the kissing, and teasing back home. I thought I could exact a small revenge. Now it's gone further than I meant.'

I could recognise a brush-off when I got one. I made a huge effort to control myself, because it would be too dreadful to break down now.

'Ian, don't say any more. I understand completely.'

We drank our coffee in awkward silence. Ian paid, we gathered up our coats and walked back along the street to the hotel. He took my arm politely, but now, there was an impenetrable barrier between us. I couldn't understand what had happened, nor why his attitude had changed, but I was absolutely and utterly mortified.

He turned to me in the lift.

'I'll ring Laura now. Is there any particular message you want to send to Peter?'

'Just say that the children are going on well.'

I tried to smile. He hesitated when we reached our doors.

'I'll say goodnight here. I'm sorry my darling, but I think it's better this way.'

He brushed my cheek with his, and went inside his room. After a moment, when I stood there, almost in shock, I opened my own door.

Now I could let the tears flow, and I struggled to control my sobs. I didn't want Ian to hear me next door. Eventually, I staggered into the bathroom and found some tissues, then I came back out and groped my way to the window. Cheerful lights bobbed on the water just like the night before, but I wanted to blot them out.

I sat down on the bed. I remembered the happy, passionate time I had spent there so recently with Ian, and almost choked, I was crying so hard. If he wanted revenge for the way I had behaved towards him in the past, he was getting it.

Once the first fierce fit of crying was past, I tried to calm myself. I stroked the figured velvet of the bed runner, hoping the action would soothe me, and the sobs slowed to hiccups, and then stopped.

It didn't make sense. He might have been the one playing games in Cheshire, but I knew he had really wanted to see me, and the kissing had not just been some calculated action. And last night – last night, he had been as keen as I was to make love. I recalled the expression on his face when we were intimate in the morning, and it had been tender, loving and blissful. It had never crossed my mind that he would turn and reject me.

If this was my punishment for having been unfaithful to my husband, I'd have to live with it as best I could. I tried to think about Peter and the children, but my mind was full of Ian, and they seemed to be background figures in some tragic story; a Greek chorus lamenting my fall from grace.

I was terribly weary. I dragged myself into the bathroom, and turned on the shower. Hot water cascaded over me, and I stood, head drooping, wishing the water could wash away my problems.

At least, I was now past the stage of crying, although a sob still erupted from time to time. I heard the murmur of the television from Ian's room next door, and resisted the urge to pound on the wall and shriek at him.

Finally, I climbed into bed, and lay there, exhausted. Again and again, I reviewed our conversations during the day. I could only conclude that he was worried I might become so caught up in our time together here, that I would demand a bigger commitment from him in future than he was able to give, although I had specifically assured him I did not expect anything of the sort. Perhaps he was afraid of being hurt again. Whatever the truth, I was sure of one thing – the rest of our time in France was going to be hugely embarrassing and uncomfortable.

Somewhat to my surprise, I slept soundly. When I woke, I lay in bed and stared at the dim light filtering through the curtains, trying to work out how I was going to endure the next few days without giving myself away. I would avoid Ian's company as much as possible where I could.

With that aim in mind, I dressed quickly. There was no disguising the fact that I had been crying, but luckily, I had thrown a pair of dark glasses into the case when packing, and I put these on to cover my red eyes. I could always say I had a migraine.

I crept quietly from the room, and made my way down to the restaurant. If he was there, I'd get my coat and go out somewhere for breakfast. But the room was almost deserted, and I scuttled to a table, head lowered.

The brioche turned to ashes in my mouth today, but I choked it down. As I was finishing, I turned my head, and saw Ian entering the room.

He walked up to the table, and I stood up, putting my cup down with a bang. He looked surprised at the dark glasses.

'Are you okay, Eithne? Don't go. Stay and have breakfast with me.'

He put his hand out, and I ignored it.

'I've finished, and I'm going for a walk. Just tell me when to be back, for getting to the hospital,' I said, my voice flat and tired.

'Won't you wait so I can come with you?'

'No. I'll be back here for midday. Is that all right?'

I didn't wait for an answer, but strode out of the restaurant, leaving him gazing after me, perplexed.

I felt angry now. How dare he behave as though he hadn't humiliated me last night? I ran to my room for my coat and bag. I couldn't wait to get into the fresh air and away from him.

My steps led me to the same path we had walked yesterday. The sunshine dancing on the water then had been perfectly in tune with my spirits, but today, the clouds were low and grey, exactly mirroring my mood. I walked slowly, not really seeing very much, churning things over internally, but unable to reach any satisfactory conclusion. Tormenting myself, I sat for a few minutes on the bench we had paused at yesterday. Then it was on, past the fish restaurant, until I reached the main beach and the promenade.

A stiff breeze was blowing, and waves smashed angrily against the sea wall. It pleased me to see the wild water boiling away beneath me. For a sudden, stupid moment I felt like hurling myself in, to be dragged down by the current and swept far away.

A grey little Frenchman paused to stare at me. He approached, and began speaking rapidly, but my schoolgirl French couldn't make any sense of his speech. I nodded and tried to smile, and eventually I murmured 'merci – thank you,' so he would understand my difficulties. He stopped talking, and his eyes rested on me with concern. Then he patted my arm, saying some final words with a grave movement of his head, and wandered away. I think he had intuited my mood, and had been trying to console me. Perhaps he even thought that I was contemplating some rash action, and felt it necessary to intervene.

Some brave souls were breakfasting behind a glass screen at the promenade cafe, and I joined them, confident that my French was at least up to ordering a drink. Spray dashed against the glass, seagulls hung uneasily on the wind, and I tried to think more clearly about what I had to do to get through the day.

A shadow fell over me, and Ian stood there.

'May I join you? I thought I might find you here,' he said.

I shrugged, and he sat down. He ordered a coffee, and reached for my hand, but I snatched it back.

'Eithne. This won't do. Please listen to me,' he said.

I turned my head away, and stared at the sea.

'I am very sorry that this has happened,' he continued. 'Not sorry that we slept together – it was wonderful – but sorry that I had to reach the conclusion I did.'

'Perhaps you could explain it a little more clearly? I'm afraid I don't understand,' I said, in an icy voice. He sighed.

'Look, Laura is aware that I may sleep with someone else from time to time, and it doesn't really bother her. She doesn't like it, but she knows I'm not going to leave her. But with you – you're a different thing entirely. Not only do we have a past, but we have a special kind of present.

'God knows, I'm still very attracted to you, Eithne. Given different circumstances, I could see myself wanting to be with you again. But your life is the Old Rectory, Peter and your children. Peter wouldn't understand this little fling. He'd be on the phone to a divorce lawyer before you could blink, and I don't want that to happen to you. Your idea of a few passionate days together and then back to real life is too dangerous. We can't take the risk. It doesn't mean I don't want you, because I do. However, I certainly can't say I would be prepared to give up everything else at the moment.'

We sat for a long while in silence. His words made me feel a little less sore about the events of the day before, and I knew he was being honest, but they also made me begin to question my own judgement — or lack of it – in a way which I wasn't sure I was ready to do.

He reached for my hand again, and this time, I let it lie limp in his.

'Don't you understand that I'm doing this because I care about you?' he murmured.

A huge wave hurled itself in fury against the promenade, and we both jumped, as foam and spray splashed over the glass screen. People were laughing and exclaiming, and waiters rushed up to swab tables and chairs which had been drenched by the surf.

'I suppose so,' I said, watching the mopping up. 'But I don't see why we can't spend another night together. You upset me so much yesterday. Don't you understand that?'

A rueful expression came into his eyes, and he smoothed back his hair.

'It wasn't a great night for me, either. I kept wanting to knock on your door, but I was afraid you wouldn't hear me, or you wouldn't let me in. However, it's probably just as well I didn't. It would be the thin end of the wedge, my love.'

I closed my eyes. I felt shattered, and would have given anything to creep back into bed and sleep for the rest of the day.

'Are we friends again?' Ian asked.

'I don't know. I suppose we'll have to be, at least until we get back to Cheshire.'

Perhaps the little meetings and lunches would cease now. I felt even sadder at the prospect.

In the end, I accompanied him on the walk back to the hotel, although it was a silent enough affair. We collected the car, lunched quickly, and in my case, without much appetite, in the tiny port of Saint-Servan, and headed back to the hospital once again.

By now, both Alex and Olivia were becoming bored and fed up with being there. After more serious and prolonged consultations with the medical staff, it was confirmed that they would be discharged the next morning, too late, alas, to catch the ferry home.

Ian tried to book them a room at the hotel, but it was full with a convention of visiting Americans. However, as we both had double rooms, Olivia would bed down with me for the night, and Alex could do the same with Ian.

I had half made up my mind to dine alone at the hotel on Wednesday night, but Ian eventually persuaded me to accompany him to Saint-Malo. Despite my fatigue and low spirits, I enjoyed walking round the ramparts of the fortified town, watching a rosy sun plunge into the sea in a blaze of fire. Conditions were calmer now, and the evening air was mild and salty. We were made very welcome at a tiny restaurant in the 'Rue de la pie qui boit'. (The street of the drinking magpie – the name caught my fancy.) The food was deceptively simple and delectable.

Ian and I were back on speaking terms, but I was too low to respond to his efforts at conversation, and much of the meal was passed in silence.

'Anyone would think we were married,' Ian pointed out, looking exasperated. I sent him a sharp glance, but took the hint, and exerted myself to be little less dour as the wine took effect.

Eventually, we parted politely at our doors, with a repetition of the cheek brushing of the night before. A message from Peter awaited me, and I threw caution to the winds, and dialled the office flat number. He was overjoyed to hear from me, and his pleasure warmed my guilty heart.

'I can't wait for my girls to get home,' he assured me, and I agreed with the sentiment. I knew I would have to quell my own demons before I could resume our normal relationship, and vowed I would do so without further regrets.

Exhausted with emotion, I slept soundly, and looked more like my normal self in the morning. The hotel was suddenly very busy with the American contingent, and Ian and I had to wait a short time for a breakfast table to become free. The Americans were a group of males in their fifties, and there was a noisy drawling in the air, punctuated with sudden sharp bursts of laughter.

When we finally sat down, one man, with distinctive silver hair, threw me an appreciative glance on his way past, and I was cheered. My ego had taken a terrible bashing in the last twenty-four hours.

'Eithne, I'll be going to collect the luggage as well as the kids,' Ian said as we ate. 'Why don't you stay here and take a walk instead? You can't really help with anything, and it's a lovely day now. We can go out for lunch with Livvy and Alex when we get back.'

This seemed like a good idea to me, and I accepted his offer. I wanted some time to myself, anyway.

I decided to walk in the opposite direction today, towards a little beach at the other end of the yacht club. I strolled slowly, trying to absorb as much as I could. Despite the trauma of the last day or so, Dinard had captured my heart, and I didn't know if I would ever be able to return.

The walk was shorter than I had anticipated, and I soon found myself gazing into the weedy depths of a sea water swimming pool. It looked very unattractive to me.

'Wouldn't fancy a dip in that.'

I looked round, startled. The silver haired American from breakfast was standing at my shoulder, an expression of distaste on his face, and I smiled politely.

'No, it's not very appealing. Perhaps it's due to be given a clean soon, because it is the end of the season now.'

He gave me a friendly, admiring glance, and held out his hand.

'Chuck Riegert. I saw you with your husband at breakfast.'

'Eithne Leigh – and he's not my husband.'

Chuck Riegert's eyebrows rose, and he looked me over with a little grin on his lips.

'I *see*.'

'No. No, you don't see at all. He's my daughter's boyfriend's father. Our children have been in a traffic accident here, and we're sorting things out.'

He whistled, and asked me a few questions about the accident and the children's state of health.

'The driving is pretty scary over here. We've all commented on that,' he said sympathetically. 'I'm glad your kids are going to be okay.'

He grinned again, showing alarmingly white teeth. 'Say, do you fancy a coffee, Mrs Leigh – Eithne? I've got an hour to kill before the coach comes to take us off to some fancy place for lunch, and it would be good to have a little feminine company for a change. I don't suppose your daughter's boyfriend's father would object.'

'It has nothing to do with him,' I retorted, deciding I would accept this impromptu invitation.

There was a small cafe at the top of the path, and we settled ourselves there. Chuck Riegert seemed delighted to have found a sympathetic ear, and I thought a little buttering up would do me good as well. He told me that he was on a trip with a number of other men who did charitable work in the mid-western town where he lived.

'We raise a lot of money for good causes, and every few years, our wives let us off the hook for a few weeks,' he said, with a smile. 'We've done Italy, and it's gay Paree and Holland after this. Sure makes a change from home.'

He was easy to talk to, and his appreciation of my company was very welcome. I told him a little about my American friend John, and he brought out photos of his children and baby granddaughter to show me. Time passed swiftly, and we realised we would have to make a speedy return to our hotel, before he missed his coach.

'Mind if I take your arm, ma'am? he enquired as we set off again. 'This path is a little rocky underfoot, and I don't want your daughter's boyfriend's father saying I didn't take good care of you. He looks a tough guy.'

When we arrived at the hotel, he held open the door for me with a gallant gesture, and kissed my hand in farewell. There was a lot of whooping from his fellow Americans, but I couldn't help laughing.

I looked across the reception area, and saw Alex and Livvy checking in, with Ian assisting them. Livvy's mouth fell open as she saw me, but Ian laughed too.

'Your mother! We can't take her anywhere,' he said, sending me a knowing look.

I gave them a brief explanation of my outing, and Ian and I waited for the lift to return. It was full with the children and their bags.

'I'm pleased to see a smile on your face, anyway,' he said in my ear. 'You've been in a terrible sulk.'

'Well, what do you expect? We make love, and then you tell me you don't want to know any more,' I hissed back.

'Eithne. You know it isn't like that. Anyway, you pulled a nice American today, and that should cheer you up.'

I restrained the desire to kick him. However, whether it was having the children back or the fact that Chuck's company had done me good, I suddenly felt a little happier. It was easier to be with Ian, too, now I was not alone with him. Alex was quiet over lunch, but Livvy chatted away with her usual gusto, and protested when we insisted that they both retired to rest after the meal. I thought Alex still looked far from well.

We dined at the hotel, and the evening passed smoothly. Livvy was put out at having to share a room with me, but there was no help for it.

'How did you get on with Ian?' she asked, as we were settling down for the night. 'I bet you liked having him to yourself for such a long time. Dad won't have a look-in when we get back.'

'Don't be silly. Ian has been invaluable. How do you think we would have managed all this without him? You should be very grateful.'

I busied myself with folding some clothes away in my suitcase.

'Oh, I am.'

She rolled over, and surveyed me with bright eyes. 'I can see that he has his uses. Alex really worships him, you know. I think it's because Ian was out of his life for so long when he was little. It's a bit sad, really.'

We put out the lights, and soon, her regular breathing told me that she was asleep. I didn't find it quite so easy to drift off. All the conflicting events of the previous days replayed themselves in my head, and it seemed incredible to think that a week ago, none of this had been dreamed of. I hoped that I might be able to forget the worst of it once I was at home. Maybe one day, I would be able to look back on it without feeling quite so ashamed of myself.

# Chapter 14

Ian had a thin time of it the next morning. He had to be up early, returning to the airport to drop off the hire car before taking a taxi back to the hotel and collecting us for the short trip to the ferry terminal.

When I went to settle my hotel bill, I found that he had already paid it, which annoyed me. He had met the bulk of the costs of our expedition to date, and I made a mental note to send him a cheque when I was home. There was no way I wanted to be in his debt, and I knew that Peter would agree.

We were all pleased to observe that the sea looked calm as we climbed aboard the ferry, especially Livvy. She was not a good sailor. Ian had reserved two adjoining double cabins, and Livvy barged into the first one, pulling Alex firmly behind her. Muffled giggles could be heard from behind the closed door.

Ian looked at me, and gave a little grimace.

'I have a feeling that was planned. Sorry, Eithne. Would you like me to see if I can get another cabin as well?'

'Oh, don't be so silly, Ian. I expect we can cope with each other's company for a few hours more.'

We carried our bags into the small cabin. It had a tiny shower room, and there were two single berths, one made up as a sofa. Movement was limited, and we shuffled around one another with a degree of awkwardness. I was relieved when Ian suggested we should go on deck to watch the coast recede as we embarked on the journey homewards.

Livvy and Alex joined us up on deck. They were both in high spirits at the prospect of getting back to home and good health, and I was envious of their relatively uncomplicated lives.

Dark glasses protected my eyes from the autumn sun, and I was glad of them, because a few tears filled my eyes as I watched Dinard disappear into the distance. It would take me time to come to terms with my visit to France, and I felt that I would never be able to recall the days without embarrassment.

A military looking man engaged Ian in conversation, and I watched them covertly as the boat picked up speed. Ian was laughing, and he looked happy and handsome, and my stomach gave a painful lurch. I was beginning to see how far I had let him back into my heart.

I loved Peter, and I appreciated all his sterling qualities, but I had never been passionately, blindly devoted to him in the way I had been to Nick. With the passage of time, I could see that Nick might not have been the most reliable of husbands, but it didn't affect the way I still felt about him.

I had loved Ian too, in my youth, although Nick had lured me away with relative ease. Now, I wondered if it was possible to love two people at once, or whether I was hoping to recapture some of that lost, exciting time, when I found myself longing for Ian's attention.

But Ian had made it clear that he didn't want to take things further, and I had to keep that fact firmly in mind. I told myself that it made life easier, but there was still a terrible ache inside.

Livvy tapped me on the shoulder.

'We're going to our cabin for a bit. Ian's asked us to book a table for lunch in the restaurant, so we'll see you then, okay?'

She looked very pretty with her windblown curls. Alex was still very pallid, but he seemed to be feeling better today.

'Look after Alex. He's not really well,' I told her firmly. I wanted to tell her that I thought it unlikely he would be able to cope with too many physical demands at present, but didn't know how to frame the sentence in a way which she would appreciate.

I wandered off, leaving Ian to his conversation. Back inside, I went to the shop and duty free outlets, and was pleased to discover English newspapers. I bought a copy of *The Times,* even though it was yesterday's edition, and looked forward to a good read later on.

Then I returned to the cabin. Ian was not there, and I stretched out on the made up berth, heaving a huge sigh for all that had passed in France. The movement of the ship was soothing, and I closed my eyes.

I came to, to find Ian gently shaking me.

'Wake up, sleepy head. It's time for lunch.'

I was surprised I had slept for such a long time. In the tiny bathroom, I adjusted my make-up and brushed my hair, wishing that I could feel as normal inside as I seemed to look on the outside.

The children were already waiting for us at the table. Olivia announced that she was starving, and the heaped plate she brought back from the buffet of hors d'oeuvres made us all grin.

'I believe in getting my money's worth,' she explained, tucking in with relish. Not that she would be paying, but we knew what she meant.

'What happened to vegetarianism?' I enquired, seeing a few prawns and slices of smoked salmon and Parma ham amongst the salady bits. She had the grace to blush.

'Well, it's been difficult here. The French don't really go in for it.'

I hoped that meant she was returning to her old eating habits, because it would make life much easier for me at home.

We all ate with good appetites, and I was conscious that my days in France were having an adverse effect on my waistline as I surreptitiously undid a button on my trousers. After two courses, I was too full to eat any more, and I sat back as Ian and Livvy went to help themselves from an array of tempting puddings. Alex reached across the table and patted my hand.

'Thanks for coming to Saint-Malo, and keeping my father company,' he said, his grey eyes warm and appreciative. 'I know it's been much more pleasant for him, having you here.'

I gave his hand a little squeeze in return.

'It's no problem. And don't forget I wanted to see Livvy – you, too.'

'Is her father really pissed off with me?'

'No. That's not his style, and in any case, he understands that you weren't to blame,' I said.

'It isn't so easy for me to accept that. What an end to a wonderful holiday.'

He looked woeful, and I wanted to console him. As I weighed up what to say, I caught sight of several dolphins – or were they porpoises? – swimming beside the boat, diving through the waves as if they wanted to join the ship on its journey. I'd never seen any before, and it made me feel elated.

'Look, Alex! Aren't they a wonderful sight?'

He leaned across to look at them, and we both exclaimed as they leapt and dived in perfect symmetry. I wondered whether they might be a good omen, but by the time Ian and Livvy returned, the dolphins had disappeared under the waves and did not resurface.

After lunch, I went back to the cabin with Ian. He sat down, and took off his shoes and jacket, looking tired, and I remembered the early start to his day.

'Why don't you have a sleep? You look as though you could do with one,' I suggested, sitting on the opposite berth, and reaching for the paper. He yawned.

'I think I shall have to. We're neither of us as young as we were.'

I ignored the hand which he stretched out towards me, and buried my head in *The Times*. He reached further, and tweaked my hair.

'Don't be so cold towards me, Eithne. This has been just as difficult for me, too. I thought we were still friends, and I don't want that to change.'

'I don't think we should see each other for a while, Ian. Whatever you may want, I feel too – too poleaxed by all this to appreciate your company at the moment.'

To my great embarrassment, a few tears threatened to fall. He moved across to sit by me, and put his arm round my shoulders.

'Don't ... don't, my love.'

I let him hold me. It was easier than pushing him away. After a minute or two, he pulled me down next to him, and we lay together, with some difficulty, on the narrow bed. His embrace was both tender and regretful. Neither of us said anything more, and after a while, I realised he had fallen asleep.

I thought that I would allow myself the luxury of being close to him for a short time. The smell of his cologne was achingly familiar, and despite all that had happened, his presence was comforting. This would be the last occasion where I would let myself be in his arms.

I slept too.

After an hour, I woke with a jolt. The ship was rolling slightly, and my arm was sore from being squashed up against Ian in the small bed, so I gently disentangled myself and sat down on the opposite berth. He was still deeply asleep, and I watched him with a heavy heart, wondering how quickly I would be able to return to my old self at home. I was afraid that it was going to be a lengthy process.

There was a soft knock at the door. Alex stood there, looking pale and worried.

'Livvy isn't feeling too good,' he said.

I took a key and accompanied him into their cabin. Olivia was lying down, looking equally pale, and my own stomach began to feel queasy with the increased movements of the water.

'Sit up,' I said firmly. 'Put your coat on. You'll feel better up on deck in the fresh air.'

Leaving Ian in the land of Nod, we gathered up our coats and went out on deck. Once there, and seated out of the wind, Livvy began to look better, and I felt my stomach settle as well. Alex was enjoying watching the waves and flying surf, and the swell didn't seem to affect him at all.

'You were all right on the way across,' he said, giving Livvy a bracing look. She groaned.

'That was a short crossing – and I hadn't eaten an enormous lunch,' she muttered.

The sea began to grow calmer as we approached the Isle of Wight. Alex asked me for my cabin key.

'I'll go and wake my father, in case he wants to see the coast. Won't be long.'

Livvy came and huddled against me. She definitely had more colour in her cheeks now, and looked well, despite the bruise on her temple, which was reaching the yellowy purple stage.

'Are you all right, Mum? You've seemed a bit down these last few days,' she said.

Down .... that was one way of putting it. If only she knew.

'I'm fine. Just a bit tired, I think,' I said. That was true. She actually linked her arm in mine.

'I will be glad to be back at home,' she murmured.

Alex reappeared, with a sleepy Ian in tow. Ian didn't seem inclined to appreciate the view or be very talkative, and after a short while, the children announced their intention to visit the duty free shop.

I sat there with Ian, watching the sea and the contours of the island. The lights of Portsmouth were beginning to twinkle in the misty distance.

He yawned, and stretched out his legs.

'I remember going on holiday to the Isle of Wight once, when I was very small,' he told me. 'I got lost in Cowes, and there was a great to-do about it. My mother was panic-stricken, but I was quite happy, sitting by the sea front and watching all the yachts. Afterwards, though, I got a real thrashing from my father. It's coloured my view of the island, and I've never been back.'

I couldn't help feeling indignant on his behalf. I'd never got to know his parents very well, but could easily imagine they would have behaved in such a fashion.

'What a shame. I've never been there, but I would like to do so. We've got lazy in recent years. It's so easy to get to Wales, and the children still enjoy beach holidays.'

'I'd like to show you our friends' house in Tuscany, where we were this year. You'd love it there.'

This irritated me. When did he think it might be appropriate for me to visit his friends' house in Tuscany, or anywhere else, for that matter? I sighed, and returned my gaze to the sea.

After a little while, he turned to me again.

'Eithne, please say you'll come out with me one day soon. I want to feel we can go on seeing each other.'

'Absolutely not.'

My tone was decisive. I had to make him understand the position. 'I think it's better if we keep contact to a minimum for a time. Obviously, we may meet socially, and that's a different matter. But I think we both know we must be mere acquaintances now.'

I was reminded of something else which was niggling me.

'By the way, Ian, you should not have paid my hotel bill. Please let me know how much I owe you. I'll want to know my share of the meals out as well, so Peter can send you a cheque to cover things next week.'

'You don't need to do that, Eithne. I feel responsible, because Alex was driving. You know I can easily afford it,' he said, looking embarrassed.

'No. If you don't tell me, I'll simply make my own calculations,' I said.

He grunted, and I thought I would probably have to take that course.

'We'll have to clear the cabin soon,' he said, getting to his feet. 'Will you come to the shop with me? I'd like to buy you a present to say thank you for your company – some perfume perhaps, or is there something else you'd like?'

'You mean in recompense for a night of *adulterous sex*? No thanks.'

I spat the words out, the bitterness of the last day or so boiling over. He stood over me, scowling now.

'You're impossible. Please yourself, then. You'd better come and get your things, anyway.'

We returned to the cabin in silence, and collected our cases without speaking a word to one another, and then met up with the children in the part of the ship where foot passengers were to disembark. His face was dark and I was selfishly pleased to think that I had managed to wound him, even in a small way.

Peter had insisted on coming to meet us. He was waiting for us as we left passport control, and my heart skipped a beat as I saw him leaning against a wall; dear and familiar, but someone I was going to have to deceive. I wasn't looking forward to that.

Olivia ran forward and hugged her father with a cry of joy, and I hung back while Peter exclaimed over her and shook hands with the two men. He had some kind words for Alex, and I saw Alex look much happier as a result. Finally, he turned to me, and hugged me too.

Ian looked across at us as he loaded cases into the car boot, his face smooth and expressionless. I averted my eyes as Peter embraced me, not knowing whether I felt glad or sorry, then climbed into the back seat with Alex and Olivia, and prepared for an edgy ride back to Cheshire.

Once we were safely on the motorway, Peter turned to Ian.

'Ian, I can't tell you how grateful I am to you for dealing with all this so efficiently,' he said, his voice warm and sincere. I wondered just how grateful he would really be if he had known what the 'dealing with' had comprised.

Ian assured him that no special thanks were required. He and Peter conversed affably about France, and I admired Ian's cool command of himself, considering all the circumstances. I stared at the back of Peter's head and neck, and felt a terrible stab of guilt. It didn't help to transfer my gaze to Ian's handsome profile, as I calculated the depth of the pit I had dug for myself.

Sighing, I shifted in my seat. Peter looked at me in his rear-view mirror.

'Are you all right, darling? That's a very glum face.'

'Indigestion,' I murmured, my hand at my throat.

The long day's journey meant that we were very quiet, and I think that all the returned travellers dropped off to sleep at some point. We had a brief stop for a loo break, and finally, we were climbing the steep drive up to Delamere Court, where Laura, Maudie and Louisa were waiting.

They came out into the light of the porch and down the front steps as the car rolled to a halt. We all got out; everyone talking hard.

Ian and Laura embraced, and he gave Maudie an enthusiastic daddy-hug. Both Maudie and Laura appeared pleased to see Alex, too, and I caught an expression of surprise on Alex's face as Laura put her elegant cashmere clad arms around his neck. They looked the very picture of a prosperous and happy family, and for a moment, I felt so terrible, I could hardly breathe. I couldn't bear the thought of Ian going back to his household as though nothing had occurred between us. Laura would take possession of him in her assured way, and I was left with the mortifying feeling that I had been some sort of substitute who had been found wanting.

I would need to make a determined effort to forget France and step back into my old life. At least it was lovely to see Louisa again, and I concentrated on fussing over her while the men unloaded the relevant pieces of luggage. As soon as I could, I slipped back into the car, hoping that no one would notice I had not said goodbye, nor uttered any thanks to Ian.

He stood on the steps, an arm around Maudie as we drove away, and I felt a piece of my heart withering.

Once at home, I discovered that Nicholas had sent a bouquet of flowers to welcome us back. This made me feel a little less sorry for myself, and I concentrated on arranging them before I turned my attention to more pressing domestic matters. It was very late, and we were all exhausted. Laura had kindly prepared us a large packet of sandwiches, and I ate a round, although I wasn't really hungry. By now, all I wanted was to slip into bed and welcome the blessed oblivion of sleep.

Next morning, it seemed strange not to hear the harsh cries of seagulls when I woke. Peter was still buried deep under the duvet, and I crept out of bed, anxious not to wake him. Funnily enough, I had dreamed of Josh, and this made me think about Nick as I brewed my tea. The upheavals of July seemed very far away now.

I wondered what Nick would make of my lapse with Ian. I could imagine him declaring that it wouldn't have happened if we were still together; that he would always have the tightest hold on my heart as well as my body, and I could believe this was true. It would not do to dwell on any of this. I must put it firmly behind me, and concentrate on being a good wife and mother in the future.

Louisa clattered into the kitchen, eager to tell me more about her visit with Laura and Maudie. She had developed a genuine regard for Laura, which I found myself resenting, saying how Laura had treated them to meals out and bought her a great new sweater when she had been clothes shopping. She brought the sweater to show me, and it was beautiful, with a designer label I couldn't afford.

'You must write her a very nice thank you letter today,' I told her. At least we could demonstrate that we didn't lack social skills.

Lou and I had a leisurely breakfast together. She asked a lot of questions about France, which I answered as best I could, and she held forth on the subject of the luxurious life at Delamere Court, while I tried to look interested rather than vexed. Peter strolled in as I was loading the washing machine with the first of several huge loads of dirty clothes. He didn't appear to be the worse for wear after his long drive the day before.

'It's lovely to have you all home again,' he said with enthusiasm, patting Lou on the back.

'Tell me more about the contract negotiations. I was too tired to take much in last night,' I asked, exerting myself to pick up the usual threads of day-to-day life.

'Oh, let's not worry about that now. It all went very well, I'm glad to say.'

He came round the table, and put his arm round my shoulder, and I recoiled, catching my breath.

'Whatever's the matter?'

Peter looked disconcerted, and I forced a smile.

'Your aftershave! It isn't your usual one,' I stammered.

'No. Livvy bought it for me on the boat. Don't you like it?'

'Yes. I just wasn't expecting it.'

It was the same one Ian always wore, and the association threatened to derail me. I gave Peter a hearty kiss to hide my disquiet, and quickly returned to my domestic duties, reflecting that I'd just have to get used to it.

Olivia surfaced much later on. Peter was concerned about the bruise on her head, and insisted that she make an appointment to see our family doctor as soon as possible, just to check that all was well. She told us that Ian had already arranged for Alex to see a private specialist, to allay any worries about his recovery.

Alex would need to take some time off work before he got the all clear. However, he borrowed Laura's car and came to see Livvy in the afternoon, which pleased her very much.

I told Peter that Ian had met virtually all the costs of the trip to France, and we sat down together to work out a rough estimate of my share before writing a cheque. Peter forced it upon a reluctant Alex as he was going, and I hoped that would put some kind of full stop to the unfortunate chapter.

Over the next few days, I immersed myself in house and garden tasks, hoping this would stop me dwelling on the events of the week before. Nicholas rang to say that he hoped to come home the following weekend, and the thought of seeing him helped me to push the intrusive memories of my lapse with Ian to the back of my mind, although it was hard work at times.

On Monday, Peter turned to me in bed with eager ardour, and we made love. It was very nice, but it didn't shake me to the core like sex with Ian had done. Forbidden fruit certainly tasted good, but it was dispiriting when it disappeared from the menu.

# Chapter 15

I was overjoyed to see Nicholas on Friday. I picked him up from Crewe station after lunch, and we enjoyed a long mother-son chat about all the things which were important to him at the present time.

He fielded questions about his academic work with practised evasion, and assured me that all was fine on that front. His flat sharing was going well, and as we neared Fenwich and home, he confessed that he had a steady girlfriend.

'She's really pretty, and she has amazing long auburn hair. Her name's Freya,' he said, his colour deepening in a manner very unlike his normal, devil-may-care self. 'She's reading English like you did, Mum, but she's not at St Hugh's. I think you'd like her.'

'I'm sure I would. I'm delighted to see you so happy,' I said, heaving an internal sigh of regret for the joys of youth.

Both the girls were glad to see him, and he was very sympathetic to Olivia's tales of French hospital life. We had a pleasant family dinner, and then he announced his intention of going up to Delamere Court to see Ian and Laura. My heart sank.

'Must you? We've hardly seen you yet,' I protested.

'Well, that's not true, Mum. Anyway, Livvy wants me to take her up to see Alex. Can I borrow your car?'

His Mini was at Oxford. I couldn't really object, but gave him the keys with slightly bad grace.

'Say hello from us,' Peter called from the sitting room. 'And tell Ian he must present that cheque.'

I busied myself with clearing up, then joined Peter, who was watching a comedy programme on the TV.

'By the way, I forgot to tell you – the Ryans have asked us to a drinks party on Sunday morning,' he said, eyes on the screen.

'Oh, no. Did you say we'd go?'

I hated drinks parties, and was not anxious to attend this one, because I was sure the Inglises would be there. He turned towards me, surprised.

'You're always complaining about our dull social life. Why don't you want to go?'

'I just hate all that standing about, and getting boxed in with people I don't want to talk to and who don't want to talk to me. You can go if you want to. I can have a diplomatic illness.'

'I expect the Potters and Inglises will be going, and you like them.'

'Well, I can see them any time.'

I sighed, and Peter observed me narrowly.

'Are you feeling all right? You've been a bit quiet since you got home from France. Was it all a bit much for you?'

'I'm perfectly all right. It's just that I'd rather spend Sunday morning with Nicholas, that's all.'

Nicholas and Olivia didn't return until after I had gone to bed. It was a nice feeling to have everyone there for Saturday breakfast, the first time this had happened for some months. As I was loading the dishwasher, Nicholas said,

'Ian asked how you were. Haven't you been in touch since you got back?'

Bending over the dishwasher would make anyone's cheeks pink. I straightened up.

'Well, I've been busy. I've seen Alex, and it's good to know that his health is on the mend.'

Livvy had informed us that Alex had been pronounced fit to return to work, and she would be spending next week in Manchester with him, job hunting. Peter had just nodded when she told him. It looked as though he accepted their relationship was serious now, and strangely, the accident had made him more accepting of Alex, not less.

Peter took us all out for lunch at a country pub not far away, and as we sat there, laughing, talking loudly and eating with gusto, I thought to myself that we must look like an enviably happy family, much as the Inglises had seemed when I last saw them on the steps of Delamere Court. And we were happy, with the exception of myself. I thought that I didn't deserve much happiness at the moment, so that was fitting.

When we returned home, Alex drove up in a new silver Clio, a present from his father, and the young ones all piled in to go for a spin with him.

'It must be nice to be able to go out and buy a car just like that,' I observed, as they sped away.

'Yes. But it's not just about money. I suspect that Ian is still making up to Alex for the years apart and the split with his mother,' Peter replied.

Next morning, I had a 'migraine'. I was surprised when Peter said he would go to the drinks party without me, and equally surprised when Nicholas upbraided me for not accompanying him.

'You have no idea how tedious these affairs can be,' I said, somewhat mutinously. 'Besides, I wanted to spend as much time as possible with you.'

'But Rick and Judy are your friends!'

'And I will make an effort to invite them here soon, but that doesn't mean I want to want to pass several hours making small talk with uncongenial bores.'

'What if I went, too?'

'No, please not, darling. Let's stay here and have a good natter before you go back to Oxford.'

Eventually, he understood that I was serious. I waved Peter off with a guilty twinge of conscience, and instructions that he was to pass on my apologies to the hosts. Nicholas made coffee, and we went to enjoy the late autumn sunshine in the conservatory.

'Ian is putting me touch with one or two people in London agencies,' he told me, his face lighting up at the prospect. 'Much as I like Laine and Laine, it would be good to be in London for a few years, before I have any real commitments. Do you think Grandma and Grandpa would rent me their Wapping flat?'

I shuddered.

'Please don't think of going there, darling. It has too many horrible memories.'

'But not for me.'

He gave me a reproving look. 'I'd like to think I was living somewhere where my father lived before me. If that's upsetting for you, I'm sorry. But I've been corresponding with Josh, and he keeps asking questions I can't answer about our father, and I feel I want to know a lot more myself. You've only ever told me little bits about him. When Josh comes over again, perhaps we can all spend some time together retracing his footsteps – my father's footsteps, I mean.'

I didn't know how to reply to him. It made me happy to think that Nicholas and Josh were in contact with each other, but the thought of bringing Nick back to life in detail was daunting.

'Mum? Won't you do that for us?'

I would do anything in my power for my son – that was one constant in my existence. I knew that I'd have to do as he asked, even if I dreaded it

'Yes, of course I will, but you must accept there are limitations.'

He nodded, and sat there nursing his coffee, eyes fixed on the decaying November garden. It seemed to me that he had grown up a good deal over the last months, but whether this was down to the fact he was in his final year, or he had faced up to some difficult personal circumstances, or the civilising influence of a proper girlfriend, I couldn't say. I relished this adult Nicholas, even though I was conscious he would be growing further away from me as a result.

'You seem a bit depressed, Mum,' he said, turning to me again. 'Why don't you look for a job or take up a new hobby or something? It looks as though Livvy won't be living here much longer, and you're going to have time on your hands. Ask Dad if he can use you in the office – or perhaps Ian can suggest something.'

Perhaps not! However, I recognised that there was a kernel of truth in what he said. If I was to get over my mishaps in France, a new stimulus would help to speed the process.

Peter returned shortly before lunch, rather pink in the face.

'You missed a good do,' he told me. 'Everyone was concerned about you. I felt a real fraud on your behalf.'

'Sorry. I've had a lovely morning with Nicholas to myself, so I don't regret not going.'

Sunday lunch was everyone's favourite: roast beef, with all the trimmings. I was sad as we drove Nicholas to Crewe in the afternoon, but consoled myself with the thought he would be home for the Christmas vac before we knew it.

'Where does Freya come from?' I murmured in his ear, as I kissed him goodbye. 'Might we get to meet her sometime soon?'

He laughed, a trifle embarrassed.

'She's Scottish, so don't build up your hopes just yet. But maybe. It's a bit early to say.'

He embraced me, and disappeared into the train, swinging his rucksack with the airy self-confidence of youth. As ever, my heart went with him.

'Never mind, darling,' Peter said, patting my knee as we drove home. 'It will be Christmas before you know it, and then he'll be home again.'

Two days went by.

I started to plan little projects. I tried very hard not to think about sex with Ian, telling myself that anything would have seemed wonderful in a foreign hotel, removed from reality, recapturing youthful dreams. It was foolish of me to think those feelings could be translated to Cheshire, and it had all been some kind of mirage, now revealed for the false dawn it really was.

On Wednesday, I was up early to mail an urgent package at the post office in the neighbouring village. As I returned to my car, a voice hailed me.

'Eithne! You're obviously feeling better now.'

It was Judy Ryan, speaking to me from her car window. I leant down towards her.

'Judy, I am so sorry. Peter told me I missed a great party.'

'You did.'

She looked smug, her round face breaking into a great moon smile of satisfaction. 'But I'll let you off if you'll do me a favour.'

'Of course.'

I wondered what she wanted. She heaved herself out of the car, and walked round to the boot.

'Laura Inglis lent me these glasses and canapé dishes. I was on my way to return them, but I'm running late for the doctor. Be an angel, and drop them off on your way home for me. It's not really out of your way, is it?'

She was already unloading the boxes, and I had no choice but to let her transfer the glass and china to my car.

'Thanks. I appreciate that. I give you a call later in the week,' she said.

I stood on the pavement as she drove off, feeling as if I had been mugged.

Wednesday. I knew that was not one of Laura's usual days for visiting her parents, so perhaps I could go to Delamere Court without running the risk of seeing Ian unchaperoned.

As I manoeuvred my way up the winding drive, I couldn't repress a tremor of anxiety. I hadn't spent any time with Laura since I had slept with her husband, and hoped she would not be able to divine that I had a guilty conscience. I stopped in the drive, and got out to ring the doorbell. Nothing happened. Oh good, no one was in – I would unload the boxes and leave them in the porch. Relieved, I was beginning to do this, when Ian walked round the corner of the house, wearing sports gear, and with a towel round his neck. He must have been using his gym equipment in the old stables.

There was no smile of welcome for me.

'Eithne. I trust you've recovered from your migraine,' he said, coolly. He came closer, and scrutinised me. 'You won't be able to avoid me for ever, you know.'

I decided to ignore this.

'Judy asked me to return these things to Laura for her,' I gabbled. 'She isn't answering the bell.'

He produced a key from the pocket of his shorts. Unlocking the door, he threw his towel down, and turned to assist me with carrying the boxes inside. It didn't take very long, and I made to take my leave, but he closed the door.

'Where's Laura? Shall I just say hello?' I enquired, hoping my nerves didn't show.

'She's gone for a spa day somewhere with Sarah Harvey.'

He was still unsmiling, but he moved purposefully towards me, and backed me against the wall. I looked round for escape, but there was none. He seized me, and kissed me with all the passion that I remembered from our night in France.

Even his sweat smelled good.

Eventually, we had to stop for breath. I looked into his eyes, amazed and unsure of what was happening.

'What are you *doing,* Ian?' I choked out. 'I thought you said we shouldn't — we couldn't —'

'I may have been wrong.'

He turned, and began to pull me up the stairs behind him. His grip was painful, and I whimpered slightly as I stumbled in his wake. He hesitated on the landing, then led me swiftly down the right hand corridor, to a room at the very end, slamming the door behind us.

I knew that I should be protesting, but the double bed was soft and inviting. He was gentle now, removing my clothes and caressing my body with tender fingers, pulling me down until I felt I would drown in the bliss of being in his arms. I wrapped my legs around him, and lost myself in the fierce rhythms of lovemaking, until we were both sated and spent.

My body throbbed, and my heart was blossoming. I knew I would have to pay for this at some point, but now, I was unutterably happy to be with him again, triumphant, because I understood how much he wanted me.

He raised himself on an elbow, and kissed my nose. We looked at each other, long, and hard, and with an honesty and openness which was new to us.

'I've been absolutely miserable,' he confessed. 'I couldn't stop thinking about you, and wanting to be with you. Surely there's some way we can make this work? Laura is away from home several days every week; you are on your own during the day now, with Olivia in Manchester. Maybe I could rent us a little place in Chester.'

'I've missed you so much,' I breathed. I didn't want to think about the future, I just wanted to savour the happiness of the moment. We lay in a peaceful embrace, holding one another close, nuzzling and nipping, unwilling to let this unexpected intimacy disappear.

But it didn't last. Suddenly, Ian sat up.

'Oh my God. The dreaded Mrs Bannister will be here any minute to do the ironing. I'm so sorry, my darling, we'll have to get up.'

He stood up and pulled on his shorts, and I turned away, and started to retrieve my clothes from the floor.

'Shall I take the sheets off?' I asked, my voice muffled in my sweater. It was obvious that something other than sleeping had taken place in the bed.

'No, we'll just make the bed up again. I have a feeling we'll be back soon, and no one else is likely to look in here.'

I finished dressing. Ian gathered the rest of his clothes into a bundle.

'Eithne, I need to shower. Can you wait for me downstairs, and we can have lunch together?'

'What about your cleaning lady?'

'I don't think she'll expect us to invite her.'

He grinned, shepherding me out into the corridor.

'*Ian!* I mean, won't she think it funny that I'm here?'

'Well, perhaps you can take some of that china stuff in to the kitchen and unload it. I'll be as quick as I can.'

He disappeared down the opposite passage, and I made my way down the stairs. As he had suggested, I brought some of the boxes from the hall into the kitchen, and began to take out the contents.

I heard a car pull up, and then there was a grating sound, and the cleaning lady let herself in at the kitchen door. She looked extremely surprised to see me.

'It's Mrs Leigh, isn't it? Didn't expect you to be here.'

'I'm just returning these things for Mrs Inglis,' I said brightly. 'She's had to go out, but Mr Inglis is at home. Do you know where this stuff is kept?'

She picked up a canapé dish and studied it, frowning.

'I think it goes in the big cupboard in the utility room. Wait a minute.'

She trundled off into a room leading from the rear of the kitchen. 'Yes, it goes in there. I'll give you a hand,' she called.

It didn't take long to transfer all the contents of the boxes. As we were finishing, Ian came in, looking spruce and smart, if a little damp around the edges. I hoped that Mrs Bannister wouldn't notice.

'Morning, Mrs Bannister. Eithne, many thanks for bringing the china back. Laura will be grateful. Sit down, and I'll make you a coffee.'

He busied himself at an elaborate machine. 'Mrs B? Would you like one?'

'No. A tea'll do for me.'

She threw the coffee machine a disapproving glance, evidently unimpressed by the shiny chrome monster. When the drinks were ready, Ian led me into his study on the other side of the hall. It was large, and comfortably furnished with squashy leather chairs in the window recess, and an oak desk. Two of the walls were lined with books, from floor to ceiling.

'We can talk in here without her hearing us,' he said.

I sank down into my chair, looking around with interest. I thought I recognised some of the books and artwork on the walls from his flat in Chelsea, and I was hit by a wave of nostalgia. There were several important looking files on the desk. Ian saw me glancing at them.

'Did you know Simon Rogers in the old days?'

I shook my head. 'Well, he's getting me involved in a nice little buy-out. I may even sit on the board. I need to have a City project on the go, to keep my sanity in this rural backwater.'

He drank his coffee, surveying me with amused eyes. 'I suppose you are my Cheshire project. I should be kept busy between the two of you.'

I wasn't sure if I wanted to be a project. Besides, there were still many things which needed an answer.

'Ian, I am really confused,' I said. 'You said all that stuff in France about how we couldn't take the risk of having any kind of affair, and now, the first time you see me, you fall on me like a sex-starved teenager. What do you want? Is it just sex, or do you have something else in mind? I need to know, because I'm not prepared to be pushed aside again if you suddenly get an attack of conscience.'

He put his mug down on a small table, regarding me with a look of yearning concern.

'Eithne, I don't know how to explain it. I know that I shouldn't be with you in this way, but I can't *not* be with you either. I want you too badly. At the same time, I have to be honest – I don't think either of us is able to walk away from our existing commitments just now.'

I was silent as I pondered this, knowing it was true. I longed to be with Ian, but I couldn't quite go so far as to imagine a life without Peter and the children.

'I thought you were worried that Peter would want a divorce. And is Laura prepared to look the other way, as you once put it?' I asked.

'Can't we take things one step at a time?'

He furrowed his brow. 'We will need to make this up as we go along. I want us to have a real relationship again, Eithne, not just hurried sex when we can manage it, lovely though that is. Think about it. We've already been spending time together as friends without anyone objecting. We can do that as lovers, too. There will be plenty of opportunities for us to be with one another without arousing any suspicion.'

He leaned towards me, eyes glowing. 'This is important for both of us. I know you want it as much as I do.'

I knew it was a slippery slope. I didn't want to be a woman who lied to her husband and children, who put her energies into planning a secret life away from home and hearth. At the same time, I understood the reality behind his words. It was impossible to be together, but given the strength of our feelings, it was equally impossible not to be. I could not resist him physically, and that frightened me. Waves of confusion crashed down on my head.

The telephone rang, and Ian glanced at the handset.

'Do you mind if I take this?'

I rose to go. 'No, stay put, it's not private.' He lifted the receiver. 'Simon, good to hear from you. I've got the files.'

I stared out of the window, half an ear on the conversation. Ian sounded relaxed and interested, and I supposed this call must concern his London activities. He tilted his chair, speaking with concentration and clarity, and I felt achingly sad that I couldn't be part of his ordinary life. I didn't just want to go to bed with him, I wanted the intimacy of silly, everyday matters. I wanted to be involved and consulted about things which affected him and decisions which he took. I wasn't sure if the Cheshire Project would manage to achieve that.

It was a long call, and I glanced at my watch. Much as I wished for his company, I decided to refuse his offer of lunch. I needed time to myself, to think.

'Sorry,' he said, finally replacing the receiver. 'I'll need to go to London next week, but I'll make sure I go on a day when Laura's at home.'

We sat there in silence for a little while. Eventually, I roused myself.

'Thanks for the offer of lunch Ian, but I'll have to pass. I'd forgotten that one of the mums from school is coming to give me some sewing for the costumes for the school play So I have to get back.'

I stood up, and after a moment's hesitation, he stood up too.

'Come here tomorrow morning, then? Laura will be going to her parents, and she is usually away by ten. If there's any change of plan, I'll ring you after breakfast.'

He came round the desk, and kissed me on the lips.

'Don't worry, my darling. We'll find a way of making this work.'

We stood there in a tight embrace. I hoped he was right, because I didn't think I could cope with being rejected again.

He saw me to my car, and waved a polite goodbye. If Mrs Bannister was watching from the house, she could observe the perfect propriety of our farewell. Once at home, I washed and changed my underwear. I hadn't told Ian, but Peter was back in Germany. Nevertheless, I didn't want to have anything incriminating about my person when I was leading my Old Rectory life.

Of course, I wasn't going to go to him the next morning. I summoned all my common sense, and told myself that I must get over this longing for him, that it would all end in an ocean of tears.

This resolution lasted about fifteen minutes – to be precise, until he telephoned at ten past ten to say that Laura had left. I drove straight to his house, and we shut ourselves away in the little bedroom, aching for each other and the physical release of making love.

There was no Mrs Bannister to interrupt us today, and we lay for a long time afterwards, kissing, making idle conversation and growing ever closer. Later on, we went to the Three Feathers for lunch, and our outward behaviour was that of two friends, although inside, we were both glowing and contented after our morning in bed.

'It seems funny not to see Olivia here,' Ian remarked. She had given her notice in before she went to France, and her replacement was a skinny girl with a worried expression. 'Alex is confident she'll find a job soon – something I hope you'll be pleased about.'

'Yes. She and I are getting on much better now we don't see so much of one another. Is that a terrible thing to say?'

'I should think it's quite usual.'

He drained his glass. 'I know you think that Olivia is very different to you, but actually, you're quite alike in being hard-headed and stubborn about what's important. And I think that Olivia will feel happier now she doesn't have to live up to your academic expectations.'

I wondered ruefully why I found this easier to accept coming from Ian, than when Peter expressed a similar sentiment.

Olivia returned home on Friday night, arriving back at almost the same time as her father. She was bursting with the news that a friend of Alex had arranged for her to have an interview with another PR firm, and I could tell this was a job which really appealed.

'I would be a bit of a dogsbody at first, but the prospects are good,' she said, with an air of importance. 'It needs energy and ideas, and I've got loads of those.'

Peter and I exchanged glances. I suppressed my disappointment that she had definitely abandoned any thoughts of doing a degree, but I was relieved that she was showing initiative and being serious about her work. I also realised that it was a long time since I had heard her refer to my supposed preference for Nicholas, and hoped she had put that nonsense behind her for good. Her involvement with Alex had matured her, and smoothed some rough edges of her nature, and I was grateful to him for that.

'Where will you live? You can't crash at Alex's for ever,' I said, knowing that Alex already shared a flat with two other young men. She fidgeted with the Coke she was drinking, cheeks pink.

'As it happens, we think we'll look for a flat together. I hope that's okay.'

'Are we likely to be able to stop you?'

Peter was laughing, as he poured us a glass of wine before dinner. The atmosphere was cheerful, and relaxed, and I was pleased that Livvy was there to divert attention from me. I felt lit up, and sparky. However, Peter surprised me by commenting on how well I was looking.

Illicit love had made my eyes shine and my hair curl in greater profusion. My skin was clear, and laughter kept bubbling up, because of my physical contentment. I made a mental note that I must rein myself in, and not show my feelings so overtly.

I tried hard to dismiss the knowledge that I was being unfaithful to my husband, telling myself that Ian and I had been together in the past long before Peter and I had married, and so my actions were in some way understandable, even excusable.

It was strange how something so out of the ordinary could quickly feel like the norm. I was coping by becoming two people; it was the only way I could handle it. At home, I was the dutiful wife and mother. When I was with Ian, I could become something freer, less defined, and I relished this almost as much as I enjoyed our physical relationship. Life was mine for the taking again.

# Chapter 16

A week went by, during which I spent two whole days with Ian, in bed and out of bed, wrapped up in the bliss of his attention. At the weekend, my parents came to stay.

Although they were in their seventies now, they were both very active and enjoyed good health. I was concerned about what they might think of Olivia's plans, but they were not at all put out, which irked me. They would not have been so accepting if I had announced my intention of setting up home with a boyfriend at a similar stage of life.

'Olivia is so grown up for her age,' my mother remarked, after Livvy had treated her to a long account of her prospects in Manchester. She had got the PR job, in the way that she usually got whatever she wanted. 'I shall never forget that terrible summer we had with you before you went to Oxford. All those tears you cried over Nick! Young people seem so much more capable these days.'

It was hard to bite my tongue, but I saw Peter send me a warning glance, and I realised it was better not to argue. On the whole, the weekend passed very successfully. My mood was sunny, and we all laughed a lot. However, as Peter prepared to drive them back to Beresford on Sunday evening, my mother drew me aside.

'Is everything all right, darling? I can't quite put my finger on it, but you are not your usual self.'

Her maternal eye ranged over me suspiciously, and I tried to smile.

'Whatever makes you think that? I'm very well.'

'Yes ... but I get the feeling you're on edge. Is everything all right with Peter? It must be difficult with him away such a lot at present.'

She looked really concerned. My parents thought that Peter was the best thing ever to have happened to their daughter. They had never fully trusted Nick, owing to our volatile relationship, and his charm, so effective on everyone else, had failed to disarm their protective instincts. Sometimes, I joked that they would always take Peter's side in any dispute we might have, but I didn't really want to put that to the test.

'Everything's fine,' I said, firmly.

She hesitated, obviously unconvinced by my response, putting out a finger to stroke the curled petals of some late dahlias in a vase on the hall table.

'This boy that Livvy is involved with – he's Ian Inglis's son. How do you feel about that?'

'We are perfectly happy about it,' I reassured her. 'He's a charming boy, and we are all friends now. Please don't go worrying yourself on that score.'

Peter and my father came in to the hall behind us, and we prepared to say our goodbyes. As she kissed me, she whispered, with prescience, 'Don't do anything silly, dear,' in my ear. But she was too late. I already had.

Ian and I managed to meet one another often over the course of the next weeks. Our assignations were mostly at Delamere Court – Laura was very obliging in her lengthy absences from home – but occasionally, Ian came to me at the Old Rectory.

I felt much less comfortable with the physical side of our affair in my house, worrying about someone calling and discovering us, but I enjoyed entertaining Ian, feeding him the things I knew he liked, and fussing over him, as women love to do for the men they hold dear. Peter's frequent absence on business at this time made things very simple for me in my efforts to lead two separate lives.

Ian and I were completely caught up in this phase of our relationship, and I could not imagine life without it now. I didn't ask him whether he slept with Laura. It was none of my business, although I did not believe he would do so with the same enthusiasm he showed towards me.

One weekend, Peter and I were asked to a party by some county people we barely knew. Our association with the Ingleses had opened new doors for us. However, I was shaken by the unexpected pain I felt on seeing Ian and Laura together in a social setting.

I drank several glasses of wine rather quickly, and made myself circulate with unnatural vivacity, because I didn't want to spend time with Ian in this environment. I was acutely sensitive to his presence. As usual, his company was in demand, but I noticed that Laura kept him on a tight leash, and did not leave his side.

I met an old friend, Vanessa, who had moved to live on the far side of Nantwich, and concentrated on catching up with her news, as a welcome distraction. But I couldn't escape him.

'Isn't that Laura and Ian Inglis?' Vanessa asked, looking across the room to where they stood, chattering and drinking with a select coterie. 'I've heard that they are renovating Delamere Court. What a good looking couple they are. Do you know them well?'

I watched Laura brush a crumb from Ian's lapel with a proprietorial gesture, and felt deeply aggrieved.

'Yes. In fact, I spent most of yesterday morning in bed with Ian,' I said, truthfully.

As soon as I spoke, I could have kicked myself. How much had I had to drink? Vanessa gave a little start, and gazed at me, open mouthed, before breaking into a bellow of laughter.

'Eithne! You are a tease. For a moment, you had me believing you. Wait until I tell Colin.'

'Don't do that, please. It was just a little joke between friends,' I begged, cursing the possessive instinct which had led me into such folly.

There was a crush of people, and I never got to speak to Laura or Ian, but perhaps that was just as well. Peter had settled himself in a corner with a few old friends, and he carried me off quite early in the evening.

'I know you don't like these kind of parties,' he said, opening the car door for me. 'But I expect you enjoyed seeing Vanessa again.'

I hoped that he put my silence in the car down to the effects of tiredness and too much wine. Actually, I was worried about my inability to cope with Ian's presence on public occasions. I hated not being able to demonstrate our special connection, and loathed the fact that Laura was still so very much in possession of what I wanted for myself. It didn't mean that I wanted to reject my husband, but I was greedy, and desired to have both of them.

I couldn't sleep that night. Despite all the pleasure I had with Ian, I began to wish that we had never become lovers again. I couldn't go back, and I couldn't see a satisfactory way forward. And although I didn't know it then, a stunning blow was about to land.

A few mornings later, I lay in bed with Ian at Delamere Court, feeling pleased to have him to myself. Having established our relationship, we did not fall upon one another with quite such desperate longing these days. Sex had become warm, sweet and empathetic, much more so than I remembered from the days when we had been engaged. Back then, I had too often felt like a possession, to be enjoyed by the possessor.

'Let's go for a walk,' Ian said, when we had made love. 'It's sunny today, and I want to check out the work that's been done on the hedging at the end of the top field.'

'All right.'

I sat up, yawning, and he reached out to stroke my breast, gently circling the nipple with his thumb.

'Ouch!' I said, moving away. The caress had been painful.

'Sorry, sweet. I didn't think that would hurt.'

He looked surprised.

'It's just that my boob feels a bit sore and tingly,' I explained. Ian examined me critically.

'They look rounder, somehow, today,' he said. 'Is your period due?'

I glanced down at my chest, and experienced a horrible sensation, as if a house of cards was collapsing around me. Gingerly, I felt one breast, and then the other.

'Ian, you have had a vasectomy, haven't you?' I quavered. He shook his head.

'Laura keeps nagging me about it, but I'm afraid I've never got round to it. I don't really fancy the thought,' he said. A faint trace of alarm flickered across his face. 'Why? You are on the pill, aren't you? You always used to be.'

'No. I haven't taken it for years.'

I did some rapid calculations in my head, and the terrible truth dawned on me.

'Oh God. I'm more than two weeks overdue. I can't believe that we've been so stupid! I was sure I heard Laura say you'd had the snip.'

Billows of panicky blackness rolled over me, and I lay back on the pillow. Ian turned over to face me, stroking my cheek.

'Eithne... if by chance you are pregnant, could it be mine?'

I thought of all the sex we had enjoyed over the last weeks – passionate sex, frequent sex, unprotected sex. I had slept once with Peter during that time, and we had used a condom.

'Well, I should think it's almost certainly yours. How could we let this happen?'

I could scarcely take in the enormity of the situation. Ian's eyes were shining.

'My darling, it would be wonderful to have a child together. I —'

'Ian! There's no way I want another baby. Just think; I'd be getting on for fifty when I had it, you'd be fifty-seven. It would probably have something wrong with it, anyway, because very late pregnancies aren't meant to happen. And how on earth would we deal with the question of paternity?'

I sat up and began to dress hastily. I had occasionally tormented myself by imagining a number of awful scenarios which might result from our affair, but this had never crossed my mind. It seemed like the ultimate punishment.

I pulled on my trousers. Visions of nappies, sleepless nights, teething – all these things I had gladly put behind me, years ago. Much as I wanted Ian, I didn't want to have his child.

We finished dressing in an uneasy silence, and made our way down to the kitchen. I slumped in a chair by the window as Ian made coffee, trying to calculate the options before me. He was unusually hesitant, as he took another chair, and gazed at me with worried eyes.

'Eithne, let's not be hasty about this,' he said, gently taking my hand. 'Are you absolutely sure this means you could be pregnant?'

'These days, you can buy a kit to test your wee at home,' I told him. 'I'll go into Chester later, and buy one. I can't risk using the chemist locally, you know how people talk.'

I could just imagine it. 'Fancy that Mrs Leigh having a baby at her age! Careless, wasn't she?'

Careless, and stupid beyond belief. I wondered whether I could conceal this from Peter, and my heart quailed within me.

'It will be impossible to arrange an abortion here without Peter knowing. You might have to help me get it done in London,' I said.

The timing was especially unfortunate. It was now the second week of December, and I knew that Ian and his family would be away over Christmas, skiing with friends. By early January, I would be nine or ten weeks pregnant, and time would be running out for me. And could I make it through Christmas and the holiday period without anyone noticing my condition?

Ian frowned, and reached across to take my hand.

'But I don't want you to feel you have to terminate the pregnancy,' he said, squeezing my fingers. 'This is a life we're discussing here. And as I said before, I think it would be marvellous for us to have a child.'

'Be realistic, for heaven's sake. You don't have to have it, Ian. You won't be the one undergoing nine months of tiring physical changes, culminating in a lot of pain. You won't be the one getting up at night and changing nappies. And anyway, how do you think Peter will react to this? I will find it very difficult to persuade him that the baby is his, given the sporadic nature of our sex life. He's not stupid.'

Ian was silent for a while, gazing out at the frosty trees lining the driveway. Eventually, he spoke, the words coming slowly, as if he was reluctant to say what he had to.

'Well, perhaps we will have to come clean about our relationship. I won't abandon you. If Peter wants your marriage to end as a result of this, then I will accept my responsibilities.'

'And leave Laura? I don't want you to feel forced into a course of action you might not otherwise have contemplated.'

My voice was very bitter. I was frightened, because I could see my world collapsing around me. Laura would put up a fight for her husband, and she might very well win, but I knew that Peter would be so appalled by my behaviour, he would walk away without looking back. If he did that, I couldn't really blame him. The only person I could blame was myself.

I swigged down my coffee. I felt an urgent need to drive to a chemist somewhere I wasn't known, so I could do a pregnancy test.

Perhaps there was another explanation; perhaps it was the beginnings of the menopause. I began to cling to that hope.

'What do you want me to do?' Ian asked, looking very wretched. I stood up.

'Nothing, at the moment. I'm going now, because I want to do a test so we know where we are. I'll call you later on with the result. It only takes an hour or so.'

He didn't try to dissuade me, but walked me to the car, before gathering me into his arms.

'Please drive carefully, darling. I don't want any more accidents,' he murmured into my hair. 'Will you ring me when you know?'

'Yes. As soon as I can.'

I climbed into my car and began the twisty descent to the lane, wondering where to find a suitable chemist. In the end, I drove to Winsford, and found what I needed there. The assistant sent me a sideways look through curious eyes as she rang the purchase through the till, and I stared at her in defiance.

Back at home, I followed the instructions very carefully. An hour later, my fears were confirmed.

'Ian?'

He had answered the telephone very quickly. 'I'm afraid the test is positive. Now we have some difficult decisions ahead.'

A long silence followed.

'Eithne, we must both think about what we want to do. Try to keep calm. I can't see you tomorrow, I have to go to London, but we'll meet on Thursday as usual. Will you be all right?'

'Yes. Until Thursday, then.'

I wandered into the sitting room and threw myself on the sofa, then I went upstairs, and examined myself minutely in the mirror. Did I look as if I was pregnant? Apart from a fullness about the chest, I thought not. I had not suffered with morning sickness during my previous pregnancies, and with luck, I would not be afflicted this time. Perhaps I could keep things secret until I was able to have an abortion.

Abortion ... I hated the word, it had horrible associations. Nick had been very unenthusiastic about my pregnancy with Nicholas to begin with. That was also unplanned, and he had felt unready to become a father. Thank goodness I had not been willing then to agree to a termination, because I could not imagine life without my precious Nicholas. What if this baby was another wonderful child in waiting? I refused to let myself think of it in that way, for I knew that once I began to consider it as a person, I would find it almost impossible to proceed.

I wished and wished that there was someone I could confide in. It was hard having to deal with this without a confidante – Ian didn't count; he was too deeply involved. Then I thought of Josh's mother. It wasn't the same situation, but she'd had to deal with an unexpected pregnancy. I wondered what support she had hoped for, how hard a decision it had been not to tell the person she believed to be responsible for fathering her baby. Many things might have been different if she had.

I'd grown used to deceiving my family over the last weeks, in fact, I was secretly appalled at my facility for deception. Now, I began to be aware that my hormones were making me extra sensitive and emotional. It made everything doubly difficult.

Peter rang from Hamburg, and was annoyed with me because I'd forgotten to book his car in for a service. This left me fluttered and teary, and Lou gazed at me with amazement as I put the receiver down.

'Mum! What's the matter? Have you and Dad had a row?'

Her face was perplexed. She wasn't used to her parents falling out with one another.

'Dad's cross with me about his car, that's all,' I said. She didn't seem very satisfied with this explanation, and looked at me with scepticism. Luckily the phone rang again. It was one of her friends, and by the time she had finished the call, the awkward moment had passed.

I had hardly decided what to do on Thursday, when Ian appeared on the doorstep early on.

'Sorry to descend on you,' he said, walking in to the hall and hugging me. 'Laura has Mrs B in all day, doing some sort of pre-Christmas house clean. Can't think why, we're not even going to be there. But I had to see you.'

I put my head on his shoulder, needing the reassurance of being held. However, I did not feel like going to bed with him today.

'Could we go in to Chester? I'm so behind on my Christmas shopping,' I asked him, hoping he would agree.

'Yes, of course. Whatever you want.'

Clearly, I required humouring in my present state. It was comforting to sink back into the leather seat, and watch the countryside passing by. The landscape was wintry now, painted with a smudgy palette of greys, browns, and greens, and the radio was forecasting snow for the weekend.

Ian glanced across at me.

'You look rather fragile today,' he said. 'How are you feeling?'

'Tearful. Confused. Worried about what happens next.'

There was no point in hiding things. He sucked his teeth, and stared at the road again.

'If you've changed your mind about having the baby, I will support you,' he said. 'Even if that means the balloon goes up. Thank God I have the wherewithal to do that.'

I assumed that he meant he could afford an expensive divorce settlement. It begged a question which I had been avoiding.

'Are you saying that you would marry me?' I queried. 'I don't want to force you to divorce Laura. You've made it very plain before this happened that you didn't want to change the status quo.'

'It all depends what you want to do,' he said, after a long pause. He hooted crossly at a van driver threatening to cut in on him. 'If you have an abortion, then I suppose it's easier; nothing need change, so long as we can conceal it. It's a good job Peter's away such a lot.'

I wanted to make him choose between me and Laura. What would it be like to return to the days of the distant past, when he was my property? Then I would be the one to brush crumbs from his jacket at parties.

But I realised this wasn't going to happen. Deep down, I wasn't really sure that I wanted it to happen. We'd made a conscious decision to pursue our relationship as an extracurricular activity, so to speak. I had to stick with that, unless I wanted to spend the rest of my life feeling that I had left him no choice but to take me on.

And in any case, I wasn't sure whether I could go through with pregnancy and bringing up a baby, especially amidst the messy break up of two families.

'I will go to see my doctor next week, and see what can be arranged,' I told him. 'I don't think we can have the baby. It's kind of you to say you would support me, but I'm not sure you want to go down that road, not really.'

He stared ahead, thinking over what I had said, but I thought he looked relieved.

'Could you tell Peter that you need to have some small gynaecological procedure? Men shy away from knowing too much about these things. It might be possible to get round the problem that way,' he suggested.

'That's a good idea. I'll look into that.'

Once we had arrived in Chester, I parked him in a cafe with a coffee and a paper – just like a husband – while I dived into the crowded shops, glad to think about something else for a change. Chester was as hectic as it had been on the day we had met so unexpectedly in July, and I was tired after an hour or so, but at least I managed to cross a few items off my list.

Ian helped me to carry my bags back to the car.

'Lunch now? Where do you want to go?' he asked, when we were back in the busy street. An arm snaked round my waist, and I jumped.

'You two again! I'd think you were having an affair, if you didn't both look so bloody miserable.'

Rick Ryan's face was screwed into a wheezy laugh. Ian assumed a look of false jollity, and I forced an unwilling smile.

'Eithne and I bumped into one another in Debenhams,' Ian explained. 'We thought we'd have lunch. Would you like to join us?'

My heart sank. I liked Rick, but wasn't sure if I could sustain a social front today. He laughed again.

'You seem to make a habit of bumping into one another. Thanks for the invite, but I have to collect something for Judy.' He kissed me sloppily on the cheek. 'Tell that husband of yours to ring me, I haven't seen him for a while.'

'I will,' I murmured. The two men exchanged a handshake, and then he was lost in the crowd.

'That was a narrow escape,' Ian said. 'I'm not sure I could have coped with his particular brand of humour today.'

We ended up in a small French bistro, which reminded me of our turbulent days in Dinard, and did nothing to improve my self-esteem. However, I was hungry, and the food was good.

'How will you cope if you start being sick in the mornings?' Ian asked me.

'I'm hoping I won't be. I didn't have that sort of problem with my other pregnancies,' I said.

I was too tired to contemplate further shopping, and Ian drove me home again. I didn't invite him in.

'I'll see you on Monday,' he said, giving me a farewell squeeze. 'Let me know how you get on with the doctor if you manage to make an appointment.'

We were both very conscious of the fact that he would be going away the following week, which would make communication almost impossible. I hoped that I would have a better idea of the actions I would need to take before he left.

Preoccupied with my problems, I had forgotten that Nicholas was due home for the Christmas vacation at the weekend. It was lovely to have him back, and his presence helped to mask my distraction, but I realised it would also make it harder for me to see Ian without detection. So I was pleased when Rosine rang to ask him to spend a night or two in Beresford, where she was visiting her father. She had decided it was time to tell Mr DeLisle about his American grandson, and wanted Nicholas to be there to help. He was happy to do this, having maintained a regular correspondence with his half-brother during the term.

I think they had found this a better way to begin to know one another than with potentially awkward, face to face contact. They could be honest and open more easily on paper, and Nicholas confessed he was now looking forward to seeing Josh in person once more. This wasn't likely to happen until the Spring.

I telephoned the surgery and made an appointment. Usually, I saw a woman doctor, Mary McIver, but I wasn't sure I wanted to consult her about my problem, because she was a friend as well as a GP. I asked to see a junior doctor instead. Unfortunately, winter ailments were in full flow, and there were no appointments available until the following Thursday. I would just have to wait.

After Nicholas left for Beresford on Monday morning, I drove up to see Ian. He was sweet and loving, and persuaded me into bed with him without much difficulty, although I hadn't been feeling particularly sexy up to that point.

'This will be our last chance to make love for a while. I shall miss you, my darling', he murmured, holding me close to him, and stroking me in the places where he knew I liked to be touched. 'I wish to goodness we weren't going away. I shall be worrying about you all the time.'

'I suppose it will be impossible for us to contact one another without arousing suspicion. You will have to trust me to make the right decisions,' I said.

He urged me again not to hesitate if I decided to have the baby, saying he was fully prepared to face the cataclysm which would result. I wondered whether he really meant this. It was good of him to be so open about it, but at the same time, I didn't like the feeling that the decision was resting on my shoulders. However, there didn't seem to be a way round it. We said a tearful goodbye, without much further discussion. The worst part of the whole affair was having to keep this to ourselves.

# Chapter 17

I exerted myself to finish my Christmas preparations over the next few days. We would be a small family group for the celebrations, as my parents had decided to treat themselves, and were spending the festive season at a hotel on the coast. Livvy petitioned for Alex to come to us, as he wasn't included in the Inglis trip to Switzerland, and I assured her we would be delighted to welcome him.

Nicholas wasn't due back home until the day before Christmas Eve. After spending some time in Beresford, he had accepted an invitation to visit Freya and her family in Edinburgh. If I hadn't had so much else on my mind, I could have been upset about this.

Rosine rang me on the day I was due to visit the doctor.

Her father had been incredulous, and then stunned, to find that he had another grandson. At first, he was upset to think that Nick had unwittingly fathered a child, but Nicholas was able to talk to him about his budding relationship with Josh, and Mr DeLisle slowly became more accepting of his American descendant. The upshot was that Josh was invited to visit both Rosine and her father in early spring, and I hoped very much that he would spend some time with us as well. This was a piece of good news amongst the gloom.

My appointment at the surgery was at two thirty, and I was early. The first blow was to find that, owing to staff illness, the consultation would be with Mary McIver, after all. I'd just have to rely on the Hippocratic oath and our previous friendship to get me through without too much condemnation. However, I entered her surgery feeling anything but calm.

She welcomed me warmly, but I cut short her enquiries about the family.

'Mary – I'm pregnant. I don't want to have the baby, and I'm hoping you can arrange a termination for me as soon as possible after Christmas.'

She turned towards me, eyebrows raised in surprise.

'Are you sure, Eithne?'

She started to look through my records. 'Have you done a test? You may just be perimenopausal. That can mean you start missing periods.'

'No, I'm sure. I've done a home test. My periods are still very regular, and I have other symptoms that I recognise.'

'I see.'

Mary sat back, and looked at me with a serious face. 'Are you certain you don't want to continue the pregnancy? There are tests and procedures we can do these days, which minimise the risk of problems with an older mother. I can —'

'No. I don't want to have it.'

Sleet pattered on the window. I could feel Mary scrutinising me closely, and she was beginning to sense that things were more complicated.

'Have you discussed this with Peter? I would like to know you both agree about the need for a possible termination.'

This was the part I had been dreading.

'He doesn't know. It isn't his baby,' I stuttered, my face growing uncomfortably crimson as I spoke. She looked at me again, her mouth definitely grim this time.

'I'm very sorry to hear that. Are you planning to tell him?'

'Not if I can avoid it.'

I took a deep breath. 'I know what you're thinking, and believe me, I wish this had never happened. There is no way I could convince Peter it's his child, and if he finds out, our marriage will be over. I don't want that. If there is a way of doing this so he thinks it's some routine gynae procedure, I might be able to save things. Otherwise, I'll have to ask the baby's father to help me arrange something privately, perhaps in London.'

Mary was doodling on a notepad, apparently thinking hard.

'And what about the baby's father?' she said. 'Does he want you to have the child? Does he have a marriage to protect as well? I assume you've discussed matters with him.'

'Yes, of course. He says it's up to me, and he will do whatever I need him to do. But Mary, it's not just the paternity question. I don't think I can go through pregnancy and bringing up a child again, because I left that stage of my life behind long ago, and I don't want to revisit it.'

She stared down at her desk. Although her manner was cool, I thought I detected a gleam of sympathy when she finally looked up at me.

'How far along do you think you are?'

'About seven or eight weeks. I know it will be a problem with Christmas looming, but I must get it done as soon as possible afterwards.'

We sat in awkward silence for a minute, before she turned to me, looking rather sad this time.

'Well, the signs are consistent with an early pregnancy,' she said. 'I'll refer you to the Termination Clinic in Chester, and the procedure can be done as an outpatient, so Peter needn't know, if that's really what you want. But it can't take place until well into the New Year. Are you going to be able to keep things secret until then?'

'I shall just have to.'

I started to put on my coat, feeling tearful. 'Mary, I am grateful to you. This has been a terrible mistake, and I'm paying for it. I just want it over with now.'

She was writing busily, but she looked up and gave me a half smile.

'Are you sure you can't tell Peter? He is a sensible man, and he may not react in the way you fear. Think about it, won't you.'

'Okay.'

I stumbled outside to my car. That hadn't been too bad. Now I just had to get through Christmas.

It was awful not being able to get in touch with Ian. I wondered how he was feeling about things, and whether he thought continually about our predicament, as I did, or if he was able to forget it for a while as he enjoyed himself on the ski slopes. I coped by making myself concentrate hard on practical matters in the run up to Christmas.

A sense of excitement and anticipation swept through everyone as the day drew near. Peter stopped work on December 23rd, and was delighted to be finished with his foreign travel for a time. Lou was still enough of a child to find pleasure in traditional Christmas pursuits, and Nicholas came back from Edinburgh laden with presents and flushed with the happiness of his burgeoning relationship. On Christmas Eve, Livvy and Alex returned from Manchester, and in the evening, we sat round a blazing log fire, and were cosy.

Peter cuddled me to him as we sat on the sofa, and I wished I did not have to keep him in ignorance of my terrible secret. I thought I might prepare the ground for my termination by telling him I had some gynaecological issues, but every time I tried to broach the subject, my courage failed me. Despite Ian's belief that men preferred to be kept in the dark about 'women's problems', I knew that Peter was someone who would want to know all the details and options for treatment, and it would not be easy to fool him. I decided to wait until after the festive season was over before tackling the subject. Perhaps I might feel braver once this special family time was out of the way.

Later on in the evening, the telephone rang, and I went to answer it in the hall.

'Eithne?'

It was Ian. My heart skipped a beat as I heard his voice, and then I felt panicky. The line crackled, and I couldn't speak.

'It's all right. I'm allowed to ring to say 'Happy Christmas' to my son,' he said rapidly. 'How was the doctor? Can you talk, or is it difficult?'

'It's okay for a moment. She was helpful, and it should be in the New Year,' I said quietly, hoping he would understand. He was silent for few seconds.

'I still don't know whether I'm glad or sorry about that,' he said. 'Are you coping with it all?'

'Just about.'

Tears came to my eyes as I realised how very far away he was, and how much I wanted a comforting shoulder. 'I'd better get Alex for you.'

Alex was delighted that his father had called him from Switzerland. Livvy told me that Alex and Ian had become much closer to one another since the accident, and this, together with his developing relationship with Livvy, meant that Alex was a much happier and more confident young man than the one who had paid a late night visit to my kitchen six months previously. This was good to see. I liked Alex such a lot, and was grateful to him, because his calming influence on Livvy had definitely made my own life easier.

Nicholas was very contented as well. He had enjoyed his visit to Freya's family, and I hoped that soon, we would be able to welcome her to Cheshire. However, I wanted to deal with the pregnancy before that happened.

I was finding it increasingly hard to behave normally with Peter. Feelings of guilt, exacerbated by my surging hormones, perpetually threatened to overwhelm me, and sometimes, I wondered how long I would be able to maintain an innocent front.

Would he really want to end our marriage if he knew the truth? Could I confess to a passing fling, instead of a passionate affair, and if so, would that make it a less serious lapse? I revolved these questions in my mind, unable to reach a firm conclusion, more unhappy and undecided with each passing hour.

The day after Boxing Day, I was conscious of some painful twinges in my abdomen. They didn't feel as if they were connected to the baby, and I thought I had probably overeaten, as one usually does at Christmas.

Two days later, they came again, a little more sharply, and I began to think I might need to return to the surgery.

On New Year's Eve, Peter and Nicholas announced their intention of doing a day long walk in the Peak District. They left after breakfast, promising to be back in time for tea. I knew that Nicholas had agreed to meet old friends in Chester in the evening, and Livvy was preparing to rejoin Alex in Manchester, but Peter and I had no special plans. I never enjoyed New Year very much, and was glad when all the hullabaloo was over.

They had been gone about an hour, when I was racked by acute spasms of pain in my stomach. I staggered to the lavatory, and found I was losing blood … a lot of blood. My head spun, and I vomited.

Thank God I hadn't shut my bathroom door. Livvy heard the noise, and came in to see what was going on. Her eyes widened in horror as she saw the mess.

'Mum! What on earth – are you all right?'

I was bent double with the agony now.

'No. I think you'd better get help.'

I lay on the bathroom floor, passing in and out of consciousness. I thought I heard Ian's voice, saying that he was sorry he could not come, but the snow was exactly right for skiing, and he was staying in Switzerland. Livvy was putting a towel under my head, and her face was chalky white. 'Just like the snow,' I told her weakly, and she stared at me without comprehension.

I shut my eyes, and tried to blot out the racking spasms. After a while, paramedics arrived, and I surrendered myself to their rapid ministrations. They gave me an injection, and some of the pain began to recede. Dimly, I was conscious of the urgent ride to hospital in Chester; of white coated figures bending over me, and the swift assessment of what was wrong. People kept asking me questions, and I tried to answer as best I could.

They told me they would need to operate. I had to sign a form, and then I slept.

Sometime later, I wavered into consciousness. The acute pain had gone, but there was a tight, pulling sensation in my stomach. A nurse floated into my field of vision, and bent over me, with an encouraging smile.

'Mrs Leigh? You're going to be all right now. Doctor will come along and see you shortly.'

Where was I? In a hospital bed, apparently, but I was going to be all right. What could have happened?

Tiny things assume an unexpected significance when you've been abruptly removed from your ordinary life. I looked at the clean white sheets, and the minute patterns on the hospital bedspread, and savoured the fresh laundry smell. I was tucked in nicely, like a child who is ready for a long sleep after a tiring day. Then I began to distinguish subdued voices and the slap of feet on the floor.

My cubicle was curtained off, and I wondered what was happening outside my shrunken world. Then there were louder voices, and the curtains were pulled back. A tired looking doctor came up to the bedside.

'Mrs Leigh? How are you feeling?'

'Confused,' I murmured. 'What is wrong with me?'

'You had an ectopic pregnancy. That means the baby was growing in one of your fallopian tubes, and not your womb. If it's not detected early, the tube may rupture, and that's what happened with you. We've had to operate to remove the tube, but all went well.'

'I'm not pregnant any more?'

'I'm afraid not.'

I digested this information. The doctor misunderstood my silence.

'I'm very sorry that you've lost your baby. You —'

'No, it's fine. I didn't want to be pregnant, not at my age. I was very careless,' I said. I tried to sit up, swamped with relief.

'Now, you lost a lot of blood, so we will keep you in for a day or two. After that, you will need to rest for a few weeks, and your stitches will come out in eight or ten days. Do you have any questions?'

'I expect I will, later on. I just feel terribly weak now.'

He began to pull back the curtains. I saw that I was in a four bed ward, but only one other bed had an occupant, who was sleeping.

'I'll ask Sister to bring you a cup of tea.'

With that, he was gone. I heard him speaking to someone in the corridor, and a nurse came in.

'Would you like a cuppa, dear? And your family are here. Shall I let them come through now?'

'Yes, please.'

I stared across the ward, not really seeing anything. I wasn't pregnant. I'd need to manage things with Peter, but at least the awful decision about termination had been taken away. And in the circumstances, there had been no possibility that the baby could have gone to term. In a strange way, that made me feel better about things.

Footsteps echoed in the corridor, and anxious faces appeared around my bed.

Peter bent down to kiss me. He was pale and tense, but my attention focussed on Olivia, whose face was swollen and blotchy in a way I'd never seen before. I stared at her, open mouthed.

'Oh, Mum. I thought you were going to die,' she said, tears welling in her eyes as she spoke. She bent down, and hugged me fiercely.

'Careful, darling. Mum's fragile,' Peter admonished her.

I was amazed at this display of affection, and it jolted all my preconceptions about Olivia and her feelings. Perhaps she had room for me, as well as her father, in her heart. The knowledge slowly filtered through and warmed me.

'I am sorry to put you through all this,' I whispered, reaching for her hand. She scrubbed at her eyes with a tissue.

'I didn't know what to do. Thank God for the ambulance service; they were marvellous. And then, I didn't know where Dad and Nicholas were, or when they'd be back.'

She sniffed. 'It's been a horrible day.'

'Not so good for you, either, my love,' Peter said to me.

He didn't seem put out, or suspicious in any way. We chatted briefly for a few minutes, and then he asked Livvy to fetch Nicholas and Louisa from the waiting room.

'We were told only two visitors at a time,' he explained. As Livvy walked off, he bent over me.

'Did you know you were pregnant, my darling?'

His tone was tender, his eyes loving. I gulped. Was this question designed to trap me?

'I thought I was starting the menopause,' I lied, feeling awful as I did so.

'I've been racking my brains. We took a chance just before you went to France, didn't we? That will have to stop.'

For a minute, my mind was blank, and then I remembered. Our normal method of contraception was the condom, but on occasion, at the very beginning or end of my menstrual cycle, we had assumed we were safe without it. In fact, I had got my last period immediately after the incident he was referring to, but I don't think he had realised.

Tides of relief swept over me. There weren't going to be any accusations or difficult questions. For the moment, I was safe.

# Chapter 18

Once I began to feel better, I basked in the attention I received from my family and friends. I pushed my guilty feelings away, and assumed the role of a needy patient instead.

I shed a few private tears when I thought about the baby. It might perhaps have been the catalyst which determined whether my affair became more than an affair; however, I knew that the outcome was probably for the best.

I spent two more days in hospital, and was glad to be discharged on January 3rd. When I arrived home, my parents were there to greet me. Peter had asked them to come to stay to take care of me, as he was due to return to work.

I walked in the house, to find the girls and my mother staggering about with armfuls of flowers and greenery.

'The Inglises have sent half a flower shop,' Louisa exclaimed. 'It's very nice of them, but we've run out of vases.'

'I'll go and borrow some from the Potters,' Peter said. 'How kind of Laura and Ian, but they do go over the top.'

I wondered how they knew about my medical emergency, but realised that Alex must have told them the news.

'Alex says that Laura and Ian send their love, and they were really sorry to hear you were in hospital,' Olivia said, fussing round me on the sofa with tea and biscuits. 'Goodness knows what all these flowers have cost.'

'You know the Inglises. Money is no object,' I replied. But I was pleased, all the same. I thought I detected Ian's hand in the lavish gesture.

It was lovely to be home. I felt surprisingly weak after my ordeal, and was also limp with relief that I no longer had to worry about the pregnancy and its outcome. I could sit back and allow everyone to spoil me.

My mother was firmly in control in the kitchen. Sometimes, I felt like a schoolgirl again, as I lounged with my feet up, whiling away the hours with a book, which I never really got round to reading. However, this enforced idleness also left me with time to think over all the events of the last months, and I slowly came to understand that things could not go on as they had before.

Despite my ruptured tube, I recognised that I had been fortunate to have come through the pregnancy incident relatively unscathed, and with my marriage intact. At times, I was determined that I should learn my lesson, and walk away from the physical relationship with Ian. I would begin to imagine what I was going to say, how I would end it, and then I would be swamped by the strength of my desire for him.

Why couldn't I be content with what I had? Perhaps I had never loved Peter deeply enough to be able to resist temptation. I could see how Ian had drawn me to him, perhaps unwittingly at first, and that a combination of boredom, flattery and opportunity had all played their part. Ian's good looks and lifestyle made him a very magnetic figure, and maybe I had tried to recreate our past, to prove that I still had power over him.

I couldn't deny the physical attraction between us, and we had grown very close over the autumn. Sometimes, I would allow myself to fantasise that we might have a future together, if there was some way of getting past the problem posed by our existing spouses and families. However, I think I always knew that this could only ever be a fantasy.

When Peter returned to work, my mother decreed that she was satisfied enough with my recovery for her to pay a quick visit to Chester with my father and Nicholas, leaving Louisa in charge. Now she had recovered from the first shock, Lou was disappointed I did not require any medical intervention on a daily basis. She would have loved to be a hands-on nurse.

I was on the sofa as usual, reading a magazine, when the doorbell rang. She went to answer it, and I heard surprise in her voice. Then the door opened, and Ian walked in.

Stupidly, I began to cry. He came swiftly to my side, knelt down, and gave me a huge hug.

I was conscious of Louisa hovering in the background, no doubt perplexed by what was going on.

'Eithne, darling, I am so, so sorry you have had such a terrible time,' he said gently, pushing my hair away from my face, and kissing me with warm affection. Lou caught her breath, and he looked round. He stood up, assuming a social smile.

'Any chance of a coffee, Louisa?' he asked.

I could see that this was designed to remove her from the room for a while. She hesitated for a second.

'Yes, do make us coffee darling. I'd like one as well,' I said, wiping my eyes.

Lou stood there, expressions of doubt and suspicion settling on her face.

'I don't want you to make her cry,' she said to Ian, after a long pause.

'I promise I won't do that,' he told her.

Eventually, she turned on her heel, and went to the kitchen. Ian pulled up a leather stool, and sat beside me, holding my hand. I had got over the surprise of seeing him, and had control of myself now.

'Alex has told me what happened. Are you going to be all right?' he asked, his face and eyes anxious.

'Yes. I'm getting over the op well. I'm afraid there was no way of saving the pregnancy,' I said.

'You are the one that matters.'

He kissed my hand very tenderly. 'What did you tell Peter?'

I lowered my voice.

'He thinks the baby was a result of something which happened much earlier on. No one suspects anything.'

Lou's footsteps echoed in the hall, and we drew away from each other. She leaned against the doorpost, watching us.

'Thank you, Ian, for the wonderful flowers.'

I wanted him to know I was grateful. 'We ran out of vases, and it's like being in a bower of blossom. It took you and Livvy ages to arrange them, didn't it, Lou?'

'Yes.'

She didn't seem to be feeling conversational. Ian turned to her.

'Maudie says hello. She and Laura are getting a flight the day after tomorrow. I've had to come home early, to see to some business matters.'

Lou nodded, looking a little less frosty. The kettle whistled, and she returned to the kitchen. Ian took my hand again.

'I don't want to arouse any more suspicion, so I'll sit further away now. Just assure me that you are all right.'

'I will be fine.'

'When will you be up and around again?'

'Well, I can't drive for a few weeks, but I think I'll try to start being more active tomorrow. I'm a little tired of the sofa.'

Although I could not hold him in my arms as I longed to do, I felt invigorated by his presence. Louisa came in with our coffee, and then sat down herself, looking for all the world like an old fashioned chaperone. The chat would have to be very general from now on.

Ian told us about the skiing in Switzerland, and how well Sam and Maudie were doing on the slopes. He talked about the food and the snow and how busy he was about to become with his City project, which was now approaching a critical stage. He knew about Lou's interest in animals, and described seeing chamois at close quarters, although she asked questions about them which he couldn't answer. After twenty minutes, he rose from his seat.

'I mustn't tire you,' he said to me. 'Laura will want to see you when she gets back. I have to go to London for a day or two, but perhaps we can meet next week, if you are feeling up to it.'

I held out my hand to him. Lou was still with us, so I could not give him the embrace I wanted to, but he bent down and hugged me, and kissed my hair.

'Look after yourself,' he said softly.

Lou got up to show him to the door, and I lay back on my cushions, wishing we could have had more time alone together. There was such a lot I wanted to say to him.

I heard the front door close. Lou came back in and began to collect up the coffee cups. As she stood by the fire, she suddenly turned to me.

'I don't think I like Ian Inglis,' she announced.

'Why? Think how kind he's been, helping Nicholas with work, sending me these lovely flowers. And he's Maudie's dad. I thought you always got on well with him.'

She paused, her face growing a little pink.

'I don't like the way he looks at you,' she said, and left the room.

I started to get up and do things about the house. Within a few days, I felt I was getting back to normal, and it was almost a relief when my parents decided to return home to Beresford. I was grateful to them for all their care, but I wanted my house to myself again.

Term time recommenced, and Lou went back to school, with Nicholas departing to Oxford a few days later. My spell of ill health had prevented us asking Freya to visit, and I hoped we might invite her at Easter instead.

I was impatient for Ian to call me to arrange a meeting, but a week went by without my hearing from him. Finally, he rang from London, and we were able to talk.

'I'm sorry I've been so tied up,' he said. 'But things have gone very well here, and I'm looking forward to working with this company. Apart from you, there's not much to occupy me in Cheshire.'

I didn't like him speaking in that way. Sometimes, I felt it wouldn't take much for him to walk away from Delamere Court, and then I'd probably never see him again. He arranged to pick me up from home on Friday.

'I assume you're out of action still,' he said, referring to the need for me to forego sex for a few weeks following the operation. 'So it will just be lunch.'

Lunch was better than nothing. I took particular care with my appearance on Friday, wishing I didn't look so washed out. I had lost some weight as a result of my health problems, and was thinner that I'd been for some time.

When Ian arrived at the house, he hugged me, and looked me over carefully.

'You look peaky. Poor darling, I wish I hadn't been in Switzerland when all this happened. But I might have found it difficult to keep my distance, and that would have made people wonder. I suppose that Peter accepted everything you told him?'

'Well, I didn't really have to say much. That was lucky.'

I collected my coat, and we got into the Mercedes.

'Chester? Let's not subject ourselves to prying eyes at the Three Feathers today,' Ian said.

During the drive to the city, Ian told me enthusiastically about the new agency buyout with which he was involved. I wished I could feel equally excited. It was becoming obvious to me that he would be away much more often in future, and I could see that things would not be so easy for us.

'How does Laura feel about you spending so much time in London?' I queried, wondering if he had considered how I might feel as well.

'She isn't happy. But I've told her that I need to do this. She has her commitments in Cheshire to keep her occupied.'

'Where will you stay when you are in town?'

'I've been very lucky. The tenants of my old Chelsea flat have given notice, so I shall camp out there.'

No wonder Laura wasn't happy. He'd effectively be living a single life again, away from the restraints of home. We drove in silence for a few miles, while I pondered on these changes.

'Of course, that means we won't have many opportunities to spend time together, either,' I said, realising that he was not going to raise the issue. I wanted to test his reaction.

'I'm afraid you're right. But it can still be very special when we do see each other.'

His tone was light and unworried, but I sensed that the goal posts were shifting as we spoke. I wondered whether the pregnancy scare had made him conscious that great sex could come with a number of problems in its wake.

'So. New job. Wife and family. Country mistress. Probably London mistress soon, as well,' I said, remembering his chequered history. 'You really are going to be fully occupied.'

'Don't exaggerate, Eithne. You know I want to be with you as much as I can.'

'But for how long?' I asked myself. Sadness began to overwhelm me. I could see that our affair was going to end almost as soon as it had begun.

We went to an upmarket restaurant close to the Cathedral. Ian was on good form, relaxed and in high spirits, and I tried not to let my feelings show, although inside, I was preparing myself for a turmoil of regrets.

'When can we make love again?' he asked towards the end of the meal, reaching for my hand and kissing it.

'In a week or so, I should think. Providing you can find a spare hour in your crowded itinerary.'

He sent me an irritated glance.

'Don't be like that, Eithne. Can you start taking the pill again now?'

'It isn't medically advisable at my age, I'm afraid. What are the chances of you having a vasectomy?'

'Absolutely nil, thank you. Perhaps you can find an alternative, because I really don't care for condoms.'

This made me furious. I was finding it increasingly difficult to reconcile the self-satisfied and egotistic man sitting opposite me with my passionate lover of the autumn, but a little voice from the distant past nagged me *wasn't he always like that?*'

His focus seemed to have undergone a radical change, and I began to suspect that I was falling way down the pecking order.

Ian didn't appear to notice that I was quiet. A smartly dressed couple paused at our table on their way out, and greeted him with loud enthusiasm. He stood up politely, and the woman pressed an invitation upon him, patting his arm and fluttering her eyelashes in a way which I found intensely annoying.

Ian introduced me as an 'old friend and neighbour', and they acknowledged me with nodding heads, before transferring their attention back to him.

'Sorry about that,' Ian said, reseating himself as they moved away.

I stared into my coffee, and finally faced the fact that I had made a cardinal error in letting Ian so far into my life again. My powers of attraction were never going to be enough to compete with all these others who wanted a piece of him. I blinked a tear of humiliation away, and then I felt belligerent.

'Suppose it had been a normal pregnancy, and I had decided to keep the baby. Just what form would your support have taken?' I asked him. 'How would I have fitted in with all these other commitments you have?'

He cleared his throat, and his gaze slid away from me across the restaurant.

'Well, I suppose we could have lived together in London. It's a theoretical question now, thank goodness.'

To be fair to him, I think he would not have walked away. But I was very thankful I had not had to put him to the test.

'You're cross with me,' he remarked later, as we retraced our drive through the country lanes.

'Not cross. Just disappointed. I remember you saying to me that we would have a real relationship, and spend a good deal of time together. Clearly, that isn't going to happen now.'

'But I do want to go on seeing you when I can.'

He put his hand on my knee, and squeezed it. I took the hand in my own.

'It won't work, Ian. There are going to be too many calls on your time, and frankly, I'm not prepared to be at the bottom of the queue for your attention. I think we should finish it now, and go back to being neighbours, without any rancour. It's the only way I think I can deal with it.'

The car slowed down behind a tractor which was trying to reverse into the entrance of a field. We sat there, unable to move forward, the car engine idling.

'I wish I could promise you more,' Ian said, giving me an agonized glance. 'I do love you – but I'm not a free agent, and the love has to fit into a complicated jigsaw of work, family, and other demands.'

The tractor cleared the road, with a muddy churning of the grass, and the driver waved us on.

'My first instinct in France was probably right,' Ian continued. 'I knew there were risks. If I followed my heart, then I'd be trying to persuade you to make a new start, just the two of us. But then, I think of everything else my life involves ... yours, too. Before Christmas, it seemed as though we could have things both ways, and we still can, if you don't mind me being less available for you. After all, we can't expect things to continue at the fever pitch of the first days. It will just be several times a month rather than every week.'

'No. I think I deserve more than that. I think we both deserve more.'

We drove in silence for a long while, and then we came to the outskirts of Fenwich.

I was thinking over everything Ian had said. Perhaps if this new business opportunity had not arisen when it did, we could have had the relationship we both wanted. But how long could we have maintained it without our partners finding out? And what else might arise in Ian's life, to shift his attention away from me? I was always going to be the vulnerable half of this pairing.

I wasn't going to risk my marriage further on such flimsy grounds.

Ian turned into the drive of the Old Rectory, and came round to open my door.

'Can you give me a cup of tea? I'm not prepared to let you throw in the towel without an argument.'

To give him his due, he looked really sad. We went in, and he sat in the rocker by the window, gazing out into the misty gardens as I filled the kettle.

'I like your house. It's a manageable size, neither too big nor too small. Delamere Court is fine in summer, when we can use the pool, and enjoy the gardens, but it isn't what I call a cosy place in winter,' he said, twiddling with a cuff link. I didn't reply, but I agreed with him. For a moment, I pictured Laura perched in her cavernous hillside home. Perhaps she was wondering how enjoyable she would find it now, with her husband so often absent from her side.

I placed a mug of tea before him, and sat down at the table. Ian looked across at me, his eyes dark and mournful.

'Are we going to have to call time on this?' he said. 'It's been important for me to be close to you again, Eithne, and I know you've wanted it too. Think of all the wonderful hours we've spent in bed together. Are you prepared to walk away from that?'

I returned his gaze, trying to clarify things in my mind. Ian was so handsome, so very desirable, so much in control of his life. He was everything which had attracted me to him in the past, but it wasn't enough. And I wasn't enough for him. He wasn't about to leave Laura, or stop doing the things he wanted to do, and whatever pipe dreams I might have had about our being together in any permanent or acknowledged way had no foundation in reality. I had taken a wrong turning when I went to bed with him again, and I needed to get back to the right path. It was dawning on me with an alarming clarity that I had run a terrible risk of losing my husband, the one person I could always depend upon.

'Oh, Ian. It will be very difficult for me to stop seeing you in the way that we have been doing,' I said, suppressing the pain which gnawed at my heart. 'But I see now that there isn't a best of both worlds, not in real life, and I think we should accept that it is better to part as friends before we get in any deeper. Perhaps we've been trying to recreate something which never had a chance, and in the future, I hope I can look back, feeling that there was something good, and valid about what we have shared; that it wasn't just a sordid little episode of lust. But I think it has to finish now.'

The kitchen clock ticked peacefully, marking the silence as we sat there, coming to terms with an ending.

'I see you're serious.'

He got out of the rocker, and put his arms around me from behind as I sat at the table.

'Can't I do anything to change your mind?'

His voice was insistent in my ear, and he nuzzled my neck. 'The sex is great, isn't it?'

Despite my sadness, I smiled.

'Yes, the sex was wonderful. You've always been an amazing lover.'

I removed his arms very gently, and stood up to face him. 'Please don't put pressure on me. It's difficult enough, as it is. There are too many complications, and I'm afraid that things just can't work out for us.'

He stroked back my hair. For an instant, his face sagged, and he looked his full age and more. I thought how well we knew one another – and also how little.

'No. They never have done.'

He gazed at me beseechingly. 'Promise me that, if we find ourselves alone when we're really old, you'll come to me. Promise me that, at least.'

'I promise,' I said.

It was a defining moment. He took his leave soon afterwards, but not before I had agreed to meet again – as friends – before too long. When he had gone, I went to my room and had a good cry. Then I told myself that it was done with, and I could not afford to look back. I was desperately sad, but at the same time, there was a sense of relief that I would no longer be party to a spreading deception.

The rest of January and February passed slowly. I chafed at being housebound. It was too cold to work in the garden, because we suffered a prolonged spell of very bad weather. My friends seemed to be hibernating too, and it was all very dull.

I missed Ian terribly. I missed the physical contact, and the excitement of being with him, and there were days when I felt so low it was hard to make myself function normally. However, I knew that the decision to end the affair had been the right one.

Towards the end of February, I met Laura outside the Post Office. She looked as classy as ever, in a fur trimmed jacket and matching boots, but I thought I detected signs of strain around her eyes.

'How is Ian getting on with his new business venture?' I asked. He had not called me since our last parting, and I was a little hurt about this. She gave a grimace, her face downcast.

'The business is doing well, but I'm afraid he's hardly been at home of late. He says he can't risk being stranded up here because of the bad weather. The trains have been unreliable, and our drive can be somewhat challenging when it's icy.'

'Yes, I can believe that,' I said.

'Of course, I'm stuck here with Maudie, because of school. He can be very inconsiderate at times.' Her voice rose in complaint.

'Oh dear. I am sorry.'

I didn't really care for Laura. She was not a woman's woman, and I'd been very jealous of her during the short time Ian and I had been lovers. I was still jealous of her, but I also carried a burden of guilt.

'Why don't you let Maudie stay with us next week? Then you could go to London and spend some time with Ian,' I suggested, feeling incredibly magnanimous. Her face opened out, and her eyes brightened.

'Do you mean that, Eithne? It would be wonderful. Maudie would enjoy herself, and I'd love a few nights in town.'

'It's a deal, then.'

We arranged that Maudie would come to us on Monday, and Laura would collect her again on Friday evening. I almost felt virtuous as I walked away, and had to remind myself that it didn't really make up for sleeping with her husband.

Peter was still travelling from time to time. He had been very tender and loving towards me since the ectopic pregnancy, and sometimes, this was hard for me to bear. But I made strenuous efforts to appreciate his care and show my affection for him, and began to feel better in a small way.

Lou was delighted to have Maudie to stay. She missed Olivia, and the two girls got on very well. I liked Maudie, too. She wasn't very like her confident father, nor did she have her mother's elegance and style, but she was a sweet natured girl, and I was relieved to discover that she had outgrown her crush on Nicholas.

Both girls were now smitten with a lad from the local stables, and I listened to the excited speculation about Harry's preferences with a wry smile, remembering similar conversations from my teenage years.

I was surprised to find both Laura and Ian on the doorstep on Friday night, to collect their daughter. Laura was carrying the inevitable elaborate Inglis bouquet, which she pressed upon me with effusive thanks. As Maudie wasn't ready, I invited them in for a drink.

I hadn't seen Ian since we parted in January. He gave me a polite peck on the cheek as he came in to the house, but he concentrated on greeting his daughter. She and Louisa immediately dragged him out to the stables, to see the new baby guinea pigs, and Laura and I retreated to the kitchen.

'This has been so kind of you,' Laura gushed, sinking gracefully on to a chair while I went in search of a vase big enough to hold the flowers. 'I've had a lovely time! Lots of shopping, and we found a divine new restaurant. And being back with Ian in his old flat brought back some very exciting memories.'

I could believe it, but I tried not to think about it.

'Where's Peter?' she continued, looking round. 'Is he still travelling?'

'No, he's in Manchester this week. He'll be home any time now,' I said. Ian returned from the stables, shivering slightly from the chill night air.

'I find it difficult to work up much enthusiasm for guinea pigs,' he explained, warming his hands at the Aga. 'But yours certainly live in a very stimulating environment.'

'That's thanks to Josh. He designed and made that amazing pen for them in the summer.'

Ian looked across at me with a reflective smile.

'Ah, yes, Josh. How is that young man these days?'

'Well, I believe. He's finishing his course at MIT.'

We had decided not to broadcast the truth about Josh's parentage unless the need arose. None of our friends in Cheshire had known Nick, and I didn't think there would be much interest anyway. When the news did filter out, it would probably be a nine days' wonder, and nothing more, and I did not feel tempted to raise the subject with Ian and Laura.

Peter arrived home as I was pouring the wine. We sat cosily in the kitchen exchanging news, and I ignored siren voices urging me to turn greedy eyes on my former lover. Peter and Laura began to discuss some affair connected with her brother's firm, and they drifted off to the study to find an article in a trade journal which Peter wanted to show her.

Ian and I were left alone. We took a proper look at one another, and the atmosphere grew charged.

'I've missed you,' he said, almost inaudibly.

'I expect I've missed you more. You are very lucky to have so much going on in your life.'

I couldn't repress a certain bitterness in my tone, and he glanced away, knowing that what I said was true.

'It was good of you to invite Maudie to stay,' he murmured.

'Yes, wasn't it? I hear you and Laura had a great week together.'

He frowned, looking as though he would like to disagree with me.

'I could be at home more often – under certain circumstances.'

Was he throwing down the gauntlet again? I decided I couldn't pick it up.

'I think we both know that isn't a good idea.'

The girls burst in amidst gales of laughter, and our conversation was cut short. The Inglises departed soon afterwards, and I turned my attention to our supper. Peter was in a good mood.

'Let's go out tomorrow, just the two of us,' he said, putting an arm round my waist as I laid the table. 'Where would you like to go?'

'Anywhere,' I thought to myself. Anywhere far away, where I could escape my unhappiness, if only for a while. I attempted a smile.

'How about the coast? I fancy a bracing walk by the sea.'

Although my enthusiasm was forced to begin with, it turned out to be a lovely day. The wind was cold, but the sun shone, and we were well wrapped up for a tramp along a North Wales beach. Afterwards, we lunched at a hotel, seated before a blazing fire, and I hoped we could spend many more days like this, content with one another's company. My husband was a lovely man, and I was ashamed that I had to remind myself that I was lucky to have him.

However, the problem with Peter being so sweet and attentive towards me was that I faltered even more under the burden of guilt over my affair. It was hard to carry alone, and there was no one else I could confide in. My parents would have been shocked beyond belief. My girlfriends might have sympathised, but condemned me at the same time. And could I trust a confidante not to gossip? Just think how irresistible it would be. 'Did you hear about Eithne and Ian Inglis? What on earth was she thinking?'

Ironically, the person I would normally have turned to with any problem was the one I couldn't tell.

A blustery March ushered in the first signs of Spring, and I made myself get to work in the garden, hoping that I might tire myself with physical labour, and sleep better as a result. My nights were broken, as I wrestled with memories of passionate embraces and scenes which couldn't be repeated. I had not fully recovered my health after the traumatic incidents of New Year, and I knew I looked peaky and tired, and Peter was beginning to be concerned about me.

One Friday afternoon in mid-March, I was digging furiously in the garden, Aconites and early primroses were blooming in the damp earth, and birds were busy building nests and singing to their mates.

The sense of a new cycle of life beginning struck me with some force, and I wished fiercely that a new cycle might begin for me.

Car wheels scrunched on the drive. As I walked round from the garden, I met Ian, getting out of the Mercedes.

'Hello stranger,' I greeted him, not without irony. My heart still skipped a beat when I saw him, and I thought that it probably always would.

'Eithne. How are you?'

He leaned against the car, relaxed and affable, grinning at the sight of my muddy boots and gardening gear. 'I see that you are managing to occupy yourself. Don't get any thinner, though, I don't think you've really looked quite right since Christmas.'

'Is this a social call, or did you just drop by to insult me?' I asked.

'Ouch.'

He was still grinning. 'Trouble is, Eithne, you send me such mixed messages. Your mouth tells me one thing, but your face says quite another.'

He reached out, and kissed me briefly on the lips. I shut my eyes. 'I've accepted that we aren't going to continue our affair, but I that doesn't mean I've stopped caring about you, and I hope you still care about me. Will you give me a cup of tea, and a slice of cake? I don't suppose you have another cherry one on the go?' he asked.

Somewhat to my surprise, we passed a pleasant hour over tea and fruitcake. After the kiss, Ian did not attempt any more personal contact, but told me in enthusiastic detail all about his work in London, and I listened, fascinated and frankly envious. Peter arrived home early, and I was glad that he found us in an innocuous situation.

'I've been encouraging Eithne to take up some form of work again,' Ian told Peter, as he rose to leave. 'She's practically an empty nester now, and I think a new interest would do her good. Don't you agree?'

Peter looked surprised. He crumbled some fruitcake, frowning thoughtfully.

'Are you getting bored at home, my darling? What do you think you might want to do?'

We had a brief discussion without really reaching any conclusions, but I thought that Ian was right. I was ready to take on a new challenge, and I was glad that seeing him had left me with some positive thoughts rather than merely sad ones.

I poured myself a large glass of sherry before supper, and Peter opened a bottle of wine to follow. Louisa was spending the night with Carly Potter, so we had the house to ourselves.

As we settled down for the rest of the evening, I found myself desperately wanting to set the record straight with my husband. Perhaps then I could really make a fresh start. I could admit my past failings, and go forward, freed from the load which weighed me down.

Peter was immersed in a book. The wine had made me bold, and I could feel the words trembling on my tongue.

'Peter.'

But before I could speak any further, the doorbell rang. We looked at one another in surprise.

'I'll go,' Peter said. I heard him open the door, and he exclaimed with pleasure. The sitting room door was flung open, and a beaming figure came in.

It was Josh.

# Chapter 19

'Josh!'

I rushed over and embraced him heartily. He was grinning, and returned my hug with an extra squeeze.

'Hi, Eithne. I hope you don't mind me surprising you like this. It was a kind of a spur of the moment thing.'

'No, of course not. There's a room here for you any time, you know that. It's so lovely to see you.'

I stepped back, and took a good look at him. The slight, diffident boy of last summer had filled out, and seemed altogether more substantial. His gaze was direct and confident, and the miserable expression in his green eyes had been replaced with laughter.

'Why didn't you let us know you were coming?' I demanded.

'I wanted to give you a surprise.'

Peter took Josh's coat, and went to get him a beer. Josh plumped himself down on the sofa next to me. 'That's a good fire,' he said, gazing at the flames flickering up the chimney. I couldn't take my eyes off him.

'When did you get to England?' I asked.

'Last weekend. I've been staying with Rosine and Andrew. My – my grandfather was there as well.'

He pronounced the word 'grandfather' with decided pleasure, and his face glowed.

'But I can't believe Rosine didn't tell me you were here.'

'I asked her not to. I wanted to take things one step at a time.'

He paused, his eyes still on the radiant coals. 'They've been just great to me. And it was wonderful to get to know my grandfather. I'm so sorry I never got to meet my grandmother.'

'I'm so pleased that they made you welcome,' I murmured, still in a state of surprise.

'I called in to see Nicholas on my way here,' he continued, giving me his special grin. 'It's good to meet, knowing where we stand now. His girlfriend's a real babe. You'll love her,' he added.

Peter returned with the beer, and began to ask him about MIT, but Josh seemed more interested in the German project. I sat back and watched them converse, marvelling at the change in our American visitor.

There was still very little of either Nick or Nicholas in his physical appearance, although I had already been treated to a flash of his attractive smile. But the ugly duckling was definitely turning into a swan, and I believed that much of this change was a consequence of his recognition and acceptance by his English relatives. Whatever the cause, it was heartwarming to see.

'How long can you stay, Josh?' I asked later on, as I turned down his bed in a motherly fashion.

'Can you put up with me for a week or ten days maybe? Nicholas tells me he's back home for the Easter vacation on Thursday, and we have a favour to ask you.'

'A favour?' I queried.

'Yes. If you don't mind, I'll leave the details until he's here.'

As I lay in bed, I realised that Josh's arrival had stopped me spilling the beans about my affair with Ian. His timing had been exemplary.

We all enjoyed having Josh back with us again. He spent hours with Peter talking engineering matters, but he also made time for Lou, and listened to her prattle with composure. He expressed polite interest in the health of the guinea pigs, and made a few tweaks to their living quarters, which were well received.

On Sunday, Livvy and Alex came for lunch, and Livvy monopolised him with her accounts of France, the accident, and her new life in Manchester. If I felt a little left out, I wasn't going to show it.

I didn't get too spend much time with him until Tuesday, because he had visited Peter at the office the day before. It was a fine spring day, and he suggested a walk. After a mile or so, we found ourselves on the bench where we had sweltered in the heat of summer. He turned to me, with a hesitancy in his voice.

'Eithne, I was very sorry to hear about you losing your baby,' he said, flushing slightly, obviously embarrassed at the personal nature of the subject. 'I hope you are all okay now.'

'Physically, yes. Emotionally ... well, that takes time,' I said.

I spoke almost without thinking, and then wondered whether I could unburden myself to him. We were close, but not too close, and I remembered how my American friend John had always been there for me in the past. Perhaps Josh could take on a similar role now.

'Peter must have been hit hard too,' he murmured.

'Josh, I'm afraid I did something very stupid. It wasn't Peter's baby,' I said slowly, looking him full in the face.

The words came tumbling out now, I couldn't stop them. 'In France, and afterwards for a time, Ian and I slept together. You wouldn't have known this, but he and I were engaged to one another years ago, and I left him to be with your father. When we met again, it was difficult ... there was an attraction, some unfinished business between us, I suppose.'

The expression of shock on his face brought me up short.

'With Ian Inglis? Alex's dad?'

He had gone very pale. 'And are you still sleeping with him?'

'No. It's over now. But it's been very difficult for me. I felt as though I was torn between two people,' I said slowly. 'And now, I wonder whether I ought to confess, because Peter doesn't know. I don't want to break up my marriage, but I'd like him to understand. It might help me.'

'What? Are you completely crazy, Eithne?'

He jumped to his feet, glowering, his green eyes hard as pebbles. I was too surprised to answer him.

'What do you think you'd gain by that?' he demanded, and I was shocked by the cold contempt of his tone. 'If I understand you, you think you'd feel better for getting it off your chest. But that won't absolve you from anything! You'd just be shifting part of the guilt on to Peter, and that's not fair. Don't you think he'd be asking himself how he'd fallen short of your expectations, to prompt you to do this? Things could never be the same for you afterwards.'

I sat there in silence, trying to take in what he was saying. His reaction had taken me by surprise, and I realised that I had made a grave error in thinking he might understand. His fists were clenched, and he almost panted as he spoke.

'Don't you understand how lucky you all are? When I was here last summer, I thought you guys had it all – the perfect family, everything I never had.'

His voice trembled. 'Now you want to throw it away. And I thought the world of you.'

There was no mistaking the scorn in his voice. I was choked with pain and emotion.

'The only thing you can do now is try to forget it ever happened, and put your husband and children first like never before.' he continued. 'I can't believe you did such a dumb thing, Eithne.'

He started to walk away from me, and I stared after him, flooded with remorse. But before he had gone very far, he turned abruptly, and retraced his steps.

'Does Nicholas know?' he demanded.

'No. Just you.'

'Please don't tell him, ever, unless you want to destroy his trust in you for good. I don't want to go on walking. I guess I'll catch the bus into Chester now.'

I watched his retreating form; tears gathering as I realised that I had probably ruined our relationship for all time. And too late, I saw that I had been very unkind by confiding in someone who wasn't enough of an adult, who didn't have enough life experience to begin to comprehend. Would I ever stop making mistakes? I seemed to be stuck in a cycle of misjudgment, and mishaps.

Chastened, I began the slow tramp back home. Josh had told me nothing I didn't already know, except for one thing. It had not occurred to me that Peter might blame himself in any way for my shortcomings. I couldn't let that happen, so my silence on the subject was now assured. Perhaps Josh had helped me without really knowing it.

The afternoon was miserable. Lou came home from school, but didn't seem to notice that I was preoccupied. Even the thought of Nicholas' imminent arrival for Easter could not lift my spirits. I felt flattened and low. At about four thirty, the kitchen door opened, and Josh walked in.

He was holding a bunch of roses, which he thrust awkwardly at me.

'Eithne, I am really sorry about what I said earlier,' he muttered, his face flushed. 'I was well out of line. It isn't anything to do with me. I just don't want you to ruin things for everyone.'

I accepted the roses, feeling equally awkward.

'You didn't say anything I hadn't worked out for myself – except for the assumption of blame,' I told him, speaking low in case Lou overheard us, although she seemed to have the television blaring loudly in the snug. 'I am really sorry to have involved you. I can see now that it wasn't fair. Can you forgive me for that?'

He shrugged off his coat, unwilling to meet my gaze.

'I suppose so,' he said, after a while. Then, his courage returning, he sent me a hesitant smile. 'I think it's a mistake to put people on pedestals.'

'It is. It's also a mistake to judge people too harshly unless you've been there yourself. I know I was extremely foolish, and I'm trying to make amends,' I said. 'At least I know the value of what I have now.'

He sighed, walking round the table, and gave me a brief hug, which I wasn't expecting.

'Luke would never forgive me if I quarrelled with you,' he said, 'Let's forget the conversation happened.'

'No, I can't do that. But I won't quarrel with you, Josh.'

After this exchange, my mood lightened, and we passed a happier evening than I had anticipated. Josh told us that he was looking forward to spending time with Nicholas. Their correspondence over recent months had helped them to a good understanding of each other, and they were beginning to feel a real connection.

I wondered what their father would have made of it all, and whether he would have been pleased that his sons were growing into confident young men. Nick had been so young himself when he died, that it was almost impossible for me to think of him as a paternal figure. In my mind, he was almost a contemporary of the boys, but I think he would have enjoyed living life again through them.

It was only as I was going to bed that another thought occurred to me.

When Nick came back into my life during my engagement to Ian, I believed that he'd saved me from making a real mistake. Now, I felt he had saved me a second time, thanks to the intervention of the son he had known nothing about.

It was strange to think how the threads of life could continue to weave their patterns, even after death. I didn't pretend to understand it, although I felt unexpectedly close to Nick again after the events of the last months.

Nicholas arrived home at lunchtime the next day, and greeted us all happily. He didn't seem to be worried by the imminent prospect of his final exams, and I hoped his love life wasn't distracting him from his studies.

He and Josh spent the afternoon closeted together in Nicholas' bedroom, and I had to repress a reprehensible pang of jealousy that they were growing closer. Josh's attitude towards me had undergone a subtle shift since the confession about my affair. I had caused the scales to fall from his eyes and I sensed that I was no longer an object worthy of veneration. This hurt more than a little, but perhaps it was better this way.

They came into the kitchen at tea time with a special request for me.

'Mum. Are you free tomorrow?' Nicholas asked me, sitting on the table edge and grabbing a biscuit. Josh leaned against the door frame, watching.

'I think so. Why?'

'We want you to come to Beresford with us. Josh wants to see where his father and grandmother are buried, and we both want you to tell us all you can about your life with our dad. You've never told me very much, and it's time that we heard the full story.

'I know you don't like visiting the grave,' he went on, cutting short my initial protest. 'But it's important that you do this for us. Can you bring yourself to come with us, please Mum?'

He got up and rubbed his cheek against mine in his special affectionate way. How could I say no to them? I was the adult here. It was time for me to put my emotions to one side, and be there for my boys.

The following afternoon, we sat on a wooden seat in the churchyard of St Peter's in Beresford. We had lunched with my parents, who had now been told about Josh, and they spoke honestly about their own recollections of Nick. I think Nicholas was a little upset when my mother gave her very decided version of the times when Nick and I had split up, and I made a mental note to balance her views with my own later on. My parents would always feel ambivalent about the boy who had broken their daughter's heart.

The boys had brought flowers for both graves, and laid them down gently on the ground. For once, the peace of the churchyard gave me cheer, rather than sorrow. We sat there in the weak spring sun, gazing at the headstones, and I began my epic tale.

From time to time, one of them would have a question, but they mostly listened quietly while I described my life with their father. I told them of the happiness of those early years, and the terrible sorrow of our last parting. I had to talk about Ian, too, and I hoped that this would help Josh to sympathise a little more about my affair. I knew that Josh would keep his thoughts about Ian to himself, as Nicholas was still inclined to regard Ian as a figure to be looked up to, and we didn't want to disabuse him. Ian might still be a useful contact for Nicholas in the future.

The sun slipped lower in the sky, and now I was recalling Nick's funeral service, and the terrible months on my own after Nicholas' birth. I hadn't cried up until that point, but remembering my awful loneliness made me very choky.

'At least I had you, darling,' I said, stroking Nicholas' cheek very tenderly. 'Life couldn't have gone on for me without you.'

He thought about this, his eyes dark and solemn.

'But then Dad came to the rescue,' he said, meaning Peter. 'And you loved him too, didn't you?'

I sensed Josh stiffen slightly as he sat beside me, and I recognised with some surprise that this was important for Nicholas.

'Yes, I grew to love him,' I said slowly. 'And I did love Ian too.'

There was a silence, while I tried to ignore a throbbing ache around my heart. Although I was trying hard to get over it, I continued to have strong feelings for Ian, and this was my punishment for having thought I could rework the past.

'But I loved your father the most of all.'

This was still true for me.

I rose, and went up to the grave, the memory of the coffin and funeral still fresh within me after all the years that had passed. I'd been angry with Nick, as well as sad, because he had slipped away from me at such an important time of our lives, but I thought it was time for me to forgive him. Nick had left me a special legacy in these two boys, and they were the ones who mattered now. I was immensely grateful to him for that.

We were all quiet on the drive back to Fenwich. I was exhausted after the effort of reliving the past, and was delighted to find that the boys intended to cook the evening meal for me.

I slumped in the conservatory with a glass of wine, reading the paper and listening to the sounds of laughter and the banging of pans which accompanied the food preparation, hoping that the clearing up would not fall to my lot later on. When Peter came in, I was almost asleep, but I jolted back into consciousness when he leaned over and gave me a kiss.

'I've had a great idea,' he said, his eyes bright. 'As soon as we can get you a visa, I'm booking you on a flight to see your old friend John in Washington. You might even get to visit Luke and Ray as well. This has been a difficult winter for you, and a change of scene is what you need. Would you like that?'

I thought for a moment, and turned to him with a beaming smile.

'I would love it,' I said honestly.

Today had been a final step in putting the sad parts of my early life behind me. Now I needed to deal with the fallout from the sorrow of recent months. I thought the trip might help me with the process of starting over, working towards different interests and a new direction, perhaps the new cycle which I'd pondered in the garden. 'But what about you and Lou?'

'Easily taken care of with friends and family. You know your mother always loves to come to stay, and Laura Inglis owes us a favour,' he said, grinning.

Another thought struck me forcibly. It was essential that I said it now.

'There's just one thing ...'

He looked surprised.

'Please don't raise any objections, darling. I really want you to go.'

'It isn't an objection. It's a request. I would like you to come too,' I said.

It was worth saying it to see the look on his face. A tentative smile hovered on his mouth, and then his eyes lit up. And I began to smile myself, as I understood that I meant it, that I needed to be with my husband, and this was the way in which I could begin to move on.

#0179 - 180416 - C0 - 210/148/12 - PB - DID1426273